OVERPROTECTED

by Jennifer Laurens

A Grove Creek Publishing Book
OVERPROTECTED
Grove Creek Publishing / April 2011
All Rights Reserved.
Copyright 2011 by Katherine Mardesich

This book may not be reproduced in whole or in part without permission.
For further information:
Grove Creek Publishing, LLC
1404 West State Road, Suite 202
Pleasant Grove, Ut 84062

Cover: Sapphire Designs
http://designs.sapphiredreams.org/
photography by Sarah Mc Arthur
Book Design: Julia Lloyd, Nature Walk Design
ISBN: 978-1-933963-00-6
$13.99
Printed in the United States of America

for Joe

OVERPROTECTED

by Jennifer Laurens

———————— CHAPTER ONE

I saw him and my heart started racing. His dark hair gleamed in the crowd at the intersection of Lexington and 89th Street. His head was bowed, looking at the street. I had to see his face. *Look up.* I blinked twice, sure I was seeing a crazy dream. Lots of guys had dark hair.

The light turned green. I wanted to turn and walk another way, but couldn't. I'd be in deep trouble if I wasn't home in ten minutes, and home was a good twelve minutes away—at a run. I'd never make it in time. Sweat sprung to my skin.

My phone vibrated in the depths of my Burberry coat. *Stuart.* I hoped he hadn't discovered that I wasn't at the townhouse. He'd kill me when I walked through the door. I didn't pull my cell out. I might miss seeing the stranger's face.

I started across the street. So did the crowd sweeping the stranger along. *Look up. I want to see your face.* His cocky stride and confident posture caused my heart to plunge. It had to be him. He'd always walked with a confidence that shouted he owned the moment and everyone in it. Closer. My pulse jumped. Twenty feet. *Look up.* Curiosity tangled with an old fear, an apparition floating like ice through my blood.

His head lifted. His dark eyes focused on something ahead, something to my left.

My heart leapt to my throat and lodged. *Look away before he sees you.* But I couldn't. As if no time had passed, his magnetism seized my attention. His wolfish gaze scanned and locked on mine. Ten feet away. Six. The look in his eyes shifted to wonder. Intrigue. *Do I know you? Have we met before?* Questions crossed his brown eyes and angular face like the wind shifting the taut planes of a sail in search of direction.

I lifted my chin, refused to look away. My knees shook but I held his inquisitive gaze and kept walking. Three feet. Bats fluttered in my stomach. One. As we passed each other, our shoulders brushed. The corners of his lips turned up in a smile, like he couldn't place me, even though he searched my face. His deep dimples flashed.

Colin's smile.

I looked away. Closed my eyes, swallowed. I opened my eyes, and stepped onto the curb, and continued up Park Avenue, curiosity gnawing at my bones. Had he recognized me? I was probably just another girl. Someone to smile at, to flirt with. He couldn't possibly remember.

We hadn't seen each other in over five years.

I glanced back over my shoulder. My heart froze. Colin stood on the corner of Lexington—crowds filing around him—watching.

His smile was gone.

I swallowed the lump in my throat, tore my gaze from his and started into a half-jog toward home. I'd lost two, maybe three minutes I didn't have to spare. Fear shifted from the run-in with Colin to what awaited me when I got to the townhouse. In the depths of my wool coat, my cell phone vibrated over and over again.

I tapped the security code into the panel beside our double front door, breath racing with my heart. Three minutes late. The green light shone and the bolt slid open. I pushed the doors and entered the townhouse.

Soundlessly, I shut the door, peering up the curved marble stairs to my left, then through the arched hallway in front of me for any signs of life. Mother was out with friends. Daddy was at the firm. Gavin was either at the market or cooking in the kitchen at the back of the house. I sniffed. No scent perfumed the air.

That left Stuart.

When I'd gone, he'd been taking his usual "nap"—something he did every day between three and four o'clock—while I was supposed to be working on homework. From the moans and grunts I heard coming from behind his closed bedroom door, I doubted he was sleeping. The thought rammed a shudder down my spine.

I reached into my coat pocket for my cell phone. Twenty texts—from Stuart. I opened one message. Then another.

WHERE R U????
U KNOW WHAT THIS MEANS!!!
CALL ME!!

Sweat drenched my skin. He'd probably gone into my bedroom once he'd discovered I wasn't there—my bedroom was off limits to him—who knows what he'd done once inside.

Hands shaking, I peeled off my scarf, gloves and coat, draping them over my arm. I tip-toed across the marble entry, heart banging against my ribs so violently, I was certain the thuds would bring Stuart from his hiding place. Invisible eyes pierced me from every direction. He was somewhere.

Maybe I could make it up to my room before he saw me, lock the door and—

"Are you out of your mind?" His hot breath hissed in my ear. I whirled around. The presence of his towering bulk pressed me into the entry wall. My pulse tripped. His green eyes glared into mine.

"What the hell do you think you're doing running off like that without me? You know the rules." His spit dotted my face and I blinked. Rage sizzled off his muscles, sinews bunched like bowling balls ready to roll and strike out beneath his blue sweater and jeans. "It's not safe out there."

It's not safe in here. "I just went for a walk," I sputtered, hating that my voice trembled.

He inched closer. "No walks, Ashlyn. No opening that door, taking a breath or blowing your friggin' nose without me."

"Get away from me." I jerked to my left, toward the safety and freedom of the stairs. His meaty palm wrapped around my arm, holding me in place.

"Do you understand?" he growled.

I wrenched free, didn't answer. I shot him a parting glare and fled upstairs, tears rushing up my throat.

I hated him. Hated my life.

After storming into my bedroom, I slammed the door. Tears sprung free. My shoulders buckled in a sob. I crossed the room, ignoring the temptation to dissolve into an emotional puddle on my bed and went instead to the window overlooking Park Avenue, giving me a view of the street below and the apartment buildings sheltering the townhouse.

My secret escape walk had turned into another humiliating slap meant to keep me on my knees behind brick and mortar and glass. Safely protected.

Below, people dressed in black, gray and plaid coats walked freely on their way like storm clouds passing through sky. No hound dog bodyguards followed them, breathing down their necks, watching their every move.

Even Colin Brennen enjoyed freedom.

Sighing, I swiped away tears. How unfair that a jerk like him walked the streets doing whatever he pleased while I lived under a magnifying glass.

The door flew open. I turned, heart pounding. In my distraction, I had forgotten to lock it. Stuart heaved in the jamb.

"You're not allowed in here," I shouted.

"I haven't crossed the line. But you did, sneaking out like some friggin' dog off a leash. Don't ever do that again or I'll tell your father."

"Go ahead." My bones quaked at the very idea. But I knew what Stuart was after, and he'd never tell my father about my outing. Stuart wanted this job too much.

He crossed his arms over his chest. "If this was the first time, I'd consider cutting you a break. But it can't happen again."

His icy gaze chilled me. He backed from the room, closing the door. I blew out a shaky breath. The sweat on my skin started to cool. Two storms raged within me, fear and desperation combining, both angry for release.

I turned, gazed out the window at the steady stream of freedom below me, and I vowed to make a change. For now, I was home, in the townhouse with the same familiar options I'd grown up with: free to do anything I wanted in the house—reading, studying, playing the piano and talking to my friend Felicity.

I headed out the bedroom door, down the dark hall to the light pouring out of the music room. In the corner of the empty music hall sat our black baby grand piano. I crossed to it and sat. My fingers danced on the ivory keys. I closed my eyes, the vigorous melody of Beethoven's Seventh Symphony in G filling the room, my head, and senses. Stress tightening my neck and shoulders gradually seeped away. It always did when I played.

When my father's suffocating grip tightened around me, the piano took the pounding I inflicted as I searched for the answer to my most desperate question: why? I'd never understand what drove him to protect me the way he did, and the question left me unsettled, lost in a dark forest with no light to show me the way out.

The echo of Mother's heels on the wood floor alerted me. The day's luncheon was over. A second set of footsteps told me that Stuart was right behind, and a flash of panic raced through me. Had he told her about this afternoon?

I didn't stop playing. I never stopped until a piece was over; everyone understood that. One of the few things I controlled. When I finished, I turned and looked at both of them.

"How was the party?" I asked.

Mother waved a dismissive hand to Stuart, who nodded at her, then proceeded to shoot me a slit-eyed look of warning. "Ashlyn. Mrs. Adair." He left the room and I took in a deep breath.

Tucking a sable fur under her arm, Mother sat next to me on the piano bench. Countless emerald beads and gemstones glittered like stardust across the bodice of her designer dress.

"Boring luncheon, darling. You didn't miss a thing." She stroked a strand of hair hanging at the side of my face. "I should have been as lucky to have stayed home. I would have saved my ear from Mrs. Jacobsen bragging endlessly about her son, Adam. Honestly, did she really think I cared? I must have yawned—discreetly of course—ten times. Did that stop her? Absolutely not."

Eyes focused on the keyboard, I remained still. "I'm sorry it wasn't what you expected."

"Oh it was precisely what I expected—a brag session." Mother rose, leaning briefly to place a kiss on my head. "Well. I'm completely exhausted. I'll see you at dinner, hmm?"

I watched her saunter across the expanse of dark wood flooring, the fur coat dragging behind her.

Frustration sunk its teeth through my soul. I turned back to the piano and pounded out Beethoven. Again. As usual, the day was Mother's: packed with shopping, lunch excursions, trips to the spa while my freedom was carefully meted out, moment by moment.

I finished the piece, then settled for an abusive banging that rang chords into the air. Even with the inflicted abuse, the piano would be there in the morning, like it had been since I was eight years old. Always in the same place—just like me.

Weary, I stood and crossed the large wooden floor before making my way down the hall to my bedroom.

Before my full-length mirror I stood for my daily ritual. Though nearly eighteen, I looked too young for my liking. Mother repeatedly promised that being petite was what men preferred, but I never knew if that applied to me because I rarely saw men. The only men in my life were "companions." That's what my parents had called them when I was younger. My bodyguards were always adult men who carried weapons. I often wondered why Daddy didn't just call a bodyguard a bodyguard. I guessed the word choice made confinement easier to live with—for him.

I'd been told over and over again that I looked like a character in a fairy tale—Sleeping Beauty. Nothing was more ironic. My life consisted of our five thousand square foot townhouse, my piano, and my music. There was no Prince Charming, not even a cat or dog or frog for company.

There, in front of the mirror I stood. And there, in the mirror I remained.

Daddy's concern for my safety began after my nanny, Melissa, kidnapped me when I was five years old. She had a crush on Daddy. It wasn't until years later when I spent hours Googling the incident that I knew what really had happened.

Melissa hadn't had a crush at all—she'd turned into a stalker. When Daddy threatened to fire her, she took me, and threatened to kill me unless Daddy 'saw the light' and left Mother for her.

Daddy moved us from our beautiful home in Southern California to the townhouse in New York City after that. My parents spoke in hushed whispers that left Mother in tears. I knew life would never be the same. That was when Kent came to live with us. There had been numerous "companions" since.

When I'd asked about it, Daddy had told me I was his *special princess*, that there were bad people in the world who might hurt me. But he would never let that happen—never.

The vow sent my spine crawling in every direction.

Why hadn't he done anything about Colin Brennen when I was younger? He'd hurt me plenty of times. Of course, I'd been too terrified to tell Mother and Daddy—or even my companions— about Colin's brutal teasing, afraid Colin would find out I'd snitched and make my life more miserable.

I pulled my long blonde hair up into a knot at the top of my head and brushed blush on my cheeks. Circles shadowed beneath my blue eyes. Before I could stop, tears slid down my face. The moment, the feeling, was too familiar. I blinked them back, swiped the tracks from my face and took in a deep breath. There were more tears these days, something deep inside of me reached out with a need that wouldn't be ignored or suppressed any longer.

I wanted things, yearned for experiences. My own apartment. A job I could give my heart to. Freedom to come and go as I pleased. Someday I wanted a man. All of that and more.

I dressed for dinner in black slacks and a white blouse. I couldn't allow my parents to control me any longer, no matter the cost.

I took the stairs down to the first floor, cold from the black and white marble reaching up my legs, chilling me in spite of the velvet designer flats on my feet. The majestic curved stair curled from the main floor to the top, framed in a half-circle cylinder-like room where Mother hung her collection of tapestries from around the world.

On the first floor, hung a portrait of me Mother had commissioned a year earlier. I hated the pretentious display. In my black dress, pearls and hair done up I looked like I was ready for prom. *What a laugh.* I'd never go to prom.

Stuart stood gaping at it. This wasn't the first time I'd seen him drooling over the massive image. He turned when he heard me coming down, and his lips slit in a grin. He clasped his hands behind his back and his eyes raked me from head to toe.

"Stunning, as usual," Stuart said.

My stomach rolled. I went to pass him on my way to the dining room, but he stepped in front of me. I stopped. His face inched toward mine. "Your sneaking out is our little secret." His hawk-like gaze traveled over my face, neck and lower, shooting hot fear beneath my skin.

Without answering, I stepped around him and opened the French doors to the dining room. Mother sat at her usual spot at the foot of the dark mahogany table, Daddy at the head. Both looked up when they heard the doors swing open.

"There she is." Daddy set aside the papers he was reading and gleamed. He wore a designer suit in deep charcoal. He had dozens made for himself, tailored to show off another of his obsessions: his manicured body. As frustrated as I was with my circumstances, his sky blue eyes melted my heart. Adoration swamped me. The moment he and I were in the same room together, the mood was as if nothing and no one was more important than me.

Daddy stood, one hand reaching out. I crossed to him and gave him a hug, his spunky cologne familiar, the feel of his slick suit firm, cool and unyielding against my body. "How's my girl?" He studied me, his lawyer-sharp gaze searching for anything out of perfect alignment in my life.

"I'm good. How are you?"

He stepped to the chair to the right of his and pulled it out for me. I sat.

"Long day. I'm glad to be home."

"That's what Mother said." I plucked my intricately folded cloth napkin from the left of my place setting and spread it over my lap.

Mother looked up from her BlackBerry. "Agatha won't leave me alone about Adam. She insists we introduce him to Ashlyn. He's in his thirties."

And bald. I'd seen photos of the guy in society trades Mother occasionally shared with me.

Daddy's deciphering gaze still scrutinized me. Did he see that I was angry at Stuart? Frustrated with my protected life? That I had disobeyed, sneaking out for a walk this afternoon?

I ate my salmon salad with my eyes downcast.

"The age difference doesn't bother me as much as his past," Mother prattled on. "He's thirty something and single for a reason— in his case, countless reasons, all of them tall, slender and money hungry."

"He's not good enough for Ashlyn." Daddy's sharp tone landed like his will: iron clad and final, over the room.

"I'm only seventeen," I said. Even though I'd be eighteen in a few months, pairing me with a thirty-something was ridiculous. And arranging my marriage? No way I was going to let them do that.

Silence followed. My stomach fisted. We'd had this conversation before, with Mother and Daddy orchestrating everything from where I would attend college (somewhere close by so they could keep an eye on me) to when I went shopping, always with Mother or Stuart—usually both.

I set aside my napkin and cleared my tight throat. "I think Stuart needs to be dismissed."

Mother's fork froze midway to her lips. Daddy's firm jaw stopped in the middle of chewing. They both stared at me. I swallowed. "He's been here three years now. He's become too comfortable with me."

Daddy's jaw rotated once. He swallowed, shifted and his blue eyes iced. "Define too comfortable."

"He…" Fear and relief rushed through me at the same time. Condemning Stuart was the first step to freedom, I was certain.

"He… touched me today."

Mother gasped. Daddy's eyes bulged. "Not like that," I clarified. "He grabbed my arm… because he was mad at me."

Fire blazed in Daddy's countenance, reddening his smooth skin. For a moment, I wished I hadn't said anything, afraid he'd explode like he did sometimes when one of his employees disappointed him.

"Why would Stuart be angry at you?" Mother whispered, her auburn brows drawing tight over her green eyes.

They couldn't find out I'd gone on a walk, not only would Stuart be fired, but the grave I lived in would be dug even deeper.

"I think he's…in love with me."

Mother's hand went to her lips. She sat back in her chair as if blown there by a gust of disbelief. Daddy set aside his napkin, reached into his breast pocket and pulled out his cell phone.

I swallowed.

After he'd tapped in a number, his gaze met mine. "Ashlyn, I'd like you to leave the dining room please. I need to speak to Stuart alone."

The double doors swung open and Stuart smiled in. He slipped his cell phone into the front pocket of his slacks. "Yes, Mr. Adair?"

I stood, set my napkin over my salmon and excused myself, passing Stuart with a smug glance beneath lowered lashes. Confusion flashed on his face. The doors shut behind me.

In the empty hall, I pressed my back against the wall and let out a sigh. It was almost over. Stuart would be fired, I was certain of that, and though I was pretty sure Daddy would want to hire another bodyguard, my plan was to convince him I was capable of taking care of myself.

Raised voices leaked out from the dining room, echoing off the cold marble floor of the empty hall. Daddy—shouting at Stuart. Stuart's pleas, at first desperate, were finally smothered by Daddy's booming commands.

The doors flew open. Stuart stormed out. I hid in the darkness of a doorway. He continued toward the entry, and took the stairs up two at a time.

Daddy appeared, looked left, then right, his piercing gaze catching me. "Ashlyn, come inside please."

Fear tripped my heart. He waited in the open door and I passed him, his penetrating gaze cutting open my back, following me to my chair. I sat. He sat. Mother's sober face was taut with disappointment and accusation.

"You went out alone today." Daddy placed his napkin back on his lap.

My throat locked. Stuart had delivered his own final punch. I knew he was in love with me. I figured he'd lie to save himself, so he could keep the job, not tell Daddy the truth.

Deafening silence. My pounding heart rang through my ears. I lifted my chin. "Yes. I went for a walk." I met Daddy's slit-eyed gaze. "I needed to be alone and I didn't feel comfortable with Stuart any longer. I told you. I… haven't felt… safe…around him for months."

Daddy rose to his feet. His fist pounded into the top of the dining room table, shaking crystal and china. I jerked back in my chair. "And you're just now telling me?" Red rage stained his cheeks. He reached into his breast pocket, pulled out a slim cigar and snapped off the tip. Then he thrust it into his lips. He dug for a lighter, his hands quaking, lit the cigar and he blew out a bank of smoke.

My pulse raced. Across the table, Mother sat ruler-straight in her chair, composed, without an ounce of surprise visible either on her face or in her body. "Charles, settle down."

Daddy hissed in a breath, his mind appearing to roll like a runaway wheel down a steep mountain. I couldn't swallow, my throat was caught in an invisible fist. Finally, he looked at me. "I fired him. Until I find a suitable replacement, you will not leave the premises without your mother or me. Understood?"

"Daddy, I can—"

"This topic is closed." He smashed his barely-smoked cigar into the rim of his salad plate, and the plate wobbled.

He sat, placed his napkin on his lap and resumed eating.

Mother's raised-brow expression sent a wave of anger through my blood. I stood.

"Sit," Daddy commanded without as much as a break in chewing.

"I've lost my appetite." I turned and headed for the door, waiting for them to call me back to the table. Sweat drenched my skin. I was sick of being controlled. Two steps from the door, and still nothing. I passed through the threshold, my breath frozen in my chest.

"Ashlyn." Daddy.

I stopped.

"You weren't excused, young lady."

I turned, cocked my head. "Do I really need to be excused from the table at my age?"

Mother's eyes widened for a moment. "Where is this attitude coming from?"

"I'm almost eighteen. You guys treat me like I'm twelve."

"Being excused from the dinner table is good manners at any age." Mother's brow arched.

Daddy clasped his hands at his mouth, his lawyer-sharp blue eyes cutting open my conscience. I felt like all of my thoughts were naked. "Let her go," he said.

Mother turned to him with an indignant tsk-tsk. Though Daddy's words should have returned some of my dignity, I didn't buy his sudden change of nature. And I didn't thank him. I held his gaze then went out the door.

My skin started to cool as I climbed the stairs. From the third floor came thumps and mumbling—Stuart, no doubt packing. Once on the second floor, I went into my bedroom and shut the door.

Nerves jumped beneath my skin. The need to flee raced with my pulse—fierce, determined and frustrated. I crossed to the window. Black towncars, limos, sedans and cabs rushed by. The occasional businessman cloaked in black and plaid scarf passed. Joggers. Dog walkers. And here I stood.

The door swung open and I turned, gasped. Stuart. His muscles bunched beneath his sweater and jeans. He stepped in and shut the door at his back, his body filling the frame.

"You're not allowed—"

"I didn't think you had the guts, Ash."

A tight pause sprang between us. "You still have to respect Daddy's rules. If he found you in here he'd—"

"I don't have to follow the rules anymore." His low voice crept along my shivering skin. "I don't work here. Thanks to you." He started toward me. "You had to know I wouldn't go without screwing your little attempt at freedom. Especially when you got me fired. You're never going to have your own life, not as long as Charles is alive."

"That's not true!"

"Truth hurts, doesn't it?" He snickered, coming closer. Panic raced up my throat. "Daddy's little princess isn't going anywhere." He reached to touch my cheek and I slapped his hand.

"Why did you do it?" he hissed. "I've given you three years of my life. I'd do anything for you. Why?" Hurt and anger crossed his face.

"Get out."

Defeat filled his eyes. "I didn't mean to hurt your feelings. Ash, I'm so—"

"Just leave." Angry tears filled my eyes.

"I wanted to help you." He shook his head, backed toward the door until his body finally bumped into the frame. His hand wrapped around the knob, his eyes latched to mine as if clinging to every second. "Come with me."

My expression must have shown my disbelief.

"Now. Come with me. I can take you away from this insanity. Come on, Ash. It's the only way you'll—"

"Get out, Stuart!" It was naive of me to think anyone living under the same roof as Daddy, Mother and I didn't see Daddy's deep obsession with my safety. Still, it humiliated me. I turned toward the window, forcing my body not to give into tears in his presence. Minutes ticked by. Finally, the door closed softly.

———————— CHAPTER TWO

The strong tap on my door was Daddy's—his signature knock—demanding and unyielding. In the middle of a novel I was sure he'd frown upon—a romance—I turned the book over and positioned myself across the bed so it looked like I was taking a nap.

"Come in."

The door swung open. Daddy still wore his suit, though he'd loosened his necktie. The faint scent of his faded cologne tickled the air. He smiled. "Princess. Am I interrupting?"

"No, I was just resting."

He shut the door quietly, then leveled me with his penetrating eyes. "Something happened today. And I'm not talking about Stuart touching you, though that was unfortunate. Did he hurt you?"

"No." I shook my head.

"What then?"

My throat clutched. "Wh-what to you mean?"

"I saw it on your face." He started in my direction and my nerves skittered. "What happened?"

Surely my accidental run-in with Colin Brennen didn't show in my expression. I swallowed, sat upright. Daddy's keen gaze shifted, focusing on my now-exposed romance novel.

My heart pounded. He reached out, picked up the book and examined it. His silver gray eyes slid to mine. "What happened on your walk today, Ashlyn?"

Hiding anything from him was as futile as a mouse hiding cheese from a rat. My day couldn't get worse, I was already a prisoner of his obsessive fear. Maybe if I told the truth, he'd let me keep the book. "I ran into Colin Brennen."

His eyes widened for a millisecond. He took in a deep breath, looked off for a long, tense moment before his gaze met mine again. "How is he?"

My pounding heart notched up. "I passed him on the street. I don't think he recognized me."

His teeth gleamed in a smile. "How could he forget a face like yours?" He handed back the book. I took it, my face heating, fingers trembling. "Colin was, what, three or four years older than you?"

Three. The bully had rubbed the years in my face. I shrugged, keeping my focus on my book. At least Daddy let me keep it.

"How did he look?"

"Older."

Daddy chuckled and sat down next to me on the bed. "The last time you saw him you were twelve if I have my facts right."

He always had his facts right. "I don't remember."

"No matter." His tone was grave. "I wish you had come to me about Stuart when you'd first felt uncomfortable. Did he do anything, ever touch you in any way that was inappropriate or—"

"No, Daddy." I fingered the book in an effort to disguise my trembling hands. "I just didn't like—"

"Explain to me what happened."

"He just got angry, so he… was forceful."

Daddy's gaze burned a line through my chest, as if trying to open my heart and peer inside. He let out a sigh of displeasure. "That's inexcusable, but his admittance that he's fallen in love with you was enough for me to fire him."

Disgust rumbled through my system at Stuart's admission. Daddy reached out and patted my head. "I don't mean to upset you, Princess."

"Don't call me that." Long, taut pause. "Please."

Daddy's finger lifted my chin, forcing my gaze to his. "I'll forgive this excursion today, Ashlyn, and I assume you are too upset by what's happened with Stuart to give me specifics. But disrespect to your mother or me is not allowed. Understood?"

I nodded.

He rose, smiled.

"I'm too old for Princess, Daddy."

"You're still my little girl."

"I'm going to be eighteen soon."

His gaze lingered, a shadow of what looked like melancholy on his face. "Since when did you like to read romances?"

A knot formed in my throat. "Oh, not very long."

"Your mother used to enjoy those." He turned and strolled to the door. There, he paused, eyeing me over his courtroom smile. "If you'd like, we can go for a walk later."

"Maybe."

"Let me know." He opened the door, went out, turned one last time. "Love you, Princess."

Frustration bubbled beneath my skin. My cell phone vibrated from the top of the table next to my bed. I crawled over and plucked it up. Only one person texted or called me: my friend Felicity Gordon. We met at Chatham Academy when we were both freshmen. Through the years as other friends had sloughed away—my parents picking who was a safe choice—Felicity had endured. Her conservative parents and, like me, her only child status resonated with Mother and Daddy. And Felicity was not what my parents considered a social threat. Few guys looked beyond her full figure and through her glasses to see how kind and fun she was. Still, Daddy openly checked my cell phone bill for phone numbers he didn't recognize. If I wanted to keep my line to the outside world, I had to carefully screen who I connected with.

hey
wanna hang?
love to, but doubt possible daddy fired stuart.
what?????
long story
calling

My phone rang.

"The watch dog is gone?" Felicity sounded as shocked as I'd been earlier. "What brought that on?"

I looked at the photo sitting on the side table next to my bed, taken on one of the few nights I'd been allowed to have her sleep over. Felicity had brought me my romance books. Did Daddy know that? I grinned. Probably not, or Felicity might not be allowed to come over.

"I told Daddy he'd been coming on to me."

Felicity gasped, then laughed. "Oh, man, he must have been royally pissed. I'm surprised he didn't shoot the guy."

"He fired him on the spot. But get this, Stuart admitted to being in love with me. Sick."

"I knew it! Ewww. That's just wrong."

"I'm so relieved. Maybe Daddy will finally come to his senses about all of this."

Felicity snorted. "Like that will happen."

Though she meant to keep the mood light, her honest words plunged me into fear. "He has to," I said. "I'm almost eighteen. I can leave if I want then."

"Yeah, I know."

Felicity and I had had this discussion countless times when I'd been so overwhelmed I was sure I couldn't take another second of Daddy's suffocating protection. As I'd watched my peers experience firsts from the sidelines, years raced by marked in milestones I could not participate in, from crushes to employment and finally driving. I'd never even been behind a wheel. Daddy insisted I be chauffeured like royalty.

Felicity and I both dreamed and talked about our futures, college, careers—but mine was as far out of my reach as the moon. I let out a sigh. Even if I left, where would I go? I didn't have a job, no way of supporting myself. Daddy refused to let me work, unwilling to expose me to any situation outside of his control.

Once, I'd approached him about working in his office. He'd merely pondered the idea for about two seconds before telling me he preferred if I stayed home and worked on my music. I did hope to compose for musical theater or film, someday. My first piano teacher, Madame Stefan, was the one who told me I had an unusually exquisite gift for music.

"Sounds like you need me to come over," Felicity said. "Ask."

"I'll text you if he says it's okay."

"K. See ya in a few."

Hopefully.

I clicked off my phone, stood and went downstairs, passing Stuart who was carrying boxes of his belongings to the main floor. The tense air between us sent a shiver down my back. He allowed me to go down the stairs before him, and I did, breaking into a half-skip to avoid being near him.

I continued to the back of the townhouse and heard him plop the boxes on the marble floor by the front entrance.

Daddy's office doors were closed, so I knocked. The low rumble of his voice, mixed with his hearty laugh, continued. He was on the phone and probably didn't hear me. I cracked open the door and stepped inside.

The scent of leather from chairs and tufted couches filled the walnut-paneled room. Books lined the walls, mixed with framed images of himself, Mother and me and the few choice paintings of African lion wildlife he had collected. Antiques and other possessions lined shelves and stood on display.

"Bring your appetite. Yes. That's right. We'll see you Saturday." He clicked off his cell phone and slid it into his shirt pocket. He'd changed into casual camel slacks and a light sweater.

"Princess."

"Please don't call me that."

"How long have you been here? I didn't hear you come in." He moved around the side of his imposing lion-head desk. The piece had scared me as a child, massive as it was with roaring lions claws carved into the legs.

"Not long."

"Do you want to go on a walk? It's not that chilly out."

"I wondered if Felicity could come over."

He stopped in front of me, considered, seeming to draw out the moment. "After your leaving the house today? No. I'm working on a replacement for Stuart."

My heart plunged to my feet. "I don't need another bodyguard. I—"

"This topic is not open for discussion." His words banged against the paneled walls surrounding us. "We've been over this."

Frustration steamed my blood. "I'm tired of having someone breathing down my neck all time."

Daddy turned and headed back to his desk, his posture erect, his demeanor cool. He pulled open a drawer, plucked out a slim cigar. He slipped the cigar between his lips and lit the tip. A stream of smoke slithered into the air around his head.

My hands fisted at my sides. I recognized the pattern: silence. Listening, but ignoring my pleas.

I turned and walked out the door. Stuart was still bringing boxes down from the upper floor, piling them in the entry. His glare locked on me when I entered the foyer but he continued up the curving staircase until he was finally out of view.

In the depths of my pocket, my cell phone vibrated. I stood in the entry, shivering, staring at the closed front doors. It felt like the marble walls were closing in. *Run.*

My heart raced.

I crossed to the front door.

"Going for another walk?" Stuart's voice boomed behind me. I placed my hand on the ornate brass knob, turned it. "Go ahead. You don't have the guts to free yourself."

I opened the door three inches before Stuart's thick palm slammed it shut with an echoing thud. His palms clasped my shoulders and he forced me to face him.

"Take your hands off my daughter." Daddy's voice tore through the tension tying Stuart and I together. He stood beneath the arch that led to the back of the townhouse, his face tight.

Stuart released me and stuffed his hands in his front pockets.

"She was trying to leave, I thought—I knew you wouldn't want her going out alone."

Daddy's steps were slow as he came toward us. One hand was in the front pocket of his slacks, the other held a smoldering cigar. "It's too late for you to redeem yourself."

Stuart's jaw turned to stone. Hanging at his sides, his fingers opened and closed. He crossed to his stack of waiting boxes.

Daddy opened the front door and held it wide. Out front, a cab idled next to the curb. For the next three minutes, Daddy and I watched silently as Stuart took his boxes out the door and into the yellow cab. No one spoke. Sounds of cars rushing, horns , and the occasional pound of music from a car radio drifted into the townhouse. When the last box was carried out, Daddy shut the door with a final thud.

He looked into my eyes, brought the cigar to his lips, inhaled and held, his gaze never leaving mine. A shiver wrapped around my spine. I didn't appreciate his overt display of power. I might be his child, but I was tired of being owned.

"Time for that walk, Princess?"

"No." I turned and took the cold stairs up.

Unnaturally charming, Mother's voice slipped under my closed bedroom door Saturday night like the artificial scent of drug store cologne, drawing my attention from the romance novel I was reading.

A smooth male tone—not Daddy's—followed. Who was here? Then Daddy's commanding voice. I flipped the book over to save my place, stood, and opened the door a crack. Their voices came from the foyer.

"You look absolutely wonderful," Mother said.

"Thank you, Mrs. Adair."

"Glad you could come. It certainly has been too long," Daddy said. "Come in. I'll get Ashlyn."

My heart leapt to my throat and lodged. The new bodyguard?

I shut the door, pressed my back against the wood and closed my eyes.

Seconds later, Daddy's firm knock caused me to jump. I turned and opened the door. His silver-blue eyes smiled into mine. "Ashlyn, can you come into the my office please?"

I rolled my eyes and Daddy's smile vanished.

"Is there a problem?" he asked.

"I don't want another bodyguard."

Daddy moved into the low-lit hall, indicating I should exit my bedroom. I didn't move. "Our guest is here. You're making him wait."

My knees locked. "I won't."

Daddy's eyes widened for a second. I crossed my arms. Daddy studied me, then smiled—a practiced move I was certain he'd used countless times with countless juries. He patted my shoulder. "Fine. I'll bring him up here."

He turned and disappeared down stairs.

A man in my bedroom? Daddy never allowed bodyguards inside my bedroom. The last thing I wanted was a stranger stepping into my sanctuary—the only place I felt truly alone and protected.

I shut the door and half-skipped down the marble stairs on Daddy's tail. He glanced at me over his shoulder. He knew I wouldn't want a stranger in my bedroom. His threat was a manipulation, I was sure of it, and frustration quickened my steps.

Mother's voice danced with the male timbre of the guest's, the intriguing melodic sound coming from the open doors of Daddy's office. Daddy slipped his arm around me once my feet hit the floor of the entry hall. He stopped me with a gentle hug.

"Thank you for indulging your father." He brought me to his side and kissed the top of my head. My heart softened a little. "I know you're not happy about having another companion, Ashlyn. But this is as much for my peace of mind as it is for your safety." He held me between his palms and looked me square in the eyes. "I promise this one will be the last."

The last? I didn't dare hope his words were true. "I don't need--"

His fingers cupped my chin. "If you really feel that strongly about this, we can talk about it later."

I couldn't deny he loved me. That was the reason he did what he did. "You have to trust me, Daddy. I can take care of myself."

He nodded. "It's not you I worry about. It's other people."

I gripped his wrists. "I won't do anything without clearing it with you and Mother first, I promise, just—"

"I know you won't," he nodded. "You and I can have a more in depth discussion later. I want you to meet your new companion."

My feet rooted to the marble beneath them. "You hired him already? Without letting me meet him first?"

"We've talked briefly about the situation. He's very interested. Come meet him."

———————— CHAPTER THREE

Mother faced us, her ivory skin glowing against her emerald green sweater and slacks. The stranger's back was toward us. He wore jeans and a black sweater. His tall, lean form, his black mussed hair sparked a memory in my head. When Mother's flirtatious eyes shifted to Daddy and me, the stranger turned.

My breath stalled.

Colin Brennen.

Dimples flashing, he grinned, shooting a sparkling of white into the room. His charisma bounced off the walls of the room like a captured star.

Mother moved to his side, threading her arm through his. "Ashlyn, you remember Colin, don't you?"

Daddy's placed a palm at my shoulder, urging me to move closer. "Of course she remembers him."

Colin extended a hand and stepped my direction. "Hey, Ashlyn. Good to see you again."

I opened my mouth, but nothing came out.

"Let's have none of this. Come now. Friends embrace when they see each other." Mother's hands waved, gesturing for Colin and me to move closer. Suddenly he was flush against me, his warmth heating me from head to toe. Citrus cologne drove a twinge through my body.

Colin's arms enveloped me. I froze, my stomach a jumble of tightening knots. His body was solid as an oak against mine. My heart banged out of rhythm, my feet itched to back away.

Daddy's gaze sharpened, but his practiced smile remained in place.

Colin released me and stepped back. He'd no doubt hugged zillions of girls—an encounter like this wouldn't faze him at all. I swallowed, hoping the blockage in my throat would go away, but his eyes, endlessly black and locked on mine, paralyzed me.

"Isn't this simply marvelous, you two reunited?" Mother gushed. "Let's catch up over dinner shall we? There's so much to talk about. We'll start with you, Colin." With that, Mother took Colin's arm, squeezing in close. "I hope you're hungry. Our chef Gavin is world-class."

My stomach, still knotted, didn't allow me to digest dinner.

Mother suggested I sit directly across from Colin, a strategic move I didn't appreciate. Every time I lifted my gaze—to pat my linen napkin at my lips or sip water—Colin's intense eyes pinned me to my seat. Nerves tied my muscles into unresponsive bundles. I didn't even know what was being said—only catching scattered sentences: that Colin was attending NYU; he was studying accounting and had had a hard time finding a job. Then, Colin set down his fork.

"Ashlyn, what have you been up to?" he asked.

I met his penetrating gaze. "Not much."

"Oh, come now darling." Mother's face gleamed. "Colin, she's too modest to say but she's a very gifted composer. She's going to graduate first in her class from Chatham and she's already been awarded the Golden Trust award for excellence. She's got Julliard knocking on her door."

"Yes. Ashlyn is exceptional," Daddy added. "She'll play for you later, won't you, Princess?"

A dense silence followed. I was sure my pounding heart could be heard over the thickening tension. Mother and Daddy routinely bragged about me to their friends, but with Colin—an old next door neighbor who used to bully and torment me—I felt like I was splayed on the table for vivisecting. I kept my gaze on my plate, spoon tearing into the delicate meringue clouds until they were nothing but mush.

"Of course she will," Mother said. "What do you think of our Ashlyn, Colin? Isn't she marvelous?"

My eyes flashed to Mother. Fiery heat burned my neck and cheeks. Why was she asking him such an outrageous question?

"Yes, she is, Fiona," Colin said.

Mother pushed her barely eaten plate of dessert aside. "It's so wonderful having you here. It brings back so many memories. Remember all of those imaginative games you used to play as children?"

I hardly considered them games.

"I'd never heard such scenarios—from pirates to slaves in haunted castles. Remember those, darling?" Mother looked at me, waiting for a response.

"Yes." My voice came out an embarrassingly weak whisper. "I remember." *I'd been the slave.*

Daddy lifted a gold box sitting next to his place setting, opened it and extended the array of cigars to Colin, who shook his head. Then, he plucked a cigar, put it in his mouth and lit it. "Do you still run?" Daddy closed the box and set it on the table.

"When I can." Colin's curious gaze skipped from Daddy to Mother to me. "How did you know?"

"I seem to remember you ran track in high school. Sounds like you could use more personal time for yourself."

I wasn't surprised Daddy had checked Colin's background. What I couldn't believe was that he was considering hiring someone he knew I despised as my bodyguard. I'd grown to hate Stuart. Now Colin?

"How much time does Phil spend on the golf course, now that he's retired from the Marines? " Daddy asked.

Colin grinned. "As much time as he can."

"We hope you'll join our family, Colin," Mother chattered. "Ashlyn's simply a doll to be around. Having a friend here will be just wonderful. You know us and we know you. There'll be no awkward moments between us. Isn't that a fabulous thing?"

"Princess." Daddy sat forward, eyes pinned to mine. "Take Colin up and show him the view from the roof."

Alone? With Colin? My nerves twisted. "Are you sure you don't want to come along?"

Daddy inhaled his cigar, then held, allowing the moment to smoke. "You take him," he said, white plumes hissing out with his words.

Colin's dark eyes were waiting for mine. The idea of him watching me sent a foreign fluttering through my body.

"Yes, sir." I stood, tossed my napkin down and silently turned to lead Colin out of the room.

Colin followed me up the winding stairway, our shoes echoing against frigid marble. What to say to someone you never liked? I remained silent, jittery, his presence pressing into my back.

"This place is huge," he murmured. "Reminds me of the Haunted Mansion at Disneyland."

We'd gone to Disneyland together once. Colin and I had shared most every ride, being the only children. The memory raced through my head like a rollercoaster. He'd dared me to ride the Matterhorn until I finally gave in, and sat with me in the front. "I'll take care of her," he'd said to our parents who waited for us at the ride's exit. Once we were strapped into the bobsled, he proceeded to tell me horror stories of kids falling to their deaths, giggling at my terrified reaction. He'd screamed along with me on the fast turns and head-whipping drops of the ride.

And when it was all over, he dared me to ride again, even as I fought to hold back gurgling nausea.

Finally, we reached the top floor of the townhouse. The long hall, lined with closed doors, spanned the width of the building. I stopped at the middle door and opened it. A small, narrow staircase awaited us.

"Wow," he said.

Everyone was impressed with the early Gothic architectural detail adorning the townhouse. The building—nestled between modern apartment buildings—was on the New York Historical List.

I climbed the narrow stair first and he followed. The space seemed to squeeze us together.

At the top of the stairs I tapped in the security code and opened the door. We came out on the flat, brick rooftop fenced by scrolling black wrought iron that edged the roof line in a lacy pattern, each post topped with spikes. Potted trees and winter-hushed plants were scattered here and there, and a heavily scrolled patio set sat near the edge for viewing the city.

Colin went to the railing and looked out. In spite of my frazzled nerves, the cold air, the view of scuttling cars on Park Avenue was exhilarating.

He turned to face me, and I stepped back. "This is incredible. Do you come up here much?"

"Yes."

"Are you okay?" His dark brows knit over concerned eyes.

I heard sincerity in his question, but didn't trust it. "I'm fine." I'd learned to say, in spite of what I really felt.

My cage closed tighter.

Leaning his back against the rail, Colin eyed me instead of the view. I remained fixed by the door. Moonlight showered him in extreme blacks and bluish white. I was reminded of the night he'd locked me in the Brennen pool house, swearing the cloistered building was haunted by the soul of the previous resident who'd supposedly hung himself inside the place. I shuddered away the memory.

His eyes sharpened. "I could have sworn I bumped into you downtown earlier this week."

"I'm rarely downtown." I looked away. A long, chilly moment passed.

"Tell me about you," he said. "You're what, a senior this year?"

I turned, pretending to examine the brick walls of the townhouse so he couldn't see my flushed face. The rough, cold blocks scratched my fingertips. "Yes."

"What are your plans after? Have you got your eye on any colleges?"

College? Julliard was Mother and Daddy's first choice. I'd secretly wanted to go back to California—my birthplace—and far away from New York, but Daddy had only approved of me sending applications to colleges in the city. "Yes, I have."

"Which ones?"

I shot him a glare. His bottomless brown eyes held mine without excuse for inquiring. Cold silence whipped the air between us. He started my direction, and my heart stuttered. I stepped back, feeling cold brick press into my spine.

He stopped so close the citrus scent of his cologne wafted through my head. Blood shivered in my veins. I couldn't answer him or snap at him if I wanted to, too stunned he still had paralyzing power over me.

"Ashlyn?" His voice lanced through my paralysis.

I swallowed. Opened my mouth. I wanted to slap myself for not having more composure. The heroines in my books had composure. Why couldn't I say something sassy? I closed my eyes a moment, hoping that by not looking into his eyes I could come up with some quippy remark.

When I finally looked at him, his brows tightened across his forehead. "Aren't you going to school? Fiona mentioned Julliard."

"Yes. Of course," I sputtered. "Everyone goes to college." I just hadn't decided because in my heart of hearts, I'd only focused on one next step—freedom.

"You going to major in music?"

His closeness was almost unbearable, causing my knees to go numb. "Yes, probably. Maybe."

He laughed, tossing his head back. "You sound like the typical anxious senior with the world at her feet." He shoved his hands in his front pockets and strolled to the edge of the patio to take in the view again. "You shouldn't ignore any possibility."

I gulped in a breath, stealing the moment to study him. Only scant resemblances remained of the boy I'd known. His eyes no longer seemed to dance with mischief; his wicked grin was just a smile. He was taller and lean under his suburbanesque clothes. How Mother had overlooked his mega-department store ensemble was laughable, except to say she was willing to ignore his poor taste in clothing—for the time being.

Trailing the black rail with my fingers, I inched in his direction, the cold metal making me shiver, my breath blowing plumes into the air. With each step closer to him, I breathed deeper, wondering if his aura would sink into me. Testing my heart for its new reaction to him.

"Take your time figuring out where you want to go and what you want to do. That's what this time of life is about." He glanced my way, and his eyes remained fastened to mine. "You sure you weren't downtown earlier this week?"

I shook my head. Pleasure trickled through me. He *had* noticed.

"It's cold," he said, moving toward me. "Let's go inside."

We ventured back down the tapered stair and once again were in the darkened hall of the top floor.

"This is where the help stays," I said. *Where you would stay.* The thought of him relegated to the status of help sent a delicious trickle of power through me. I made it halfway down the flight of stairs before he paused in front of my life-sized portrait. Stuart had drooled over the painting, the look in his eye causing my stomach to roll. Colin's head tilted and his gaze swept the painting but I didn't see any lust in his eyes. More study. A warm sensation flooded me from head to toe, almost as though I stood under his inspection, rather than an oil paint likeness.

I cleared my throat.

"This is beautiful," he said. "When was it done?"

Why did I tremble inside when he looked at me? I took a deep breath. "Two years ago." I started down the stairs.

He didn't move.

I continued on, clearing my throat again.

When he finally caught up to me, we were on the main floor,

heading back to the dining room. His fingers grazed my elbow. "How do you feel about me working for your father?"

My elbow singed as if burned. I tried to steady my frantic heart. "Well, I… you… it's you're decision. It's your life." I turned. At that moment, I was relieved Mother and Daddy were only a few feet away.

———————— CHAPTER FOUR

Up and down the piano keys my fingers pounded scales, a habitual exercise I engaged in for therapeutic reasons as well as for fine tuning my craft. I let out a slow breath. When I'd exhausted myself, my gaze lifted from the ivory and black keys. Daddy stood quietly by the door. I slammed out the rest of the exercise, too angry to acknowledge him.

He crossed to me, a cigar in one hand; the other he kept tucked in the front pocket of his slacks. "Was that display your way of telling me that you don't want Colin here?" He remained standing, shooting his stare down at me. Sucking in some smoke, he held it. "He's always been harmless." He blew the gray plume out the side of his lips.

My fingers played with the keys, creating a soft, light melody. I said what he wanted to hear: "Of course Daddy."

Listening to the strains in my head, feeling waves of emotion lightly stroking my heart, I let the melody take me to another place—a place of solace and privacy, of relief from the overbearing attention focused on me. The tune was romantic and sweet, though it was Colin's face drifting through my mind.

"The fact is you should have outgrown this dislike of Colin a long time ago."

"Of course."

"Will you work on this?" Daddy stepped closer.

I nodded, my fingers continuing to glide along the keys, the melody deepening with haunting tones.

"I've hired him. He's perfect for the job."

Perfect? I detested him. And how was he perfect for the job? He

ıe FBI. If I argued with Daddy about his
mature enough to move on and handle
storm inside of me, I continued playing
head. Daddy watched my hands move over
ʒak a language he could never understand. I

.d out of the room and shut the door behind
him. I farı.   ɔitter smoke out of range and continued to play.
The melody haɑ taken over, was growing and swelling within me. I
heard notes yet to be played as well as those that simultaneously
came from the tips of my fingers. In my mind I saw Colin— the way
he'd looked at me across the room when I'd first walked in. His
eyes—the color of rich espresso, smiling and sparkling at the same
time.

With yearning fingers, the song reached deep into my soul. I
thought of when his arms had wrapped around me. The memory
sent a pleasant yet unfamiliar stirring through me, causing the tune to
take a dramatic turn.

I yanked my hands from the keys.

Irritated with the fluttering, I pushed away from the piano. How
could I create such a beautiful piece with thoughts of someone who
had been the source of such misery?

I jerked to my feet, rubbing my arms to ward off a chill. But the
chill wasn't real. Underneath the bumps covering my flesh, warmth
flurried.

The window beckoned, and I crossed to it. Often, the view of
the city calmed and comforted me. Alive even at the late hour, the
neighborhood trickled with people whose lives I could observe and
wish for their freedom.

Colin was out there. He would become a part of my life again.

With a finger I traced the outline of a pane. In spite of fears,
the melody echoed inside, crying from within the recesses of my
soul. Billowing, wave after wave; it became a force I couldn't ignore.
I paced next to the piano until my creative side won out and, afraid
of losing the tune, I sat down and scribbled the notes and chords on

paper.

I hadn't been this enthused about a piece in a long time. Every cell bubbled and burst. The race of instruments began, mingled, and peaked in my head, the melody traveling through every cell of my body before shooting out of my fingers in harmonious strain. Whatever else became of the evening, whatever the future held even though the past we shared was tumultuous, opposition created the most beautiful masterpieces.

From the moment Colin entered the townhouse, the air, the mood, the scent of home became infused with his magnetic aura. As if one of the bright signs on Times Square had been dropped into our living quarters, its light penetrating and lightening every hall and room with enthusiastic color you couldn't ignore. Part of me was annoyed by his charisma. Another part of me was jealous I wasn't the same way—drawing people to me for reasons they didn't understand.

The following afternoon, I heard the front door shut, followed by Daddy's charming tone, then Colin's melted crème voice. The sound wound up the stairs, slipped under my closed door, and swirled around my body, causing a tingling sensation to sparkle from my head to my toes.

I took one last look in the mirror. My pale skin had pinked at the sound of his voice. A grin tried to work its way onto my mouth, twisting my lips upward. *Why are you reacting like this to him?* The white velour workout outfit I wore only made me look paler, but I didn't care. I wanted to soak up some sun. I grabbed my romance novel and opened my bedroom door, headed to the rooftop patio.

Daddy's voice and Colin's foreign presence—invisible yet strong as a waft of seductive cologne—greeted me in the hallway. Daddy was dressed in casual khaki slacks and a designer plaid shirt in Christmas greens.

Colin wore jeans and a light blue shirt and had a jacket tucked under his arm. His arms weren't as hairy as Stuart's. I disliked excess body hair on men—I'd always told Daddy so.

"Colin's here, Princess," Daddy said.

Colin's brown eyes sparkled. "Hey, Ashlyn."

Daddy's gaze gleamed with pleasure. He leaned and kissed my cheek. "Ashlyn isn't fond of my insistence that she be protected," he explained.

Colin's hands wrapped tighter around the two suitcases he held. "I can understand that." He rocked back on his heels. "Don't worry, Ash, I won't crowd you."

Heat flashed to my cheeks. "Oh." My gaze went to my feet. My brain stumbled over words when I was in Colin's presence.

"Ashlyn, why don't you to show him around? Give you two a chance to get to know each other again."

"Uh…" I swallowed. "I was just on my way up to the patio to read."

"It's cold outside." Daddy's gaze skimmed my clothing. "I'd appreciate it if you could show Colin the house." *In other words, stay in.*

I hardened my gaze. "Okay. But afterwards, I'm going to read on the patio."

"Is that Colin I hear?" Mother blustered across the hall from the her bedroom. Her Chanel running suit warmed her wrinkleless complexion to silk against her auburn hair. Her arms extended, she fastened her eyes on Colin and wrapped him in a hug.

"Fiona. Nice to see you again."

"Lovely, isn't it?" Mother drew back, her hands remaining on Colin's arms. "That color is fabulous on you, dear boy." Her scan slowly swept him in an appraisal that left Colin shifting feet. "We might have to do a bit of clothes shopping."

Colin swallowed. He glanced at me as if to verify Mother's comment. I kept my face void of confirmation.

"Ashlyn's going to show Colin the house." Daddy produced a cigar, broke off the tip and held the cigar ready at his lips. "I'll be in the library. Colin, after you've unpacked, come down and we'll talk."

Colin nodded.

Daddy excused himself and headed downstairs.

"If there is anything you need, let me know." Mother's right hand remained glued to Colin's bicep, her other floated expressively in the air around her as she spoke. "I've had the room cleaned and everything is like new. Make yourself at home."

Colin's contagious smile flashed. "I will, thank you."

Mother's hand slid slowly down Colin's arm to his wrist and lingered. "And I'd be happy to have Gavin pick up a few of your staples for the kitchen. Anything you like to eat, just give me a list. All right?"

"Great. Thank you."

Why a twinge of discomfort lodged in my stomach, I didn't know. Mother had been friendly with Stuart at first, but over the years had come to practically ignore him. Colin accepted her cordial hostessing and Mother excused herself.

Colin's bright smile met my gaze. "So, where to from here?"

I turned, relieved that his enigmatic aura was out of my line of vision, even if only temporarily, and led him up the next flight of stairs. Was he watching me? Examining my hair? My butt? How close was he? My nerves jangled.

I escorted him to Stuart's old room, which Mother had had our cleaning service scour from floor to ceiling. The room had a single dormer window that kept the space in perpetual shade, but what did he expect? He still had a nice view of Park Avenue. The room was furnished with a queen sized bed, dresser, oversized chair, and tasteful lamps. A few silk plants and a wide-screen TV made the room homey.

I stepped inside. "This is it."

He crossed to the bed, and a soft clean scent breezed by me. He plopped the suitcases and his jacket on the mattress and went to the window, the A-frame of the dormer barely tall enough for him to stand in. "Another great view."

He turned, his gaze meeting mine. "This is nice." Hands on his hips, he moved to the center of the room, surveying. "So, the other guy stayed here? What was his name, Stuart?"

I nodded, suppressing a cringe.

"You were glad to see him go, I take it?"

"Why do you say that?"

"The look on your face just now. You two didn't get along?"

I took in a deep breath. "Not really."

His piercing gaze was so tight on my face, I had to look away. "Anyway, this is the room," I said. "The bathroom is down the hall. If you'll follow me."

He chuckled. I started out the door, the hair on the back of my neck standing upright because he was so very close.

"You miss California at all?" he asked.

"I hardly remember it," I lied.

"Palos Verdes is still the same. Man, I miss the beach. The views here are great, don't get me wrong. But the coastal views… I miss not being able to park up on Via Del Monte and just sit and stare at the coast, all the way up to Malibu. You know?"

I remembered. Early afternoon, when the fog finally slunk back out to sea and the view from our house in Malaga Cove stretched for miles showing off curved beach line, Pacific Ocean and endless city, the sight was a cause to take a deep breath and hold it, hoping the view would last more than a day.

"Do any other employees live here?" He eyed the closed doors lining the hall.

"No. Our cleaning service comes in three times a week. Gavin lives in Brooklyn. Eddy, our chauffer, lives in Queens."

"I see."

"There's a den here." I paused at another open door and let him peer into the room Stuart had used to hang out. A plasma TV hung on one wall, complete with gaming options. Couches sat in an inviting L-shape, a walnut coffee table between them. This room also had a dormer window, but the view faced the towering apartment buildings behind the townhouse.

"Your dad's obviously doing very well." Colin scratched his head and let out a chuckle. "This place is… really spectacular."

I lifted my shoulders. I was used to visitors being taken in by an opulence I now passed by with second nature.

Uncomfortable with us sharing the close space, I left the den and went out into the hall for a breath. Colin followed, his scan taking in each door.

He stopped at the one that led to the roof and touched the security keypad. "Every exit on the same code?"

I nodded. "Daddy will have you change it once a month for security."

Colin continued down the hall, eyeing windows and casings. "Is that the only way in up here?"

"Yes."

"Mind if I take a look at it in the daylight?"

"Sure." I recited the code. He continued to the roof exit, entered the security code and opened the door. This time, I followed him up the steep stairway. He had a nice body, but I felt ashamed watching him. *So what, he probably stared at you. Get over it.*

Unlike me, he seemed unaware that I was behind him and that I might be taking the time to check him out—like I had felt him do. He was probably used to girls staring at him. The thought registered a frown on my face, a frown I quickly dissolved, disliking that I'd even had the thought.

On the patio, he set his hands on his hips as his gaze swept the rooftop area. A soft breeze always sung between the tall buildings, and the current lifted the dark hair from his face.

He crossed to the corners, looked over the edge and then upward at the tall apartments flanking us. "Has the emergency ladder been kept in working order?"

I shrugged. I had no idea—security had been Stuart's job. His sweeping gaze finally settled on me. His midnight eyes sent a fluttering through my system. Would I ever not have a reaction to them?

"Has it? Or do you know?" He started toward me, his gait as confident as it had been when we were children and he'd been intent on making my day miserable if he felt like it.

For a second, I couldn't speak. He stopped inches away, waiting for my reply.

"Uh…" *You sound like an idiot. Don't let him think he still gets to you.* "I'm pretty sure it is. But you'll have to ask Daddy."

I turned and took the stairs down, relieved when my feet hit the hard wood inside.

I crossed to his bedroom and heard him close the roof door sometime later. He studied the hall again on his way. He passed me in the door jamb, his lips curving up a little when he brushed by. "The other rooms up here, can I see them sometime?"

"Sure, they're not locked."

He opened his suitcases and let out a sigh. "Guess I should unpack."

There was a knock at the open door. With a swish of fabric and a wave of perfume, Mother sashayed in. "Knock, knock…" She surveyed the area with a smile. "I just wanted to make sure everything was satisfactory."

"It's fine, thanks," Colin said.

Floating directly to his suitcase, her long fingers combed through his wardrobe. "This will never do. Ashlyn cannot be seen with anything less than a man who is completely put together. If *Socialite* got a photo of this… well. We'll shop this afternoon. Meet me at three o'clock in the main foyer." She grazed past him, her shoulder brushing his arm as she swiveled to the door. A trickle of discomfort and embarrassment caused me to itch at her behavior. She paused, grinned. "I'm so glad you're here. It's just like old times, isn't it?"

With some major exceptions—like the fact that Colin and I weren't kids anymore.

Mother swiveled out the door.

Colin's cheeks had pinked from Mother's visit. He scratched the back of his head, something I'd seen him do before when he seemed uncomfortable. "Is she serious about taking me clothes shopping?" His voice squeaked.

I suppressed a smile. Why did his discomfort cause me to feel vindicated somehow? "I'm afraid she is."

Colin glanced at the jeans and blue sweater he wore. "I've been told I have lame taste in clothes."

"Mother's very particular." She was more than particular. She was an unabashed snob about what she wore, Daddy wore, and I wore. Anyone seen with us—who she could control—wouldn't be seen in anything less than designer perfection.

"Wow." Colin shrugged. "Okay then." His grin sparkled like a rising sun. "You'll come, right?"

——————— **CHAPTER FIVE**

The melody arranged itself in my mind.

After pulling on my pink robe, I secured my hair in a claw at the back of my head. It was past midnight, the grandfather clock chimed two. But I had to play.

The music room welcomed me, its double doors spread wide like open arms. After entering, I closed them, even though the music would carry. The need to play pulsed through my veins, and I abandoned concern for satisfaction. Thoughts of the day rambled through my mind flashing pictures of Colin, of being out in the city. I couldn't remember when I'd had so much fun shopping. No traces of the old Colin seemed to exist. Even though Mother preened and primped and fluttered around him like a peacock, he had patiently endured her hours of insistence that he try on dozens of pieces. He'd been accommodating, charming and agreeable. I'd watched with speechless admiration.

My fingers tapped over the cool ivory keys. Music filled the room now: a slow, delicate melody that forced me to close my eyes and completely submit to wherever the tune took me. Images of Colin filled my thoughts, spun around my heart, and flowed to my fingertips, a melody so overpowering I dismissed any negative thoughts attempting to enter my mind. My heart lured me in a mysterious direction, and Colin was at its center. Tonight, I was willing to go there.

So taken by the sweetness of the creation, I was startled by a movement when at last I opened my eyes. My fingers stalled.

Colin.

He wore black sweats and a long sleeved tee shirt in black, the color electrifying. With the hushed stealth of a panther, he crossed to the piano.

"That was amazing," he whispered.

Flustered, I quickly tapped *Fur Elise* on the keys.

"Oh, I'm sorry. I thought you were done."

"I... I am." I felt exposed—naked. He'd witnessed something so deeply personal, something he had been the inspiration for. Could he see that? The idea flushed me with embarrassment.

He came closer, as if wanting to see for himself the keys I used to create. "Keep playing. Please."

I took a deep breath. I reached for some sheet music paper to make notes, wishing he'd leave but glad he was there at the same time.

"How do you do that—create like that?"

"I just hear it."

"I could never hear it let alone create music in some organized way. I'm impressed."

I accepted the compliment with a nod, and tight muscles began to relax. "Thank you." I pressed my fingers to the keys again.

"I *felt* the music." His eyes followed my fingers. "I guess I was exposed to another side of music."

I tried to deal with the emotions flooding my system. To be spontaneously taking him in as the tune ebbed from my soul took my heart to a dangerously vulnerable place. "I like contemporary music, too. Mom's favorite is disco."

He laughed. "I can't see your mom liking disco."

The sound of his laugh relaxed the taut muscles of my back. I continued to let the tune out, even as I stole glances at his face. The musical chords changed. The gentle expression in his brown eyes comforted my exposed nerves, and caused my fingers to find minor chords in enticing harmony.

"Dad tolerates my music," I said, fingers chasing each other up the shifting keyboard. "He'll listen because he wants to support me, but I catch him checking email on his phone a lot of the time." I replayed the tune still fresh in my head—Colin's song.

He listened, and when I finished, our eyes met. Silence echoed after the music.

My heart pounded so hard, I thought it might be visible through my robe. My robe—I forgot what I was wearing. My hair. No makeup. I was getting ready for bed when I'd been compelled to create. Aghast, my cheeks burned. I stood. Had he purposefully come in to see me like this, to catch me with my guard down?

"You reminded me of when you were little, just then," he said, joining me. "With your hair back like that."

I gathered my notes and went around the other side of the piano to avoid him. He caught up with me, skimming my arm with gentle fingers. "Is something wrong?"

"It's late. I'm going to bed." Brushing past him, I was out the door before he could say anything else.

"Ashlyn," he whispered in the darkened hall, staying right at my side. When I didn't respond, he reached for my arm. I froze and he dropped his hand. "What? What did I do?"

I swallowed. The dim lighting of the hall cast half of his face in a soft light. Had he really forgotten how he'd treated me? Did he think I had forgotten?

I continued to my bedroom, ready to bolt inside, ready to slam the door in his face, but he stepped into the opening.

"I don't understand. Did I say something wrong about your music? I'm sorry." His expression twisted in confusion.

My pounding heart wouldn't slow. His presence boomed with his every breath, each flash of his eyes. I'd read scenes like this in my romance novels. The heroine cornered by the hero, the two of them locked in a love hate heat.

Colin's hands lifted, and held in the door jamb. "Whatever I did," he said softly, "I apologize. I really enjoyed your music. I—"

"This isn't about my music," I blurted.

He cringed, glancing around as if to signal to me that my voice was too loud and might carry. His expression shifted from confused to sober, and his brown eyes stared into mine. I couldn't feel my heart beating. I wasn't sure I was even breathing.

"What's wrong?" His whisper slipped into my soul, just like it had countless times before, and wound around my tender heart.

"You really don't know?" I forced sarcasm into my tone.

He shook his head.

I finally had the moment to hurt him, or try to, like he'd hurt me so many times before. But when I thought about bringing up the way he'd teased me, I realized how childish I would sound.

He waited, his hands tightening on the wood. He had no clue the damage he'd caused when we were children. None. I was baffled. How does someone trudge through life so narcissistic that they toss people and their feelings aside without care or thought or comeuppance? Or was I over sensitive, taking good-natured teasing too seriously?

"Forget it. You need to leave," I said, frustration bubbling.

"But I don't know what I… Ash, please talk about this."

"You can't be in here. It's a rule. Daddy's rule. He'll fire you."

Surprise flashed across Colin's face. "Charles was serious?"

I nodded.

"Then let's take this back to the music room."

"I'm going to bed." I crossed to the door and wrapped my hand around the knob.

Colin didn't move. His eyes narrowed. I locked my knees, refusing to be the first to concede. Hot seconds popped by. The rise of his chest gradually grew more rapid beneath his black tee shirt.

He swallowed. "So, we're good then?"

I nodded.

He reached for the knob, his warm fingers enfolding mine, eyes never leaving me, and he brought the door closed.

I stared at the door. A twinge of pleasure echoed inside of me.

I dreamed of him that night. Instead of walking out my bedroom door, he pressed me against it, and kissed me. His body was strong, warm. His hands—those long fingers—touched my face, skimmed my neck then wound around me. So tight.

I woke with a longing that lingered in my body in an unattainable, delicious gnaw. When I got out of bed, I felt light. I stared at my silly smile in the mirror and covered my pink cheeks with my hands. *You're seriously pathetic.*

Colin's dream kiss played over and over in my head, like his melody. I showered quickly, threw on my uniform so fast I almost forgot to button the blue and green plaid knee skirt after I zipped it. I tore into the dry cleaning bag covering my white blouse and slipped on the crisp shirt.

I flat-ironed my blonde hair, brushed some tulip-pink blush on my cheeks and sprayed my favorite perfume at the nape of my neck and my wrists.

Above, I heard movement. Colin's room was directly over mine, and the thought sent a tingle through me, stirring the insatiable hunger the dream had left behind. Was he getting dressed? After the shopping spree, my imagination easily conjured him slipping in—and especially out—of clothes.

I took the stairs down to the entry, glancing up to see if Colin would emerge. He didn't.

Mother slept in, so I ate breakfast alone. Stuart had waited for me in the kitchen. Lately, he'd even gone so far as to toast a bagel for me and pour me a glass of chocolate soy milk. I'd grown to hate mornings and breakfast, feeling obligated to eat what he prepared whether I wanted the meal or not.

What would Colin eat for breakfast? Excitement drifted through me and I stepped into the walk-in pantry in search of a box of Kashi cereal.

"Health nut, huh?" Colin's chipper voice came from behind me, causing me to jump.

"Uh, yeah." How had he made it into the small space without me hearing him? He didn't move, only grinned.

A few seconds later, his gaze swept the pantry shelves, but his body remained blocking the entrance. Delicious fantasies of his kiss against my bedroom door drizzled into my head, causing my cheeks to heat.

"Excuse me." I squeezed past him, his shoulder pressing briefly into my chest as I turned and slid by.

Out in the opening of the kitchen, I let out a breath and gathered my thoughts. Bowl. Soy milk. Spoon. I collected all three and sat at the black granite counter top.

"Wow. This pantry looks like Dean and deLuca. Impressive."

I smiled around a chew.

"Maybe I'll have caviar on toast, or… hmm, Scottish oatmeal? Or one of these bagels. I'll bet there's cream cheese in that massive fridge over there, right?" He turned, his dimpled smile lighting the white kitchen with even more brilliance.

He wore a pair of black slacks and a black sweater, the hint of a light blue shirt skimming the collar around his neck. "What? Is this too dressy?" He gestured to his clothing. "Your mom picked it out."

He looked… hot in all black. "No. You do realize that you're only escorting me to school. You're not coming to my classes."

"Repeat high school? I hated it the first go round. I'll wait in an obscure corner somewhere."

Through the years, Daddy had insisted my bodyguards stay at whichever school I was attending, and they all had—sitting in the lobby with the newspaper or a laptop until I was finished.

One other girl had had a father as paranoid as mine: Sophie Caruletta, whose father was supposedly linked to organized crime. In seventh grade, our bodyguards had stood like sentinels outside the gray-stone exterior of Our Mother of Holies School for Girls until the two of us emerged at the end of each day, both of us whisked away in our black town cars.

Like me, Sophie was tagged as odd. Though everyone quietly respected or feared her father, no one dared tease or mock Sophie for his extraneous efforts at protecting her.

However, my father was simply a lawyer—albeit a successful one. Lots of my classmates' fathers were lawyers and none of them had bodyguards following their children's every move like me, which left me in the center of the 'bizarre' target.

Stuart, being younger than previous 'fatherly-aged' bodyguards, had taken me from being odd to interesting because lots of the girls at Chatham thought he was hot. A few of the more aggressive girls had baited him on a daily basis, coming out of the building ripping off their coats, tucking their blouses in a tie at their midriff and unbuttoning until their colorful bras peeked out.

Would they be as brazen with Colin?

He'd settled on a box of Shredded Wheat—Daddy's morning ritual food—and then he pointed to various cabinets, watching me for confirmation of which one held the bowls.

When he finally pointed to the right one, I hid a grin behind a mouthful of cereal. He pulled out a bowl, eyeing it. He whistled. "Nice."

Joining me at the island counter, he gingerly placed the bowl down. "You sure we can eat off this stuff?"

I nodded. "It's our everyday china."

"That's right." He shook Shredded Wheat squares into the bowl. "I seem to remember gold plates in the dining room." He grinned, poured milk.

"Mother likes everything just so."

He spooned a bite of cereal into his mouth, nodded. "I can see that."

The sound of rustling drew my attention to the door. Mother, fully made up and dressed in a lush, apricot velveteen workout suit fluttered in. Her emerald eyes latched on Colin. "Good morning."

Mother never got up before eleven. Gavin didn't come into the townhouse until nine, and the cleaning service didn't come until after noon so as to allow Mother the time she needed to prepare privately.

Colin swallowed. "Morning."

"You look marvelous." Mother circled Colin. I couldn't believe she was looking at him so critically, so unabashedly. She flicked at his shoulders, smoothed his sweater down his arms and back.

Colin's eyes widened, but she didn't see them. He looked like he was going to choke on the cereal in his mouth but he swallowed it down.

"Very nice." Mother stood back, appraising him. "How did you sleep?"

"I slept fine, thank you."

"Good." Her gaze slid to me. "Darling, you have circles under your eyes." She came to me and reached out to press her hands to my cheeks but I stood, grabbed my bowl and headed for the kitchen sink.

"Are you feeling all right?" Mother asked. "I don't want you going to school if you're at all under the weather, not with the flu going around. I'm sure they don't sanitize the knobs and surfaces like they should at that place." Mother shuddered.

I dumped my remaining cereal down the garbage disposal. "I'm fine."

"Charles gave you your instructions about Ashlyn and school?" Mother's attention shifted back to Colin and a wave of relief coursed through me.

Caught in the middle of chewing, he nodded.

"Mrs. Harrington is the headmistress of Chatham. She's very good about accommodating our wishes for Ashlyn's safety."

I cringed. "Mother." A low burn of rage started at my feet and raced up my legs and through my body. "It's ridiculous that you go to these lengths. It's embarrassing."

Mother froze, eyeing me through a cold stare. Colin's chewing stopped. He glanced from Mother to me.

"Your safety is not open for discussion, young lady."

Young lady? I wanted to scream. My fists opened and closed at my sides. I glared at her. "I'll be waiting by the front door," I growled, then stormed from the room.

Humiliation flooded me. I wanted to break through the front door and never come back. I opened the coat closet and retrieved my book bag, yanking it over my head so the strap crossed my chest. Then I flipped my hair over my shoulders and let out another growl of frustration.

"It's so embarrassing," I muttered, adjusting my skirt. I dug for my powder compact, opened it and dabbed my chin and forehead. "They have *no* idea."

"You ready?"

I turned. Colin stood with his hands in his front pockets. Had he heard my grumblings? This couldn't get worse. "Yes," I mumbled. "You eat fast."

"When I need to, yeah," he said.

"Bye darling." Mother waltzed into the entry, her smile aimed at Colin. "Have a wonderful day."

Oh. My. Did she have any idea how ridiculous she looked?

Colin nodded in acknowledgement, his tweaked smile an obvious expression of the awkward moment. He entered the security code into the pad next to the door and a buzzer sounded. He opened the door and held it so I could pass.

"Bye you two!"

The door thudded closed and I took the stoop down to the street where Eddy, Daddy's driver, waited in our car. Colin opened the door and I slid in. He followed.

"Mornin', Miss Adair." Eddy's thick accent always warmed me inside. He wore the typical navy slacks and matching sweater with shirt and a tie tucked beneath that most drivers wore.

"Morning, Eddy." I slunk down in the leather seat, unable to shake the utter humiliation I felt.

"Hey." Colin slid forward, his hand extended over the driver's seat. "Colin Brennen."

"Pleasure to meet ya," Eddy said. He pulled into traffic. "Mr. Adair briefed me about you this morning on his way to work."

Briefed? Did Daddy ever step out of lawyer mode? Was I simply another case to him? I crossed my arms over my chest, partly to quell the frustration boiling inside of me, partly to show my displeasure. Colin eyed me from across the backseat. I felt childish, acting like a brat. Casually, I sat up and clasped my hands in my lap.

"So you're an old friend of the family?" Eddy asked.

"Yep, that I am." Colin's right leg jittered incessantly. Was he nervous? That would be a first. Soured by Mother's insensitivity, I whipped out my phone to send her a text, then thought better of it. I wouldn't put it past her to call me and lecture me on the spot. For sure she'd call Daddy, and we'd go the 'your safety is important' lecture round yet again. She might even call Colin and tell him personal things she didn't like about me—she'd done that with Stuart, telling him I wasn't capable of making a simple decision—and he'd used that against me.

"How long have you been here in New York?" Eddy asked.

"About a year now," Colin said.

"Ya like it?"

Colin's shoulders lifted. His gaze was out the tinted window. "Now that I've lived here, I see the city differently."

Eddy chuckled. "Yeah, that's New York for ya."

We drove along Park Avenue to Freemont Street in silence. I was tempted to pull my iPod out of my book bag, and would have if Stuart had been with me. That's how I'd kept him off my back for the drive to school. I watched Colin out the corner of my eye, unable to take my attention from him. His energy was raw, like having a powerful electric cable exposed, ends frayed and yet vulnerable.

His leg continued to jitter. He appeared ready to leap from the car and, what, I wasn't sure. Did he regret the job already? Had Mother's attention given him second thoughts?

He caught me watching. He remained silent, but his brown eyes stayed fastened to mine in what? Curiosity?

School was easy for me because, through the years, my narrow life made learning something to look forward to. Outside of music, English and History were my favorite subjects. I loved to dream about life outside my world, and both of those subjects facilitated my fantasies.

Knowing Colin waited for me in the school somewhere caused my mind to wander. The dream of him pressing me against the door, kissing me, streamed through my brain to the soundtrack of his aching tune. Three of my teachers took me aside after class and asked me if I was feeling ok, telling me that I looked distracted.

My cheeks heated even thinking about what my teachers must think of me to notice distraction in their perfect little student.

I couldn't wait until lunch.

Most of the other senior girls left campus for lunch, choosing to hit Joe's Deli down the street or Indian Palace on the corner. I wasn't allowed to leave, and Felicity kindly remained with me.

"It's so boring we have to stay here and eat," she mumbled. A twinge of fear trembled inside of me. Was she getting tired of living with my restraints? If she chose to take off without me, I'd be alone. The thought made my stomach crimp, yet, I could hardly blame her.

"It's ridiculous," I said. "What burns me is that everyone thinks I'm this perfect conforming student. 'She has one day of distraction and—call her parents—sound the alarm.'"

The scent of fried food and Italian seasonings filled the archaic, wood-paneled halls of Chatham as Felicity and I walked to the cafeteria.

A tingle of mischief shot through my blood. "Let's go."

Felicity came to a halt beside me. "Your dad will kill you."

"He'll fire Colin for not doing his job and I'll finally be free of all of these bodyguards." I tugged her sleeve down the hall and turned right, taking an empty corridor which led to the gated exterior of Chatham.

Felicity snorted. "Like that'll ever happen. I don't know, Ash, I love you and all, but if your dad finds out I was along for the ride and he'll probably ban us from seeing each other. Think about it."

She was right, Daddy would do just that. I stopped at the glass door and gazed out onto the cement courtyard of Chatham where groups of girls stood in clusters eating lunch. Some hung by the chain link fence, taunting the occasional high school boy or two who happened by from the private boy's school two blocks away. Losing privileges with Felicity would pretty much cut off the minuscule vein I had feeding me anything social. Yet the drive I had to continue reaching for freedom wouldn't let me stop trying.

Mother, with her weird interest in Colin would probably give me the silent treatment for weeks. Daddy would just find someone else to come work for him. If Colin lost the job because of me—I didn't like carrying that weight on my shoulders.

I'd thought of running away before, but knew how stupid that irrational choice really was. I had no way of supporting myself. The picture of me coming back because I'd failed was worse than being stuck.

"You're right," I sighed. I was surrounded by the fences, doors, and windows I perpetually observed life from.

"But so what," Felicity taunted.

"We'll just make sure we don't get caught." I flashed a grin at her and tugged her through the door.

We snuck along the exterior brick and stone walls of Chatham, peering around corners, dipping beneath windows like fugitives. The forty-five minute lunch period clicked away, but I didn't care. Finally, we reached the front of the building.

"You sure you want to do this?" Felicity giggled behind me.

Adrenaline pumped my blood. "Totally." Frigid winter air bit through my blazer and whirled up my skirt. "Should have brought our coats." I chattered.

"We'll freeze before we're halfway down the block," Felicity joked. "But at least we'll be frozen and free, right?"

I didn't see Colin anywhere, and figured he was inside the building in this cold November air.

We made a beeline for the opening in the chain link fence and started on a jog down the street. I laughed, enjoying the cold air rushing past me, fueling the excitement bursting from the inside out. At my side, Felicity laughed along with me, the two of us running like kids ditching school. Not that I'd ever ditched before.

We came to a stop at the second corner we passed. Our breath heaved in and out, shooting white smoky plumes into the air. Restaurants were the other direction. In our haste we hadn't navigated our escape with food in mind, only freedom.

"Here we are," Felicity blew out with a perfunctory glance around. "All dressed up and nowhere to go."

"I don't care if I eat. This is great."

"Ashlyn."

The male voice startled me, and Felicity and I whirled around. Colin stood five feet away, at the corner. He'd followed us? He wasn't even out of breath.

"How did you find us?" I gasped.

He started toward me, his eyes sharp. "It's my job to protect you, remember?"

A tingle raced across my skin when he said the words **protect you**. At the same time, the word babysitter flashed in my head. Colin held my gaze long enough to pin me like a butterfly in a shadow box before he looked at Felicity and nodded. "Colin Brennen."

"Felicity." She tilted he head at me. "Ashlyn's BFF." They shook hands. Felicity's cheeks pinked. "Forever, or until her Daddy finds out about this."

I frowned, whisked past Colin and headed back the direction we'd come. I glanced back. Felicity hung a few feet behind, and Colin was gaining on me. The harsh wind searing the streets and buildings chilled me to the bone and I wrapped my arms around myself.

Seconds later, Colin's presence pressed against my side. He had the decency not to interrogate me in front of Felicity and that was good, because anger surged through my body. If he had, I would have slugged him in the face, or at least fantasized about slugging him.

When we arrived at Chatham, Colin took hold of my elbow. His grip sent a wave of electricity through me. Felicity paused at my side, looked at Colin's hand and then at me.

"Felicity, will you give us a minute, please?" he said.

Felicity nodded. Since lunch was wrapping up, crowds of junior and senior girls paraded into the school, coming back from their off-campus lunches. Groups slowed to watch. Whispers floated in the air. A chill teased my spine.

Colin's piercing gaze remained on me. I was sure he felt the stares, heard the whispers.

He slipped his arm around me so his hand pressed at the small of my back, and he escorted me to a private corner of the Chatham courtyard. There, his right arm shot up to the stone wall, partially caging me in. Out the corner of my eye, girls congregated, curious.

"Want to tell me what that was about?" He kept his voice low, which I appreciated; even if I was humiliated at being caught doing something every other girl had the freedom to do.

"We were trying to go out for lunch. Lots of girls do it. See?" I swept my hand in the direction of the students behind him. He ignored them.

"You're not allowed to leave campus."

I shrugged, and forced indifference on my face. His cologne, faded now, lightly filled my head and caused my stomach to rumble with want. The bell shrilled. He remained anchored to the wall, making me feel frustratingly vulnerable. The dream of him kissing me floated into my brain, leaving my mesmerized by his power to undo me.

"Okay." I glanced away unable to look him in the eye. "I know."

"Don't do it again." He moved into my line of vision. "Understood?"

He sounded like Daddy. I worked to control my frustration. "Yeah, I understand." My voice tripped. "So, we're good then?"

He stepped back with a nod. "Yeah."

I passed him without looking back, merging into the girls standing and watching us. Catty, curious whispers followed me to class. Stares stole after me, faced me when I went to my locker, visited the bathroom and trailed me when the bell rang signaling that school was over.

Felicity caught up with me at my locker. "Everyone wants to know who the hottie is," she whispered, her green eyes following the girls walking by staring. "He's gorgeous, Ash. Daddy done good this time!"

"Fel!"

"I know you hate him, but if you have to hate him, you might as well *like* hating him, right?" She lifted a shoulder.

I slammed my locker shut. "So what if he's good looking? He's a hound. A Rottweiler." My cheeks fired with the lie, and I quickly turned and started down the hall hoping to hide the truth from Felicity. But she knew me better than anyone else—better than my parents, who only knew their Park Avenue princess. A façade.

"Oh, I see." Felicity's tone held jest.

"Ash." Danicka Fiore, a tall, leggy, teen model draped in designer accessories, stopped me in the hall. "Who's the hottie you were with at lunch?" Her brow arched. "Boyfriend?"

"Uh, no. A family friend."

"Oh, cool. Is he single? Maybe you could introduce me." Her side-kick model minions nodded in agreement.

"Maybe," I muttered, shouldering through the stickly pack of girls. Felicity remained at my side. Once we were clear of Danicka and her pals, I turned to Felicity. "How annoying. She's never talked to me before. What would she have done if I'd said, 'Yes, he's my boyfriend'?"

"Probably asked to make it a threesome." Felicity snorted. "I've heard some outrageous stories about that girl."

I walked out the front doors of Chatham shoulder-to-shoulder with hordes of other girls anxious to get out. I stopped on the stoop, searching for our black town car, lined up with a dozen other idling cars there to retrieve students.

Eddy stood at the hood chatting with another driver.

Where was Colin? My stomach filled with hummingbirds. Would he tell Daddy about lunch? If Daddy found out, he'd ground me from Felicity. Take my phone away. Maybe I could convince Colin not to say anything.

His black-clothed form came through the throngs of uniformed-girls on the sidewalk like a celebrity tearing through a mass of female fans, some of whom slowed and watched him as he passed. A cat call pierced the air, followed by a, "Hey there," and a whistle.

Colin's quick stride continued without hesitation. Across the maze of busy bodies his gaze met mine.

"Ready?" he asked once he was beside me.

Girls slowed around us, eyeing him. Everyone knew Stuart. They probably wondered what had happened to him and who the new guy was. I contemplated lying and telling everyone he was my boyfriend, but I'd already blown that possibility by being stupid in front of Danicka. She'd spread the word about Colin faster than a blaze in a dry forest.

"Yes." I started down the remaining stairs to the sidewalk. Colin stayed at my side, both of us dodging oncoming pedestrians as we threaded through Chatham students on our way to the car.

Thankfully, he didn't ask me how my day was—like I was in kindergarten. I tried to keep a good two feet ahead of him, my stride fast, but his extra height and long legs soon had him walking by my side. In my peripheral vision I caught him glancing at me.

Eddy ended his conversation with the other driver and came to the back of the car, ready to open my door.

"Miss Adair." He swung open the door and the scent of leather and coffee wafted into my nose. I slid in.

Colin got in after me and Eddy shut the door.

I kept my gaze out the window, embarrassed to have tried to do something as simple as go off campus for lunch and then have to explain myself. Of course, it wasn't Colin's fault. Daddy's insistence that I keep ridiculous rules was the problem.

Still, I didn't know what to say to Colin after such a fail. I wasn't sorry, so I wouldn't apologize. I'd do it again if the opportunity arose. But what if Daddy tightened the reins even more?

My insides crumbled. *You shouldn't have broken the rules. You should have continued to bide your time.* When my birthday came, life would change whether my parents wanted to accept me turning eighteen or not.

Eddy rarely made small talk with me on the drive home. Today, he remained silent, sipping his Starbucks. Had Colin discussed what had happened with him? Would Colin tell Daddy?

———————— CHAPTER SIX

My cell phone vibrated and I pulled it out of my book bag. Felicity.

let me kno what your dad says k

k

Colin was watching me, his look halfway between curious and annoyed. "What?" I snapped.

"Nothing." He turned his gaze out the window. At that moment, I wanted to jump into his head and read his thoughts. Bugged that I cared, annoyed that I didn't know what he was thinking, I yanked my iPod from the depths of my book bag, shoved the earbuds in my ears and cranked up the music.

Eddy dropped Colin and I off in front of the townhouse and then merged into traffic to go pick up Daddy.

My back to Colin, I stood at the door, and tapped the code into the security pad. The door beeped and Colin reached around me, his chest brushing my arm when he thrust the door open. I shivered.

Without meeting his gaze, I entered the townhouse. I took the marble stairs up two-at-a-time. Was I imagining his intimidating gaze following me? Or was guilt making me paranoid? I didn't have the nerve to verify with a glance.

I slammed my bedroom door. Then cringed. *He's going to think you're a baby, slamming doors and acting like a prima donna.*

I tossed my book bag on my bed, unzipped it and pulled out what homework awaited me. I flopped on my stomach, opened my folders and stared at my assignments. And sighed.

Colin. Pressing me against the door. Kissing me.

Mother's voice floated from downstairs. I jerked upright. She was never here when I got home, always out with her friends, shopping or attending some event. Colin's voice mixed with hers.

I hopped to my feet, ran to the door and cracked it open.

"Did Ashlyn behave?"

I covered my mouth to quiet a gasp as I crept to the stairs so I could hear better.

"She was fine, Fiona."

"Good. I don't approve of feisty behavior. We simply do not allow it."

I remained poised at the hall corner, where I peered down the curved stairs and saw the back of Mother's head and Colin's face. Colin shifted, appearing itchy. He crossed his arms over his chest. His gaze flicked from Mother's face and caught me. I jerked back. *Oh no.* I clenched my fists. *This day couldn't get more humiliating.*

Only one thing truly soothed every emotion plaguing me. I quickly headed to the music room and shut the double doors.

I sat at the piano and let out a sigh. When my fingers touched the keys, my eyes closed and frustration ebbed on contact with the instrument. Even the familiar repetition of scales soothed. Over and over my fingers played up and down the keyboard. How long I played, I don't know, but when I looked out the large, floor-to-ceiling windows facing Park Avenue, the sky was dark and lights glowed from the buildings.

My cell phone vibrated in my pocket.

what did u r dad do?

not home yet

ate chinese gonna barf now cya

I laughed. Felicity's parents ate Chinese food three times a week. Felicity often joked that her hair was starting to grow in rice noodles.

"Ashlyn?" Mother stood in the open double doors of the music room. Today she wore a cinnamon colored suit from Dior—one of her favorite designers. "Come down for dinner, please."

"I'll take it in my room tonight."

She cocked her head. "Whatever for?"

"I've got tons of homework. I'll be up all night."

"And that's why you're playing?"

I stiffened. "I'm unwinding."

"Dinner." Mother's chin firmed. "In five minutes. In the dining room." She turned and vanished, leaving the doors open.

Would Colin eat with us? Mother had rarely allowed Stuart that luxury. My empty stomach growled, but not for food.

Mother and Daddy insisted on three things: manners, respect, and compliance. Obedience was my middle name. As I matured, I understood why Mother and Daddy had only one child: going through the process of raising another human being was more time and energy consuming than they had expected. One child graduating through the steps meant they could get it right the first time, the only time, and be done.

Had I opted to not go down to the dining room for dinner, Daddy would have gotten an earful from Mother, then come upstairs and, in his lawyer-mode, explained to me that he made the effort to be home for dinner—not always an easy task—and that I should show my love and respect for his efforts by joining them.

We'd had this discussion when I was younger.

I stood at the top of the stairs, ready to burst from the combustion of frustration, anger and tears. Cold black and white marble stairs curved in a soft spiral below me to the entry.

Chances were that Colin wouldn't be eating dinner with us, since Stuart hadn't. At least I could eat without worrying about the meal becoming a part one of yet another lecture series on my safety.

Mother's sing-song voice bounced off the walls of the entry and flew out the open glass doors of the dining room. Who was she blabbing to on her cell phone?

I came around the corner and stalled in the doorway. Colin sat at the table.

"Gavin cooks a lot of French cuisine because we absolutely adore it. The duck is marvelous, Colin. Trust me. Oh, Ashlyn darling."

Mother's smile glittered from across the room. If Colin hadn't been sitting there, she'd be giving me the silent treatment.

Colin's presence pulled me. I couldn't help staring at him. He still wore the black clothing he'd worn earlier. The contrast caused his dark hair to shine against his smooth skin. His eyes held mine like dissecting pins.

"I talked Ashlyn into dining with us." Mother sat across from Colin.

Colin's brows lifted slightly. "Really?"

I cringed inwardly and crossed to my chair—on Mother's right, also across from Colin—and sat.

"Apparently she has a lot of homework." Mother poured herself some water from a crystal pitcher. "But family dinners are not optional in our house, are they young lady?"

Humiliation heated my cheeks and ears. I didn't dare meet Colin's gaze. What did he think of Mother calling me 'young lady?'

"I think that's great." Colin reached for the pitcher, his long fingers wrapping around the delicate handle. I lifted my gaze. His brown eyes watched me intently. "Family time is becoming extinct."

Don't let him intimidate you. This is your house. You can do dinner.

I sat erect and held my hand out, indicating I wanted the pitcher when he was done.

"Ash-lyn." Mother's tone checked the air. "Ask for the water properly."

Another flash of fire heated my cheeks. I swore pity veiled Colin's expression as he handed me the pitcher. Or was it contempt?

"May I have the water, please?" I asked squeezing out words between teeth.

"What's gotten into you?" Mother sat erect, her forearms poised on the edge of the table.

I poured water into my goblet, and the sound of ice clinking against glass broke the tense air. "Nothing."

"Well." Mother's brow arched in that I-don't-approve way. "Lose the attitude before your father comes to the table."

I let out a slow, controlled breath. Had I really expected Mother to change the way she treated me—even in front of an old family friend like Colin? *Fine. I'll spend the meal in Stepford mode.*

"Good evening." Daddy entered the room in a swift walk. I'd never seen him in the courtroom but had imagined him often gliding in, commanding the attention of everyone in the room in the magnetic, powerful way of a ring master.

His blue eyes smiled even as he assessed the situation in the dining room with one efficient sweep. He didn't remove his ice-gray suit jacket, merely unbuttoned the buttons as he leaned over and extended his hand to Colin.

"Colin."

"Charles."

Daddy came to me and kissed the top of my head. "Princess." Then, he sat at the head of the table. With a smooth flick of his wrist, he plucked the cloth napkin and laid it in his lap. I glanced at Mother—Daddy hadn't even acknowledged her. Her attention was riveted to Colin.

Spices filled the air with a soothing aroma. I hadn't looked at the artfully displayed meal sitting in the center of the table, too distracted with Colin and the inevitability of him dropping the bomb of what had happened at lunch today.

As food was passed and dished up, my fisted nerves tightened even more. Why doesn't he just tell Daddy and get it over with? I glanced at Colin, my gaze caught helplessly on the way his cheeks creased as he chewed, hinting dimples.

Dinners were usually silent with the exception of Daddy asking about my day. Tonight, Mother talked more than she ate.

"How do you like the meal?" Mother asked Colin.

"It's the first home-cooked meal I've had since I moved here."

Mother cleared her throat at the term 'home cooked.' "Have you spent much time on the Upper East Side, Colin?" she asked.

Colin swallowed. "Not really. School's kept me pretty busy."

"Is that where you lived?"

He nodded.

"Some of those areas are charming. Where was your

apartment?" Mother seemed uninterested in meal. Her elbows were planted on the table and her eyes were glued to Colin.

I glanced at Daddy, eating in silence, like me. Every now and then his light blue eyes rested on Colin with interest.

"I have a place on Charles Street."

"Have?" Mother's brows arched. "You're keeping your apartment?"

As if he sat on hot coals, Colin shifted.

"A smart move," Daddy piped. "The sign of someone who is prepared."

"Yes, but he's employed here. As long as it doesn't have anything to do with your level of commitment," Mother said.

I rolled my eyes.

"I'm committed, Fiona." Colin reached for his water goblet. He seemed jittery, like he had been earlier in the car. Was he uncomfortable in the spotlight? A grin slipped onto my lips just as Colin's eyes met mine.

My smile vanished, but I held his querying gaze until his attention shifted to his half-eaten meal.

"Are you dating anyone, Colin?" Mother asked.

His fork paused before cutting into the duck flesh.

"Fiona, we don't need to interrogate the boy," Daddy chuckled.

"I'm not interrogating." Mother finally picked up her fork. "Just catching up with an old family friend."

"It's his business, not ours." Daddy's tone sharpened even though he smiled. I knew the silent encoding well: topic over.

"How did it today go?" Daddy waited for Colin's answer. My nerves prickled.

"Everything went well," Colin said without a hitch.

"I expected as much. Ashlyn's an obedient girl. You won't need to report to me unless something comes up." Daddy's firm tone was meant to remind both Mother and Colin of Colin's job—in spite of sharing a meal with us and being an old family friend.

Colin nodded. "Yes, sir."

Rebellion scraped my spine raw. *An obedient girl?* And why did

Colin refer to Daddy as sir? Stuart had, but Colin had called Daddy Charles. When had that changed? For some reason, I didn't like Colin using the term.

"Sir?" I quipped, reaching for my water.

Daddy's head tilted my direction. Silence engulfed the room.

"He called you Charles when he arrived. And Charles just now when he shook your hand."

"Ashlyn." Mother's edgy tone warned me I tread on glass.

I held Daddy's curious and amused gaze. "You don't like him calling me that, Princess?"

"It's a term of respect," Colin interjected, seeming embarrassed that I'd singled the issue out.

"One I insist on from my employees," Daddy reminded me.

"Oh, and from your daughter," I snapped at him. "I call him that too. Hard to believe, right? He's my father after all. But he insists on it." I jerked to my feet and tossed my napkin to the table. "Excuse me. Sir."

Mother's eyes bulged. "Ashlyn!"

"I asked to be excused." I left the room, half expecting Mother's whispered indignation to snatch my ankles and pull me back to the table. I took the stairs up, fury pumping my legs. My bedroom door slammed behind me, and I cringed, knowing full well that the sound echoed throughout the house.

A few minutes later one firm knock followed, and the door opened. Daddy stood in the frame, his face stony. He stepped into the room and shut the door at his erect back. "You want to tell me what's bothering you, Princess?"

"I told you not to call me that."

The taut skin on his face softened and he stepped closer. "My mistake. I'm sorry. What's wrong?"

A jumble of emotions rolled through me: confusion at my feelings for Colin, frustration about my protected life, and the strongest yearning I'd ever felt urging me toward… what? Freedom, yes, but something more…

"Is it Colin?" Daddy moved closer, I felt him—powerful and

commanding and immobile as a sequoia—at my side.

Yes, it was Colin. Partly. But I couldn't admit *why* it was Colin.

"I know you two didn't get along, but that was in the past, Ashlyn. Try to put it behind you."

I closed my eyes. I *had* put it behind me. But I couldn't help myself. His face, smile, the way his eyes probed me… stirring that deep yearning.

"You hate him that much?" Daddy's gentle hand took my chin and turned my face to his lawyer-sharp gaze.

What did he want to hear? Accustomed to telling him what would make him happy, I searched his eyes for the answer.

I nodded.

Was that relief I saw pass through his irises? A shudder rambled along my bones. His lips lit in a smile. He wrapped me in a hug meant to comfort, but I was too astounded at the look I'd seen in his eyes to be comforted.

"I know he teased you when you were children, and I know you disliked him. Hated him even. But this will work itself out," he murmured, his hand in soft strokes against my head. "Why don't you go to the music room and play?" He eased back, hands on my shoulders. "It's been ages since I've heard you play my song."

Eyes closed, I released my anguish and angst into the piano. After Daddy had left, I'd played Beethoven, but the melody now trickling across the keys was light, ethereal, and mysterious. Colin's tune. Even as the song echoed off the walls, each note threatened to envelop and monopolize me with beauty. I couldn't stop. The tune pushed itself from my soul, swung around my heart, and sprung from my fingertips. I played it over and over again.

I opened my eyes, jolted. Colin. Next to the piano.

"I keep doing that, I'm sorry." His cheeks flashed with pink, his dimples deepening.

"It's okay," I sputtered. "I'm usually in here alone."

"That song...it's..."

"What?" I asked.

"I like it."

I took a deep, fluttering breath. I was grateful Colin hadn't told Daddy about lunch today. And, after I'd played for Daddy, I'd spent a good portion of the night telling myself I could be in the same room with Colin and not let his charisma make my knees weak and leave my tongue speechless.

"Charles asked me to take you on a walk," Colin said. "You want to go?"

"Take me?" I gritted my teeth, stood. "Like a dog or something?"

Colin dipped his head. "I'm sorry, I shouldn't have put it like that."

"It's not you," I said. "It's..." Hopefully, Colin didn't see that Mother and Daddy treated me like I was an incapable child. "Sure. That'd be great." Maybe I could run away while we were out, Colin would get busted and fired and Daddy would... I frowned.

Daddy would hire an ape—an old, ugly ape.

Colin watched my face closely. "You okay?"

"Yeah." I pushed around him and headed for the double doors. "I'll get my coat and meet you in the entry," I mumbled.

We walked west to Central Park, the brisk wind biting our cheeks and noses. I was glad I'd brought a knit hat and mittens. The white down jacket I wore kept my body toasty. Colin wore a black wool coat and black knit beanie. He looked hot in black. Mother had insisted he wear one of the extra Ferrigamo scarves she kept on hand in the coat closet, which Colin had reluctantly agreed to.

"Sorry about Mother," I said.

"She's a mom." He shrugged. "That's what moms do."

"Moms maybe. She's a mother."

Colin laughed. The sight caused a jolting buzz to break loose down low in my stomach.

Central Park, with its maze of walkways, rocks, trees, and bushes was an endless black abyss at night. I didn't want to walk into the park. I wasn't allowed there after nightfall. Every warning I'd heard from Daddy about safety screamed to stay out of dark places.

At my side, Colin's stride was sure and strong. As we approached the fringes of the park, he studied the dark depths. "Let's stay out here."

We continued west, passing homeless people crouched along the low rock wall surrounding the park. Some slept, some begged for a handout. Further along, we came to a handful of men carrying big green garbage bags full of designer knock-off bags, wallets, hats, and other accessories. Colin shook his head at each attempt to stop us. When one man nagged me in the face, Colin put his hand at the small of my back. A jolt of wired heat shocked through me.

He shouldered the man aside and guided me away from the vultures, our pace quickening, and we continued on.

His jaw tensed. Steam blew from his tight lips.

"What?" I asked. "Those guys back there?"

He gave a sharp nod. "They don't know when to stop." His hand slipped away from my back, and the vacancy shuddered through me in cold emptiness.

"How about the bookstore?" he asked, gaze lighting on the Barnes & Noble up ahead.

"Yeah, I love bookstores."

"Me too."

Shoppers crowded into the building on the corner of 66th and Broadway. The smell of fresh coffee and book paper gusted at us as we herded inside. Colin's gloved fingers grazed my elbow. "What do you want to look at?" he asked.

"Don't worry about me." The last thing I wanted was for him to follow me around like a babysitter. "I'll be fine. Really. I won't split, I promise." His brows knitted for a moment. He seemed satisfied, but he waited until I started in the direction of women's romance.

I couldn't stand in one place—*forget browsing.* My mind drifted repeatedly to Colin. I decided to see where he was.

I found him nose-deep in a psychology book. I didn't have the heart to interrupt, so I stayed half-hidden, an aisle over, my eyes trained on him.

He leaned a shoulder against the shelf, one hip cocked. The way his long fingers cradled the book, one hand gently turning the pages, caused the fantasy of him pressing me against the bedroom door, kissing me, those fingers touching my face to play across my mind. His mouth…

Suddenly, his face lifted. His eyes met mine. My heart rate skyrocketed. He started over. "Everything okay?" he queried, studying me.

"Uh. Yeah." I shook my head, flushed with heat from head to toe. "I was just… looking around." *Looking at him, you idiot. You sound so stupid.*

I grabbed the first book I could, then my eyes widened when I read the title *Men: Is There a Mystery?*

Colin's gaze flicked to the book. He grinned. "Okay, well, if you're good, I'll just—"

"Yes, I'm good. Great. Thanks." I turned and shoved the book back on the shelf in a vain effort to appear preoccupied. He paused a moment.

Finally, he headed back to the book he'd been reading.

Another title caught my attention: *Guys: Insider Edition.* What I knew about males I'd first heard from Mother, her version was always coated with saccharine and dipped in diamonds. Ideals she hoped existed for me but, from what I overheard in school and the scraps Felicity shared, I figured her version of men was as unreal as happily ever after. My romance novels had been covert text books of sorts. Some men preferred a woman who dominated with her advances. While others enjoyed a more submissive woman. Kissing should be an exploration, an extension of deeper feelings.

Like sex.

I glanced around, face heating. What details I knew of sex I'd read in magazines, romance novels and what Mother had briefly—and with much discomfort—shared with me, and the brief chats I'd snuck in with Felicity on the subject. These chapters were technical, fascinating, with illustrations that left my eyes wide.

Colin's face came to mind; his smile, his eyes, the way his lips moved when he spoke. I imagined those lips against mine. Hot tremors swirled from my mouth to my center. No doubt everyone in this room had experienced these feelings before. The woman in the red coat and candy-striped scarf standing next to me—had she felt this flush of excitement? The teenager wearing the shaggy fur hat and round black glasses, had she felt these exhilarating feelings?

Invigoration settled into disillusionment, wrapping heavily around my heart. What would life be like if I was allowed to explore them? Colin wouldn't see me as some child in need of babysitting. I pictured myself admired, held, and kissed.

Loved—loving, would be a gratifying, unrivaled experience.

I could use this book. I slipped it under my arm for safe-keeping until I could purchase it.

Hearing Colin's laughter, I looked over. He stood next to a tall, sweater and cords college type. The guy playfully slugged him.

"Yeah, we'll get a drink sometime." The stranger paused when I stopped next to them. "I'll see you around." The guy walked away.

"Who was that?" I asked.

"A friend from school. Are you going to get something?" He glanced at the book in tucked beneath my arm.

"What? Oh, just this."

He tried to eye the book and I stuffed it deeper. When we checked out, I cringed when he plucked the book and handed it to the woman behind the counter so it could be scanned, paid for, and bagged.

Colin held the door open as we left the stuffy store and went out into the biting cold. A slight grin lifted his lips.

"What?" I asked.

"You don't need that stuff."

We came to the corner and waited for the light to change.

"What if I do?"

His dark eyes studied me for a moment. "Everything you need to know about love is already inside of you, Ashlyn." He held my gaze until the light changed. Then his warm hand was at my back again as we crossed the street. Was he right? I'd read a lot in magazines and books in an effort to feel more at ease about intimacy, but here he was telling me that my instincts, no matter how naïve, were all I needed.

We walked in silence for a while. I savored every person we passed looking at us, thinking we were a couple. A stupid fantasy, but I indulged anyway. He enjoyed watching a group of street dancers doing stunts to the thump of a loud boom-box on the plaza just outside Central Park. I was entranced with the way his jaw moved when he laughed, the strong yet fragile look of skin over bone. What would that skin feel like to touch? He had a nice profile. I liked the straight tip of his nose, now turning pink from cold.

"Those kids are good." He didn't look at me. I was glad—looking at him kept a warm simmering alive inside me. A shadow was forming on his jaw where he shaved. The contrast of roughness over his finely angled face created a shivering of want through me. The brisk wind picked up the ends of his hair, tossing the dark waves as though invisible fingers played in it. My fingers rubbed together in the depths of my coat pockets.

"Do you like to dance?" He looked at me then, startling me. I turned my gaze toward the bouncing, twisting teens.

"Yes."

He brought me in for a quick side-hug. "Ash, come on. We're friends."

Awash with frustration, I left his embrace and walked away. Being alone, when my side or back didn't feel the heat of a companion, was unnerving. I didn't slow. I didn't want to be friends with him. Friends don't make each other feel this way—like I can't wait to get up every morning to see him.

"Hey," he called.

I had read scenes like this in books, lovers in a disagreement. But we weren't lovers. We weren't friends—not yet, anyway—and he was there for one reason only. He was my companion, nothing more. As romantic as the moment looked, as exciting as it felt, it wasn't real.

When he took my elbow and gently turned me to face him, I dismissed the skittering inside as a ridiculous overreaction.

"I…" He glanced at his hand on my elbow before he tucked his fingers back into his pocket. "Did I say something wrong?"

Wind whipped around us. "No. It was me. I'm…" *I'm a lonely, repressed, pathetic wannabe who doesn't know the first thing about love, men or relationships.* Blood drained from my face. I turned from his piercing gaze.

Colin dipped his head down and looked into my face at eye level. "You okay?"

"Everyone treats me like I'm a baby."

"That wasn't my intention. But you are my responsibility."

"I'm not a baby." Annoyance forced me to start walking again.

"No, but you are…" He fell in step beside me. "There is something about you that is—"

"What? Tell me."

He shook his head. "There I go again, saying things that get me in trouble," he stated lightly.

"I'd say it's a little late for that, Colin."

"Yeah, I suppose it is."

We walked in silence for a block. Why *are you acting like a baby if you want to be treated like an adult?* I wouldn't waste what precious time we had together wound up in pride. "May I ask you something personal?"

"Ask away."

"How come you're not with someone?"

"I'm with you." He shot a twinkling grin.

"You know what I mean."

He shuffled back and forth on his feet to keep warm while we waited for the green light. Then his hands cupped his mouth and he blew. "I broke up with a girl just a few months ago."

A pang of jealousy rang through me. *Who was she?*

We crossed the street and headed up 78th toward Park. A sinking feeling came over me. In a few minutes, I'd see the dim lights of the townhouse. This night would be over.

"Why… what… oh, it's none of my business," I stammered.

"She was someone else once I got to know her," he said. "And I couldn't open my mouth without saying something stupid."

No one's past had ever mattered before. Now, his past prickled like an itch that had to be scratched.

We turned the corner and were on Park. Home loomed in the distance. I slowed.

"What about you?" he asked.

"Me what? And guys?"

"I can't believe Charles doesn't keep a golf club by the door to beat away the droves."

"I don't date much."

"Why? Or does Charles not let you date?"

We waited at another corner with a small crowd. The townhouse was on the next block.

"He—well, Daddy wants me to wait."

"Wait?" Disbelief sparked his tone. "For what?"

Aggravated by my circumstances, angry that he was getting close to figuring out the twisted puzzle of my life, I sighed. "He just wants me to be… older, I guess."

"What about what you want?"

I'm working on it. I shrugged, not sure how to answer. I wanted to change the subject. "Anyway, I haven't found anyone worth spending that kind of time with."

"You will," he said.

When we reached the townhouse I paused at the bottom of the stairs.

He stopped. "What is it? Aren't you freezing?"

I haven't been cold all night.

I laid on my bed like a bottle of soda, shaken and ready to pop. The grin on my face wouldn't leave, no matter how I tried to remind myself how horrible Colin had been. Once. *That was forever ago.*

Mother's voice trickled down the stairs. So did Colin's. His bedroom was above mine, I heard his movements in soft, teasing shifts overhead, wispy sounds beckoning to me. I rose and opened my bedroom door.

"Darling, you don't have to cover up for me. We're like family."

What was Mother doing? I crept out into the hall so I could hear better.

"Mmm, I'd like to see you in this. Why haven't you worn it?"

"I will. One of these days."

"That would be appropriate. You wouldn't want to hurt my feelings now, after all the trouble I went to replacing your wardrobe."

I cringed. Mother somehow believed whatever she said was okay to say, present company be damned.

"I just had to thank you for the marvelous job you did with Ash today. I haven't seen her this happy in years."

Oh no. I nearly crumpled against the wall.

"I'm glad she enjoyed herself."

"Oh, she enjoyed herself. You're wonderful with her."

With her? Like I'm a two year old in need of entertaining. I stormed into my bedroom and slammed the door. Then cringed. I shouldn't have done that. Knowing Mother, she'd be knocking on my door to see what was wrong.

When the knock never came, I cracked open the door and listened. Nothing. And no sound overhead.

Wrapping my pink robe around me, I tied the sash and crept to the music room. My body shook with irritation that would only leave me with the melodic playing of the piano.

I shut the double doors and crossed the wood floor to my sleek friend, awaiting me by the window. I smiled, bunched nerves uncoiling as I approached her.

I sat, and my fingers rested on the keys, anger shifting to anticipation as I began to play.

Colin's melody. Feelings collided inside of me, questions surfaced. Fantasies danced with reality. The end of the tune was coming, and I didn't want it to… As long as I played the song, his face, his eyes, his smile stayed present in my mind, even as conflict twined with the pleasant images. I played the song over and over, in higher octaves, then lower for more drama. Finally, my fingers laid to rest on the ending chords.

"That was amazing." Colin's voice.

My eyes flashed. My quickened breath echoed off the mahogany walls. The melody still sung in my head, mixing now with the sound of his rapid breathing, stirring me. He moved around the piano. "It hurts you when you play that song."

"Yes."

"Why?"

"I think of things that will never be."

"You can have anything you want, Ashlyn."

I shook my head, eyes pinching closed. "No."

"That can't be possible."

More than anything, I wanted someone to understand what was inside me. The bench rocked. Heat pressed into my side. He was sitting next to me, I felt his eyes beg me to look at him. I did. Frightened my face might give away my heart, my hands barely moved away from the keys.

His hand shot out and stopped me. "Play it again."

I looked at his hand, wrapped around my right wrist, and he let go. I placed my hands back on the keys. When I struck the first note, he closed his eyes.

My arm brushed his and as it did, my body moved to the swells of the music, the melody reaching inside of me. Each note, each chord and progression pierced deep, opening places that hadn't flickered with sensation so overpowering before.

Out the corner of my eye, his head turned. He watched me play. Did he know this song was his? My body writhed, fingers demanded, fighting the message of the tune. Tiny beads of sweat budded at my hairline, in the hollow of my throat where my heart beat. Playing the song was bitter. Sweet. Torture.

Colin wrapped his hands around mine. He squeezed. My breath

caught. I savored the strong feel of his fingers cuffing my hands. His eyes shifted to my mouth, then to my eyes. His body inched toward mine.

A cough startled us.

———————— CHAPTER SEVEN

Colin whipped around. Mother stood in the doorway dressed in a black with a sheer robe barely tied at the waist. Remnants of surprise vanished from her face, replaced by wary amusement.

She crossed to the piano, her eyes narrowing even though a faint smile slit her lips. "That was lovely, darling. But why did you stop?" Her eyes slid down to the keys, to Colin's hands clutching mine. "I see."

I broke free of Colin's grasp and stood.

"You don't like her music, Colin?"

Colin joined me. "I think it's outstanding. It just—she looked unhappy when she was playing." His careful gaze swept my face. "Like it hurt. I wondered—"

"And yet you asked her to play it again."

Colin swallowed. "Yes." He glanced at me, apology in his eyes. "I'm sorry. I shouldn't have done that if it—"

"That's just silly, isn't it Ashlyn?" Mother drove on. "She's a composer. Her pieces are just creations. Like an actor playing a part. It's not her."

How little Mother knew me. I caught a glimpse of confusion, maybe irritation, on Colin's face at Mother's comment.

"Anyway," Mother glossed over the topic. "I could use your help for a moment if you don't mind."

"Sure," Colin said.

I passed Mother and caught her perfume—freshly applied. This time of night?

In my bedroom, I closed the door, but was curious what Mother was doing—what she needed Colin for. When their voices grew soft enough that I was sure they were both far away, I opened the door and crept out. I heard Mother's voice from her bedroom down the hall. Mother and Daddy had had their own bedrooms ever since I could remember. I never thought anything of it until I'd had Felicity over and she'd told me it was weird. What would Colin think?

Tip-toeing, I followed their discussion until I was outside Mother's bedroom.

"You like the painting?" Mother asked him.

When she'd had my painting commissioned, she'd also had one done of her. It had hung out in the main entry up until last year. Then she'd had it moved into her bedroom. Now, it hung over her massive four poster bed.

"It's nice," Colin sounded respectfully neutral.

"Thank you. I'm dreadfully tired. But I want help moving this desk. I'd like it right under the window so that when I'm sitting here, I can look out. Can you manage that for me, dear boy? Usually, Charles helps me. But he's late tonight and I simply haven't the energy to wait up for him. I want it ready tomorrow morning."

Mother had occasionally asked Stuart to help her with odd jobs like this. Still, it had been years since she'd approached Stuart wearing only her negligee. Uncertainty twisted my stomach.

I heard tinkering, sliding, and finally a heavy thud.

"Thank you."

"No problem."

"Where are you going?" Mother's voice dropped to a low purr. I so wanted to peek around the corner and see what was going on. Afraid Colin would come out and discover me, I ran silently back to my bedroom and stood behind the partially closed door.

"I guess this is goodnight." Mother's tone had sharpened.

"Yes, it is," Colin said. "Goodnight."

His footsteps sounded on the stairs going up. I couldn't believe Mother had actually come onto him. Did she think he would respond to her advance? The idea thrust my stomach into a roll of disgust.

Mother's door closed with a slam.

When Eddy dropped Colin and me off at Chatham the next day, I was surprised to find Danicka Fiore and her skeletal peeps clinging to the curb. The minute our car pulled up, she snapped to attention, posing. Her friends mimicked her plastic stance.

Did Colin like über skinny girls? Covertly, I watched him out the corner of my eye and my stomach took a slug when his gaze lit on the frail bunch. I let out a snort, bringing his attention to me.

A wave of stupidity nearly drowned me. I wasn't doing much to earn his respect. His eyes narrowed, studying me briefly, before Eddy opened the door. Colin waited for me to get out.

The second my feet hit the sidewalk, Danicka sauntered over, flipping her long, straight hair in a practiced, smooth move. "Hey, Ash. What's up?"

Danicka's attempts to chat grated on my self esteem. I ignored her, something I'd never done before, deeming her attention god-like before now.

She continued talking behind me and I turned. "I'm Danicka." She and her friends surrounded Colin like starved cats around a bowl of cream. *What a joke.* But deep down, I figured he was like every other male. Why wouldn't the sight of beautiful prep school girls in uniform be a turn on?

He smiled, his dimples flashing, and he gave Danicka a nod. No hello. Just a nod, before he said, "Excuse me," and broke through them, his eyes on me.

My cheeks flushed with heat, and, inwardly, I cheered. *How does that feel, Danicka?*

Colin soon climbed the stairs beside me. I felt comforted, having him next to me, even though I shouldn't have.

He opened one of the heavy wooden doors to school and I swooshed inside with the other girls. Colin got stuck holding the door open, a smile on his face for every lash-batting female who passed him.

Felicity joined me inside the school main entrance. "Wow, he's holding the door open?"

"Yeah," I snickered, "he's a real Prince Charming. He totally brushed Danicka and the skeletons off though."

"Snaps for him." Felicity continued to glance over her shoulder. "She's not giving up."

I stopped, and was bumped, nudged and nearly run over by girls on their way to class. Sure enough, Danicka stood poised in the open door, one leg artfully bent at the knee, her hands behind her arched back while she flirted with Colin.

A flash of fire shot up my spine. I gripped the straps of my book bag until I couldn't feel my fingers anymore and started toward my first class. Another day of not being able to concentrate. Another day of Colin's dimpled smile like a searchlight flashing in my head, over and over taking my thoughts from academics to him and his song. Another day of doodling the notes of his song in my margins.

Lunch came and Felicity and I stayed in the lunchroom. I kept my eye on the opening, wondering if Colin would come looking for me, but he remained stationed down by the main entrance of the school.

I confirmed with a peek.

"I have got to stop spying on him," I blew out, after peering around the corner, spotting him sitting reading the New York Times in one of the main hall chairs.

Felicity giggled next to me, then stole a peek for herself. "I don't know, Ash. He's really hot. I can see why you've got a crush on him."

Eyes wide, I glared at her. "I do not have a crush. He's annoying, just like the rest of them."

"Annoying like a luscious itch that has to be scratched," Felicity swooned. "Crap, he's looking. Oh, no. I think he saw me."

Just what I didn't need. I started down the hall at a half-jog, Felicity laughing at my heels. We rounded a corner, nearly bumping into Danicka and the skeletons.

"I've been looking for you," Danicka said.

"Me?"

"What's your cell number? I want to invite you to a party I'm having this weekend at Ninety-Nine. You've heard of it, right?''

Who hadn't? For being seen by anyone who was someone important, Ninety-Nine was the current place for five-star hooking up. Or so I'd heard. "Yeah."

"It's gonna rock. What's your number?" She held out her diamond-encased cell phone.

If I gave her my number Daddy would blow a fuse. He'd make me delete her later, after a thorough background check, and he'd wonder what I was doing even talking to someone as celebutante as Danicka.

I recited my phone number.

"K. Cool. I'll text you later." She swung away, hips swaying in unison with her runway friends as they strolled down the hall.

"She never stays here for lunch," I mumbled.

Felicity shrugged. "Guess she's decided to have Colin for lunch."

An image of Danicka seducing Colin flashed in my head, causing surges of jealousy to vibrate through me. I wanted to slap myself for caring, for being jealous, for having him suddenly in my life—a distraction so overwhelming, five minutes didn't go by that his name didn't whisper into my consciousness.

"Your Dad's going to pee his pants," Felicity whispered, laughed.

"Yeah." He'd do more than that if he found out about Danicka's party. But going would be the gutsiest thing I'd ever done.

Danicka texted me on the drive home. I angled my cell phone screen so Colin, if he was looking, and I was sure he wasn't, wouldn't be able to read it.

so this sat, 99 @10 u kno where it is?
Ya
cool. will colin b coming?
The real reason she was inviting me.
um yeah.
cooool he's soooo hot.

I grinned. I couldn't wait to see her face when I walked into her party—alone.

i'll leave ur name with Carlos — the doorman. K? cu then.

I deleted the thread of texts. Daddy regularly asked to see my phone—an irritation that sent injustice screaming through my head. I sighed.

The days before Friday dragged. I couldn't stop thinking about how fun it was going to be alone at Ninety-Nine. I imagined dancing with hot guys, being the center of attention in the center of the dance floor. I stopped talking to Felicity about it, because she kept reminding me Daddy would blow an artery. I didn't care. I wondered if she was jealous, and I felt bad. We both knew Danicka would never invite her to one of her parties, and Felicity didn't have Colin as bait. I did. If that was enough to open a door, I'd take it. The excursion wasn't so much about the party as it was about being out on my own. I was navigating the entire evening myself. I would ditch the bookstore, and Colin, go to the party and return to the bookstore before it closed.

When Friday night finally came, I put my plan into action. After dinner, I dressed in sheer leggings, a skinny black turtleneck and a pair black boots and a ruffled plaid French skirt. I sprayed on some perfume and went in search of Colin.

Music overhead signaled that he was in his bedroom. I took the stairs up and knocked on his door.

"Hold on." Seconds later, the door swung open and Colin, dressed in jeans and a well-worn baby blue sweatshirt with the remnants of California silk-screened on the chest, greeted me. "Hey." His gaze swept me from boots to head. "We going somewhere?"

"Yeah. Barnes & Noble. I need to pick up something."

He seemed to ponder my words. "Sure. Give me a minute."

"Meet downstairs?"

He nodded and shut the door. Thrill quickened my steps down to the main entry where I waited.

Step one—done.

The townhouse was its usual tomb-like quiet. Friday night meant

Mother and Daddy were out together at a restaurant or dinner party.

Tonight was my night.

I did a double take when Colin came down the stairs. He wore sleek black pants that hugged his toned legs, a fitted periwinkle shirt. He was slipping into a black leather jacket Mother had picked out for him as his feet hit the marble floor.

"You didn't have to dress up," I said around a thickening throat.

He shrugged and crossed to the front door. He tapped the security code into the panel and the dead bolts slid in their casters. He opened the front door and held it for me.

"Charles and Fiona have Eddy for the night. You want to walk or catch a cab?"

I checked my cell phone for the time. Almost nine o'clock. I couldn't show up at Ninety-Nine too early. A chilly January wind brushed my cheeks as we took the stoop stairs down to the sidewalk. I didn't want to get windblown before the party but I only had cash for a two cab rides, not three.

"You have cash, right?" I asked.

He nodded. "Let's catch a cab."

I waited under the protection of our small vestibule while he stepped out into the street, his hand raised to his lips. He blew out a piercing whistle. Four cabs whizzed by before one pulled over.

Colin opened the back door and gestured for me to get in.

"Barnes and Noble on Sixty Sixth and Broadway," he told the driver. We were whisked into traffic at a speedy pulse along Park Avenue.

Casually, he glanced over. My hands gripped each other in my lap. Surely he couldn't see that this was all a fake.

We didn't speak on the short drive. At the bookstore he hopped out, rounded the car and opened my door. Guilt pinched me. He was so gentlemanly. Conscientious. My plan to leave and come back after being at Ninety-Nine for only a half hour was going to ensure that neither he nor Mother and Daddy know about my spree into freedom.

Colin paid the cabby and we entered the bookstore. He stopped.

"So," he said.

"So." My voice warbled. *Control, control.* "I'll be in the young adult section," I said, then turned and headed up the escalator to the next floor. I didn't dare look to see if he was following me. There was no rush. I'd sneak out soon enough.

Giddy chills tingled through my arms and legs. After fifteen long minutes of wandering around the store, I went back down the escalator, my scan of the first floor not finding Colin's tall form anywhere.

I left the building. The bitter wind seared my cheeks. I hailed a cab, told the driver where to take me and we took off. I checked over my shoulder, amazed, thrilled and shocked I was on my way.

And Colin was still back at the bookstore.

Ninety-Nine vibrated from a block away. The stainless steel looking building gleamed against the city lights. Lines of partiers waited out front on a purple and red carpet that stretched down the block. Strings of giant bulb lights swayed slightly in the icy breeze, lighting the gaudy red carpet leading to the entrance.

"To the front of the line, please," I told the cab driver, my stomach a bouquet of popping bubbles.

———————— CHAPTER EIGHT

Shapes moved in shadows colored by streaming lights from the dance floor. I'd never been to a club, only seen them in films or read about them in my romance novels. Raucous music shook the dark, purple and red mirrored walls. Sweaty, thick air forced itself into my lungs, nearly causing my gag reflex to start. The combination of perfumes, smoke and bodies overwhelmed me. I had to remind myself why I wanted to do this.

Carlos told me to follow him, but I walked into a fog bank of cologne and sweat. A wall of gyrating bodies suddenly seemed to converge on me. I felt suffocated. Couldn't move. Heads turned. Some stares lingered. One guy came up and started rubbing himself against me. Panicked, I stepped away, only to smack into some girl dressed in see-through netting. She smiled and swung her hips my direction in a dance that caused my blood to shiver.

Carlos must have figured he'd lost me, for suddenly he was there, scowling. He jerked his head as if for me to hurry and follow. He led me to a raised area, curtained by red and lavender sheers blowing in a soft breeze made by gold fans hanging overhead.

Fat purple and red velveteen couches sat in a circle on the raised, curtained-off area. Sprawled on the couches were dozens of skeletal chicks—some from school, others I didn't recognize—with Danicka in the center. Smoke wafted up from burning cigarettes cluttering ashtrays made to look like East Indian treasure chests.

Carlos left me at the billowing opening of the enclosure. Danicka was in the middle of sharing a smoke with one of her anorexic friends when another girl elbowed her and nodded at me. Danicka craned her dazed look around me as if looking for someone else.

Then she stood, wobbling for a second on her glittering platforms. Her tight sapphire mini dress skimmed her panty line. Glitter adorned her bare shoulders, bird-like arms, and neck. She stepped over her dazed friends and headed my direction.

My heart tripped. Danicka parted the purple veil and entered. I took one step onto the raised red platform and felt heat at my back.

"Where's Colin?" Her breath stunk of sour mint. "Thought he was coming with?"

I'd never seen her or her friends so listless. Dead-eyed. Shocked, I fumbled for words. "He'll be here," I lied.

"Cool. Have some." She gestured to the table laden with treasure boxes where cigarettes smoldered like incense. Lines of white powder striped the black glass table top.

My elbow was locked in a vice grip.

"Ashlyn." Colin's voice cut through the club muck like a trumpet. No trace of humor lie anywhere in his face. His bottomless black eyes cut me open, reached into my soul and grabbed hold. He jerked his head in the opposite direction of Danicka's party tent.

"There you are." Danicka's sour breath blew the side of my face. She leaned into Colin for balance but he barely glanced at her. "I was hoping you'd come." Her long arms wound around his neck and she lifted up to kiss his cheek.

In a swift jerk, he was free of her and leading me away from her and her minions. I didn't appreciate being dragged. I yanked, but he swung around, faced me. Somebody bumped into him, pushing his body against mine. Before we both fell into the dancing crowd, he took hold of my arms and steadied us. To my right a sweaty bald guy started rotating his hips against mine.

Colin shoved him away. Bald guy glared, but gyrated against the next available body. Frustration drew Colin's features tight. "Why didn't you tell me you were leaving?" he yelled over the music.

"I wanted to come alone."

His eyes swept the crowd, his posture ready to pounce. "You're supposed to stay with me. Do your parents know about this?"

I averted my gaze for a second. Colin's chest lifted in an

exasperated breath I couldn't hear over the music. "Let's get out of here."

Colin took me by the arm, his fingers a steely grip.

"I'm not leaving," I yelled over the grating beat.

"Ash, if your parents don't know about this, then we're not going to be here." This time he took my hand. I couldn't stop the fire that raced up my arm. He pushed through the packed crowd again, his fingers tightening around mine. More eyes, more curious stares—this time from women—watching him. Jealousy unhinged inside my heart.

He's with me. A lie, but we looked like a couple—didn't we? I shot a glance over my shoulder at Danicka to see if she was watching. She and her friends stood beneath the parted veil, their now-alert interest fastened on us. She'd probably tell everyone at school about Colin dragging me out of the place. Tears of humiliation threatened to burn my eyes and I tugged on Colin's hand, bringing his attention to me. Purple and gold lights flashed over his face.

"Colin—please—I can't leave like this," I said.

He dipped his head closer so he could hear me without me having to yell. His cologne mixed with the thick air in the place, the scent drifting into my head. He studied me a moment, then his gaze went over my shoulder—to Danicka? I wasn't sure, but he gave me a nod.

He glanced at his watch, then his attention was on me. Again. A luscious feeling of ownership, though false, temporary, and brought on by fantasy, filled me.

"How did you know I was here?" I asked.

"Your friend, Danicka, told me about the party the other day at school."

"She's not my friend." And she stood scowling at me from across the dance floor.

"I can see that."

Was she that obvious? Or was it me? I cringed inwardly, wondering what he really thought of me.

"Can I get you two anything?" A wiggling blonde bartender

dipped and shimmied next to us. The tray in her hand balanced perfectly with eight empty glasses even with her dancing.

Colin shook his head.

"I'll take a scotch," I said.

Colin's eyes widened for a moment. "We'll pass, thanks." He took my elbow. I pulled free. He brought himself tight to my chest, his warm breath at my ear when he hissed, "No drinking."

"Everyone does. They don't check ID here."

"Ash." He thrust a hand through his hair. "What's going on with you?"

"I just want to have fun."

"Okay, I get it, but underage drinking shouldn't be on your agenda. It's against the law."

"You never drank when you were underage?" I taunted. "Ever?"

He shifted. Looked at me then out—where? At the dancing couples? I didn't know what he was thinking, but he was so beautiful in the carnival-colored lights. A buzz wound low inside of me.

"Yeah, I did," he said finally. "I'm not proud of it. Look, this place is… it's not the kind of place you should be in."

"What does that mean? You think I belong at a playground or some pizza place with a jungle gym instead?"

"No, Ash, no. You're too good for this place." His hands appeared itchy hanging at his sides. Like he wasn't sure what to do with them. "Let's go."

"I told you, I like to dance."

"With these idiots? No way in hell."

"There are plenty of nice guys here." I crossed my arms over my chest.

"Like baldy? Come on." He reached for my elbow but I stepped back.

"I'm not leaving. I came to have fun and I'm going to dance."

"These guys'll eat you alive. You don't know what they're capable of."

"I'm talking about one dance, not sex," I protested. How naive did he think I was?

His hand threaded nervously through his hair, leaving it mussed. His brown eyes blackened with challenge, sending heat through my bloodstream. He snatched my hand. In a half a dozen long strides we were in the center of the dance floor.

White, purple, and red lights flashed up at us from the glowing floor. I couldn't believe I was going to dance with him. Colin. A violent tune sliced and chopped the air with insatiable teeth, cutting away the veneer of clothing, stripping bare. The song grabbed hold of my body and didn't let go.

He danced less than a foot away, his protective gaze jumping around the surrounding bodies scouring faces of both women and men with suspicion. For the first time since I could remember, I was pleased to have a bodyguard.

The leering from older men sent a scratchy creepiness across my skin. And the glaring women—I felt like Colin and I were dancing in a lioness' den rather than one of New York's most posh clubs.

Danicka scowled from the tent.

The song ended, but another layered over it, this one sensual. Slow. Like a heartbeat readying for bed.

Colin stopped. An uncontrollable urge to touch him surged through me, and I stepped close. Black flecks in his eyes deepened. My arms trembled as I slid them up and around his neck.

"Ditching me was not cool, Ash." The corner of his jaw knotted. He didn't move. One second passed. Three. Then his arms caged my waist. I saw a million questions in his eyes. Or at least I thought I did. *What does this mean? This one. Slow. Dance.*

His piercing gaze narrowed—unyieldingly aimed at me as though he was not pleased.

Shamed that I would manipulate him for my own enjoyment, I couldn't look at him anymore. His arms tightened, so fleeting—yet undeniable.

I felt his gaze on my face, and my cheeks heated. The moment was dark. Stormy. Slowly, we swayed. His thighs brushed mine. The buckle on his belt grazed my stomach. Heat from his neck, and his soft hair brushed my wrists locked at the back of his head.

I looked up.

His arms drew me closer. Conflicting sensations both taunting and frightening weaved through my body. *Please don't end, song. Please.*

I'd read about heroines in my romance novels letting their fingers play in the hair at the nape of the hero's neck. I allowed my fingers to explore Colin's thick hair. His eyes narrowed, and his tongue grazed his lips. At my waist, his fingers kneaded. He inched back.

Submerged by confusion, I broke free of his embrace, blinking back tears. His palms snapped around my upper arms. My heart skipped and nearly skidded to a stop. Heat rushed my cheeks. I tried to break free, but his hands held me firm. He didn't say a word, just stared me down, causing a quiver of the unknown to drip through my center.

In a swift move, he had me by the wrist and he tore through the dancing couples on the floor, making our way to the front entrance.

I kept my head low, sure every attendee could see that I didn't belong there. Carlos opened the door for us, and the icy air burned my hot skin when it made contact.

I tried to keep up with Colin's long stride, but barely kept at his heels in a near jog. Disgrace started to boil in my gut. I yanked my arm, but he whipped around, pulled me to his chest. His eyes fired.

The line of waiting, chatting patrons went silent. Whispers and whistles filled the air. Colin's steely frown shot to those in line. The daggers of warning in his eyes left them quiet.

My cell phone vibrated in my pocket. I couldn't move. I barely dared to breathe. Colin finished staring at those waiting in line and, my wrist still captive in his hand, dragged me to the curb where a beefy bouncer waved a cab to the curb for us.

Colin yanked open the door and firmly urged me inside. The door slammed behind me. I was so angry, I opened my mouth to tell the driver to drive, but Colin's door blew open and he got in, the door banging shut after him. His eyes sparkled like black fire.

"Twenty-Twenty Nine Park," Colin told the driver without taking his gaze from mine.

Sticky moments choked by. His leg jittered like he was ready to bolt. Tear someone apart. I bit my lower lip, panic sending a chill over my skin. His eyes slit, and lowered to my mouth for a blink I might have missed if we hadn't been in a glare-down.

"Are you going to tell him?" I demanded.

I could barely endure his puncturing stare. "You ran off. Again. I have no choice."

My stomach plunged. I wanted to beg him not to. I didn't want to face what I knew would come, if Daddy found out I'd broken the rules. The look in Colin's eyes troubled me. He had no idea what telling Daddy really meant.

I couldn't sleep. I waited in my bedroom for Mother and Daddy to come home so I could talk to them. I wasn't looking forward to the fireworks that would inevitably follow, and as the hours wore on my courage started to waver. I hadn't heard any sound overhead, and I wondered where Colin was.

I crept out into the hall and peered over the winding stairwell, about to take the steps down to search for him when I saw his long legs extending from a chair Mother kept next to the entryway table.

He was waiting for them?

My heart sunk. I'd behaved like a diva, and had probably lost any thread of respect that might have been woven between us up until this point. My behavior tonight was the excuse he'd been waiting for to be free of this job.

Finally, I heard voices echo off the marble floor.

"Colin, darling, you didn't need to stay up. Whatever it is, I'm sure it can wait until morning." Mother's voice was amazingly chipper for the hour.

"Charles, we need to talk," Colin said.

A short pause followed. Maybe Daddy was too tired. If they put off the discussion I could try to talk Colin out of telling them what happened.

"Of course. In my office."

Mother bid them goodnight, and I closed my bedroom door and turned off the light so she'd think I was asleep. After I knew she was in her suite, I took the stairs down, crossed to Daddy's closed office doors and stood as close as I could.

"Ashlyn and I went to a party tonight." Colin's voice started strong, but had a crumbling edge to it.

My stomach lurched in fear. Silence followed.

"What kind of party?"

"A club party. One of her friends was hosting it."

"A club party? Where?"

"Ninety-Nine."

"Ninety-Nine?" Daddy boomed. "Who invited her to such a trashy establishment?" His lion's roar vibrated with the power of a volcano before eruption. "I can't fathom Ashlyn in that filthy place."

"I'm sor—"

"You say a friend of hers invited her? What friend? The only friend we allow her to associate with is Felicity. Was it her?"

"No. Another—"

"Who?"

"Danicka Fiore."

A pause followed. My stomach tore in two.

"Charles, we didn't start out going to the party. We went to the bookstore."

"I see." Daddy's tone changed. Colder. The sweat coating my skin iced over.

"So you accompanied Ashlyn to the bookstore, and then what? The two of you decided you needed to go to a seedy nightclub?"

"No, that's not—"

"What, damn it?"

"We… started off at the bookstore and she left from there."

"*Left? Alone?*"

"Yes sir."

"Ashlyn took a cab to Ninety-Nine. Alone. Where were you when this happened?"

"She was in one section of the bookstore and I was in—"

"That was your first mistake, leaving her by herself. I thought I made myself clear when I hired you that I didn't want her unprotected out in public. Ever. What part of that don't you understand?"

"I'm sorry, you're right. I take full responsibility."

"You're damned right you'll take full responsibility. Do not leave her side. She's not allowed to attend such functions."

"She's... not? Ever?"

My heart pounded. A choking silence seeped through the closed doors.

"What distresses me most about this is that she'd sneak away from you. She never told you that she intended to go to Ninety-Nine?"

Oh no. The truth would punish us both. "No, sir. Again, I apologize."

Silence followed, and my nerves bunched tight wondering what was happening. I wanted to open the door, but fear paralyzed me.

"After you discovered she was gone, how did you know where to find her?"

"Danicka had invited me to the party. I declined. But she'd mentioned that she'd also invited Ashlyn."

I covered my mouth with my fingers.

"How long had she been there when you arrived?" Daddy asked.

"I got there just as she was escorted into the building."

"I see." Daddy's voice sounded calmer now. I took a deep breath. Maybe this wouldn't be a big deal after all.

"So." Daddy's steady courtroom tone returned. "Ashlyn had just entered the establishment when you found her?"

"Yes."

"Thank god for that. One of my partners handles the owners. Ninety-Nine might be decent enough for the average idiot in New York City, but the place is far too vile for Ashlyn."

Colin didn't respond.

"I don't want anything like this happening again," Daddy

commanded. "Frankly, I'm surprised at your lack of professionalism."

"I understand. Again, I apologize."

"Her behavior—sneaking off —is inexcusable to say the least. I'm going to talk to her."

A lump choked my throat. It wouldn't be long before I'd see Daddy. I quickly took the stairs up, closed my bedroom door and locked it. Though locking was futile.

Whenever Daddy knocked on my door, I opened it.

After turning off the light I got into bed. My heart raced in my chest. Fear ran side-by-side with panic. Moments later, the knock came. Faking that I'd been asleep wasn't something I could do. Daddy could see through my performance.

I flicked on the lamp next to my bed, got up and crossed to the door. Daddy's stony expression sent a shiver through my bones. He didn't ask to come in, he stepped over the threshold and closed the door. "What happened tonight?"

I remained silent.

"Ashlyn?"

"I went to a friend's party."

Daddy's eyes widened for a millisecond—almost as if he couldn't believe I'd told him the truth. Or that I'd had the nerve to defy him and go to a party.

"Where was it?"

"At Ninety-Nine. It's a club."

"I know damned well what it is," Daddy ground out. His skin began to redden at the base of his collar. "Give me your phone."

I lifted my chin, turned, retrieved my cell phone from the stand at the side of my bed and plopped it into his open palm.

His eyes flared. "Apparently Felicity is not the friend we thought she was, if she invited you to such an event."

He knew Felicity hadn't invited me. Anger and hurt burned the back of my neck. Was he determined to strip me of every friend I had?

"Felicity didn't invite me."

"Oh? Then who?"

I didn't respond, too furious.

"You're angry?" he asked. "Were you running away from Colin? I know how much you hate him."

Is that what he wanted? I glared at him.

"Did you fire him?" I asked.

"Is that what you want?"

"I want you to let me do things everyone else my age is doing."

"You have the best this world has to offer."

"Not freedom."

His expression remained unchanged. So controlled. Another round of anger raced through my blood but I mirrored his controlled demeanor. He seemed to ponder my words for a few uncomfortable, quiet seconds, then he tucked my cell phone into his pocket. "We'll finish this discussion in the morning."

He left.

———————— CHAPTER NINE

I wanted to stay buried beneath my covers the next morning. Gray light streamed through the tiny slits of the large shutters covering my windows. Instinctively, I reached next to my bed for my phone, but the spot on the side table was empty. I hoped Felicity was smart enough not to send me any Mother and Daddy bashing texts. For sure Daddy would read whatever came into my phone.

Soft sounds overhead lured my thoughts to Colin. In spite of the fact that I knew I'd face some sort of retribution for last night's outing, dancing with Colin… his nearness… the music… his attention so riveted to me… a warmth flurried and spread throughout my body. I closed my eyes, reaching for the feel of him next to mine. Of his arms around me.

A smile lit my lips.

Upstairs, a thud. Another.

I threw back the covers, stood and wrapped my robe around me. The clock by my bedside glowed eight AM. Mother and Daddy wouldn't be awake for hours. Cracking open the door, I crossed to the stairs and peered up. Colin's bedroom door was shut, but I heard another thud.

What is he doing?

I took the stairs up, arrived at the landing and thought better of sticking around, curious or not. I was the last person he wanted to see after last night. If he caught me spying on him, he'd really think I was weird. I turned, ready to head back down the stairs and to the piano when his door opened. I froze.

"Ashlyn?"

Oh no. This can't be happening. I turned before realizing I hadn't even washed my face yet. Ugh. He was dressed in grey sweats and a soaking-wet tee shirt. The moist tips of his hair hung in a muss around his face like, a dark halo. He held a sweat shirt in his hands, poised to pull the garment over his head.

"Um. Hi."

"Everything okay?" he whispered, glancing down the stairs. He stepped out into the hall, and I caught his musky scent.

"Yes, of course."

"I'm going for a run." He paused a second, and I thought a scant wariness—maybe from my behavior last night—flickered in his eyes. "Want to come?"

The last thing I wanted was for him to ask me because he felt obligated, or because he didn't trust me. I shook my head. He lifted the sweatshirt over his head and his tee shirt lifted, baring ripped lower abs. I bit my lip. The sweatshirt fell into place, his dark hair popping out, his eyes sparkling in a smile that sent my pulse skipping.

"So, you work out?" *Duh. Didn't he just say that?*

"Yeah, here and there. Hey, about last night." His scent swamped me: damp and male. He inched closer, to keep our conversation from traveling.

"Yeah, I—I'm sorry if you… got in trouble," I said.

"Ash." His tone cut through me like a hot spoon through cream. "I'm here to protect you. That's what your father wants. You taking off like that last night—"

"I really am sorry you got caught in the middle of Daddy and me. He doesn't understand how I feel." *Helpless. Caged.* I looked away.

"He's concerned about your safety."

"He's more than concerned," I muttered.

He eyed me. He seemed to hem a moment, like he wanted to say something more. "Clubs have the 21 age limit for a reason."

"I know." My gaze fell to my feet, afraid of what I'd see in his eyes. When the silence between us thickened, I looked at him. Curiosity veiled his face. He stuffed his hands into the front pocket of the hoodie.

"Do you know any self defense?"

"A little. They had a class in PE once."

He nodded. "When I get back, I'm going to teach you a few moves. You cool with that?"

I swallowed. *He's talking about self defense, get a grip.* "Sure."

"You positive you don't want to run?"

Did he think my life was sad and pathetic now? Is that why he offered an opportunity for freedom again?

"No thanks."

"You're going to stay here, right?" His dimples flashed in a teasing grin. But the scant wary trust I'd seen in his expression seconds ago resurfaced. I felt guilty about the whole incident. His dark eyes penetrated me. I could barely tolerate his scrutiny—deserving as I was of it.

He jogged down the stairs. I blew out a breath when he went outside, the stairwell echoing with his absence.

What had I done? I'd made myself into this complete idiot, running to that stupid party. I sunk to the stair and buried my face in my hands. Now, Colin didn't trust me. Who knew what I had coming from Mother and Daddy. I wanted freedom, yes, but now that Colin was here, I wanted him to see me as… what?

Not a baby.

Not a girl.

Not a self absorbed teenager.

I don't know what I'd expected from Danicka's party, but seeing her and her model minions high, surrounded by drugs and drinks, and being accosted by gyrating older guys was not what I'd pictured when I'd envisioned myself at a club. My fantasy was more like me being the in the spotlight, dancing and flirting.

I showered and dressed in jeans and a striped pink hoodie-shirt, and decided to spend the day on the patio with a book. Maybe Mother and Daddy, when they sought me out to hand down punishment, wouldn't go ballistic with hundreds of eyes watching from surrounding apartments.

Colin's bedroom door was open, and as I took the stairs up I caught his scent sneaking out, as if teasing me. I took a deep breath, grinned and continued up the narrow stairs to the patio.

Unable to concentrate on my novel, I set my book aside and crossed to the railing. I gazed down at the street in hopes of catching a glimpse of Colin on his way back. Sundays were a little quieter on Park Avenue. Traffic streamed at a less hurried pace. Instead of dark suits and dressy jackets striding down the sidewalks, runners in sweats jogged and the occasional little white-haired lady walked her white, perfectly coiffed Maltese.

A soft breeze streamed between the buildings. The wintry air lifted my hair and tossed it around my face so I tied the long, honeyed strands into a knot. I gazed left and didn't see Colin. Right. In the distance I saw his lanky form in an efficient, rhythmic run, sweeping around the random pedestrian as he headed toward the townhouse.

A tingle skittered over my skin.

He slowed and stopped in front of the townhouse, his gaze glancing up, catching me. I waved, trying to appear casual. He waved back.

Yes, I'm watching your every move. I shrunk, grabbed my book and plopped back into the chair. The patio door opened and my heart somersaulted in my chest. I jerked around.

Daddy, dressed in a casual pair of slacks and a sweater, strode toward me.

"You're up already?" I asked.

"Yes, I am." He towered over me. I kept my eyes on my book. "Your mother doesn't know about what happened last night. I'm giving you the responsibility to tell her. I have an engagement, so I will discuss this with her later. Understood?"

"Yes, sir."

"The most distressing part of this is that you'd go to such a low-life establishment."

The back of my neck started to burn. I only nodded.

His hand reached out and I jerked back, thinking he might rip the book from my hands. His outstretched hand remained poised between us, the look in his eye shock and hurt. "I was only going to touch your head, Princess." His tone carried a wound.

"Oh." I swallowed.

His hand slowly fell to his side, and he studied me a moment before leaning over and gently kissing the top of my head. Then he left.

A pang of guilt slapped my heart. I'd hurt his feelings, reacting like that. But, an eye for an eye, right? Did that make me a bad person?

The door opened and Mother teetered out. She had on her black, bug-eye Prada glasses, a silky white jogging suit, her hair mussed like she'd just torn herself from bed.

"Ugh," she groaned, falling into the lounge chair I'd just fantasized seeing Colin and me in. "I need a Rockstar. My head is throbbing."

I chuckled. Mother kept a stash of Rockstars in the kitchen. "Why didn't you get one?"

She reclined in the seat with a heavy sigh, and I was certain her eyes were closed behind her sunglasses. "Go get one for me, will you darling? We need to talk about the Christmas party and I need my brain clear. Go. Go."

"Mother."

"Ash-lyn," she commanded.

She didn't want to get the drink because she didn't want Colin seeing her smashed. I let out a loud sigh, set my book down and rose.

"Spare me the attitude, young lady."

"Maybe when you quit calling me that." Yanking open the door, I made sure it slammed behind me. On the third floor, I couldn't resist a glance toward Colin's bedroom. The door was open, and the fresh scent of soap tickled my nose, luring me.

I continued on down the stairs, a grin on my face as I imagined Colin—just out of the shower.

Gavin was in the kitchen, his humpty-dumpty presence

lumbering about in the space, made the area feel smaller.

"Morning Miss Adair."

"Morning."

I opened the refrigerator and snagged a chilled Rockstar for Mother, turned and smacked into Colin's chest. The dampness of his fresh, clean skin sent a wave of bubbles through my stomach.

"Hey." His eyes teased. "Those are bad for you, you know."

"That's why they're irresistible," I quipped, batting my lashes.

His grin slowly faded, and his eyes drew sharp. He stepped back, swallowed. Had I said the wrong thing?

Gavin cleared his throat, drawing our attention to him.

"The items you requested are on the third shelf, left side of the pantry," Gavin said flatly, cocking his brow at Colin. "In the future, I would ask you to leave me one of these," Gavin pointed to a stack of yellow Post-It notes on the counter, "on the face of the refrigerator every Monday."

Colin nodded. "Sure. Thanks, Gav." He crossed to the pantry and disappeared inside. Gavin rolled his eyes at Colin's shortening of his name, but I liked that Colin felt comfortable enough to step forward with the nickname. The cold Rockstar sent chills up my arm, but I didn't want to leave. *Go, or he'll think you're a loser with nothing else to do.*

"Thank you." Mother popped open the can and the sizzle sighed into the cold, breezy atmosphere. "Ah," she took a long drink. "Nectar of the gods."

I snorted. She handed me the can and I took a sip.

"Now." She settled into the chair like a minx on a blanket. "What are you going to wear to the party? And if you say that black Betsey Johnson thing you've got hanging in your closet I will lock you in your room that night. I want you in something classic."

"Something that makes me look forty, you mean."

"Ashlyn, we have very influential guests…"

Blah, blah, blah. I'd heard the influential, carefully-selected guests lecture before. Mother wanted to dress me up and show me off— again. But she wanted to parade me only if I wore what she deemed classic and elegant without keeping in mind that I was a teenager.

"I'll have to remind your father to talk to Colin about security. I'm certain Colin can handle things. He's very adept. He'll look marvelous in a tuxedo, too, won't he? I'll have my contact at Prada order one in for him."

"Maybe he owns one," I suggested, just to ruffle her. I could easily envision Colin in a tuxedo.

Mother laughed, sipped. "Even if he does, I'm sure it's a cheap, tacky thing. I couldn't have that at my party."

"You're such a snob," I teased, reaching for the Rockstar.

Mother's face froze. I couldn't see past the dark glasses covering her eyes, but I was sure she was glaring. She held the Rockstar in a tight fist. "Excuse me?"

"It's true and you love it." I waved my hand for the Rockstar, which she finally handed to me.

"It's in the genes, darling. Be careful where you toss those stones. They have a way of landing close to home."

Throwing stones reminded me that Daddy had left me the joyful responsibility to tell Mother about what had happened last night. My stomach turned over, anticipating the admittance. But, if I didn't tell her, she'd hear it from Daddy and that would be far worse.

"I went to a party last night," I said, steeling my voice.

Mother's head pivoted my direction. "A party? With whom?"

"Um. This girl at school invited me. Danicka."

Mother slipped the Prada glasses down her nose so her eyes could lock mine in that you-did-what way. "I take it your father doesn't know about this."

"He knows."

Her right brow arched. "My. I'm surprised he didn't blow the roof off the townhouse."

"He was pretty calm about it." I stretched the truth in hopes that she was too hungover to care.

"Was he now?" She slipped the glasses back in place, shielding her eyes. "And we'll all live happily ever after in Neverland." Mother let out a snort. "Yet you didn't ask for permission to go, at least you didn't ask me for permission."

"No, I figured since it was a friend's party and I'm almost eighteen it wouldn't be a big deal."

Mother laughed.

"It's true. Millions of girls go to parties. Why shouldn't I?"

"Because you're not like millions of girls. Colin was with you?"

"Of course."

"And he didn't speak with your father or me about it first? How odd."

"Like I said, millions of girls go to parties. I'm sure he figured it wasn't anything out of the norm."

Mother wagged her finger at me like a slow metronome. "Your nose is going to start growing, young lady."

"Stop with the 'young lady'. Okay, maybe Daddy hadn't had the chance to tell Colin how ridiculous you guys are about my safety."

"So you took advantage of that?" Mother asked. "Ashlyn. I'm disappointed in you."

"I apologized to Daddy. He got over it. Can you?"

"I'm still digesting the fact that you went to a party without our permission, do you mind? I feel like I just ate a jar of cheap caviar."

"Mother."

"Where was this party, anyhow?"

"Ninety-Nine."

Mother laughed and brought her coat tighter around her chest. "Oh, I bet that got your father's jockeys in a bunch. What did he do? Take your phone?"

"Yeah," I mumbled.

She nodded. "That was very generous of him. The punishment could have been much worse."

The door opened and Colin stepped onto the patio. "Morning, Fiona." He nodded at me.

"Colin, darling." Mother sat upright and fussed with her hair.

"You're seeing me very unkempt, I'm afraid."

Colin clasped his hands behind his back. He wore jeans and a black sweater. The simple outfit fit him with the perfection Mother had intended. "You look lovely, Fiona," he said.

Mother's cheeks pinked. "That's very kind of you to say." I half expected her to extend her hand to him for a royal kiss. "Ashlyn and I have been discussing her adventure last night."

Colin and I exchanged glances.

"Not to worry, dear boy. Is that why you were waiting for us in the entry last night? Hmm?"

"Yes."

"Well." Mother's admiring gaze swept him from head to toe. "Very admirable. I won't ask you what Charles had to say on the matter, that I can figure out on my own. Colin, I want to tell you about our traditional Christmas party. We invite about two hundred of our closest friends, so, you'll need to hire some additional security, but I'll let Charles discuss that with you. My only question for you is, do you own a tuxedo?"

"Uh, no, I don't."

Mother stood. She flicked at Colin's shoulders, her hands slowing to gentle caresses as they swept down his arms. "I'm going to order one for you. It will fit your physique… perfectly."

I stole a gulp of Rockstar to choke back an embarrassed laugh.

Colin shifted. "Okay."

"Are you going to be here for Christmas? Or home?" I finally interjected, annoyed Mother assumed he'd be staying.

Mother's jubilant expression faltered. "Of course he'll be here. He works for us." She turned to Colin. "I need you here."

A tricky silence spread between us. "I appreciate you thinking of me." He shot me a glance, then returned his attention to Mother. "I—I'm not sure where I'll be."

"What?" Mother nearly shrieked.

"Mother, people—even employees—go home for Christmas. It's only fair." Though thinking about Colin absent from the townhouse left me with a hole inside.

"Not employees who are integral to our home," Mother snapped.

Colin cleared his throat. "I can probably stay, if—"

"I insist. Charles will too. What would we do with Ashlyn?"

I wanted to laugh. *Heaven forbid they spend some time with me.*

Mother continued, "I realize that Christmas is a family time of year, but Barb will understand. I'll call her myself." Snagging the Rockstar, Mother gulped. "Now, I need you take Ashlyn to the Christmas Spectacular tonight. We have tickets—gifts from one of Charles' clients—but I've got too much to do to go. Besides, I've seen it a million times."

Colin nodded. "Of course."

"Wonderful. Ashlyn. No more partying, hmm?"

I nearly rolled my eyes, but Colin looked over. His lips curved up a little, his eyes narrowed with… what? Warning? Challenge? A zing of wonder trembled through me.

"Don't forget our lesson," Colin said. Mother's brows cocked from behind her dark glasses. "Self defense lesson. Before the Spectacular," he clarified with a grin. "Meet me in the music room in ten minutes. Wear something comfortable."

——————— CHAPTER TEN

My palm drenched in sweat, I grabbed hold of the doorknob ready to meet Colin in the music room. Colin. Touching me.

I cracked open the door, peered in. He stood alone, gazing out the window. After tip-toeing in, I closed the door and pressed my back against it, my heart beating like a hummingbird.

"What are you going to do to me?" I asked, voice squeaking.

He turned. His dimples beamed. "*Do* to you?" He strolled my direction and my nerves jangled. "I'm going to show you how to defend yourself." He stopped close. His scent swamped me with nervous fluttering. "First, always be aware of your surroundings. Know where exits are. Keep your eyes open for anyone out of the ordinary."

"Like, all the time?"

"When you're out in public. Anywhere but home."

"I've never had to do that before."

"Well, it's time to start. You won't always have a bodyguard looking out for you."

Nice dream, but I doubted I'd be independent anytime soon. "Yes, you're right." I nodded.

"Along with being aware of your surroundings, you should know some defense basics." He stepped behind me, his nearness sucking the strength from my muscles. "If you're grabbed from behind," his hands latched onto my shoulders, and my knees nearly buckled. *Get a hold of yourself. Show some dignity.* "You've got a couple of options." His body pressed against mine. His arms wrapped around and pinned me. Panicked, I wondered if I'd be able to keep breathing. He was so strong.

Wait, this feels good.

My head tilted back. "Okay." My reply rasped from my throat.

His warm laugh tickled my neck. "You're supposed to resist."

Resist? I brought my head upright. "Oh, yeah. Okay."

"Slam your foot against his instep," he said.

I tapped my heel on his foot. He laughed. "Come on, harder."

My blood was so warm swarming uncontrollably through my veins. I started to sweat. I lifted my foot and jammed it down. "Good," he said. "Use all of the force you can. Again."

I stomped on his instep until he approved. His arms remained in a vice grip around me. "Another way is to head butt."

I savored how tight he held me, how close he was. The way his lips moved next to my cheek. "Throw your head back as hard as you can."

"But I—"

"Don't worry about me," he said, positioning his body so that my shoulder blades pressed into his chest, my buttocks was flush with his pelvis. "Do it."

I sent my head back once. Twice. Three more head thrusts and his arms released me. "Don't hold back." He stepped away, scrubbing his jaw.

Standing alone, I was cold.

"We're not done, are we?" I asked.

"Go for the eyes, Ash." In a snap he was wrapped around me again, squeezing the air out of my lungs, our faces inches apart. "Gouge."

"I—I can't." His eyes flashed with determination. My gaze dropped to his mouth. *Kiss me.*

"If he gets you like this, go for his eyes." He commanded. I nodded, muscles melting in his embrace. *I could never hurt you.*

For a moment he studied me, and his brows creased. I felt the slightest stiffening in his body, the minutest tightening of his arms around me. He released me, and stepped back. A shudder wracked my bones.

"Those are some basics," he said.

"Okay."

"I don't know about you," his gaze slipped to my lips, "but I'm hungry."

Yeah. "I'm starved."

Hot bread and spices scented the air from delis and restaurants along 57th Street. Even though it was chilly outside, I kept the window in the back of the car down so I could breathe in the aromas of the city.

Looking at him stole the grumble from my stomach, replacing it with a deep gnaw that had nothing to do with food. "Do you like Indian?"

"Yes, I do."

"The Bombay House on Forty-Ninth is pretty good," Eddy piped, his eyes flicking to us in his rear view mirror. "I've taken the wife there. They got good stuff."

"Oh yeah?" Colin's gaze shifted to Eddy.

Eddy drove us to the tiny hole-in-the-wall restaurant, pulled the car over and opened my door. I waited for Colin on the curb. He leaned close to Eddy, whispered something to him, patted his arm and Eddy nodded before he got back in the car and drove off.

Colin chuckled. "Why are you laughing?" I asked.

The sparkle in his eyes wasn't malicious, it was mesmerizing. "It's just that you don't have to be Park Avenue when we're together."

"I'm not." But Park Avenue was the only way I knew how to be.

He slung an arm around my shoulder and kept it there for a moment as we walked to the restaurant door. My body stiffened, but my knees melted into butter.

"You can relax around me, okay?" When his arm slipped away, emptiness sunk to my core. I hid the vacancy behind a nod.

The Bombay House was tucked at the top of a narrow, dark flight of stairs just off 49th Street. A whisper of red and gold paper lanterns lit the dark room, painted with murals of elephants carrying beautiful women and children on their backs. From hidden speakers, a woman's voice chanted to sitar music. A mix of cinnamon and curry perfumed the musky air.

We sat at a window table overlooking the street and its hub. How ordinary we looked together—if only people knew. But I was glad no one did—including him. This was my first date. It really wasn't a date, and guilt pinched my conscience categorizing it as one. Daddy had allowed me to go to a dance with one of his law associate's sons, once. My then-bodyguard had chaperoned, a detail the boy hadn't planned on and found strange enough that he ended the date early.

This qualified as a date for two reasons: my parents weren't along and Colin had planned it—at least the dinner part. I'd picked out my favorite berry blue silk sweater, pewter slacks and Jimmy Choo heels for the occasion; though Colin hadn't done anything more than skim a glance over me when I'd met him in the entry at home.

He wasn't glancing now. His eyes watched me intently. "There's that smile of yours again."

I'd never seen such light in anyone's eyes—like stars blinking in a midnight sky. Set against his black sweater, his dark hair and white teeth were even more brilliant. "What do you mean?"

"You looked the same way the other night when you were playing the piano. What do you think about when you play?"

"Lots of things."

"What inspires you?"

"Stuff." I cringed at my simple answers. I may look normal but that's where the similarity ended.

A woman with honeyed skin approached the table. Pressed in the center of her forehead was a red bindi dot. A colorful sari wrapped around her body. After a welcome, she gave us menus and excused herself.

"I've been here before, I think." Long ago, when we'd just moved to New York, before life became so protected even meals out were meted.

"I like the Chicken Tikka Masala," Colin said. "Ever tried it?"

It had been too many years for me to remember, but I didn't admit that, too afraid of what he would think when he finally realized the extremes Daddy went through to keep me safe.

"I'll try it." I closed the menu and set it aside.

"You sure? You can pick anything you want, you don't have to take my word for it."

I appreciated his efforts to encourage me to expand my horizons, but he had no idea that I had floated on an iceberg in the Antarctic for so long, I was numb to certain things—like choices. He seemed befuddled by my lack of response, and after we ordered, he sat forward, hands clasped on the table, nearly knuckle-to-knuckle with mine.

"Ashlyn." His tone told me something heavy was coming. "I have to confess, when Charles first told me about the job, I was… well, I knew he was… serious about your safety. But, how do you deal with his… overprotection?"

I reached for my water glass, keeping the icy glass between my fingers. My reflection in the window caught my eye. *Normal.*

"I love Daddy," I said. "But, I'll be honest, his emphasis on my safety is hard to live with."

He studied me, his gaze almost intolerably intense. "But he lets you date and stuff, right?"

I swallowed. If he knew the depths of Daddy's fixation, he'd split. Where I didn't want a bodyguard, Felicity was right: if I was going to have to have one, I might as well like him. And I did like Colin.

"Ash?"

"Well, I don't have a boyfriend." My hands shook, so I picked up my napkin and set it on my lap, securing my fists together. I glanced at his face for a reaction. Why was he watching my every move?

"How has it worked in the past? Your bodyguards go on dates with you?"

I bit my lip, nodded. His gaze slid to my mouth for a second. He shifted, reached for his water glass, drank, set it back down. "That'll be interesting," he murmured.

"Like I said, there isn't anybody in my life like that. I can't wait to be out… to go to college. How did you get done so fast?"

"I took AP classes. Like you, I was ready to move on to the next phase of my life."

"Do you regret doing it all… fast?"

"Nope. I was ready."

"Did you always plan on the FBI?"

He grinned. "Yeah." He leaned forward, resting his forearms on the edge of the table. "It intrigues me. But, I needed to work some, first. Which brought me here."

I bit my lower lip, smiled.

Again, Colin's gaze slipped briefly to my mouth. He swallowed hard, shook his head.

"What?" I asked.

"Can't believe you don't have a boyfriend."

Warmth rushed to my cheeks. I averted my eyes behind fluttering lashes, shocked at what he was saying to me.

Something in his eyes changed then, I wasn't sure what I saw. A myriad of thoughts ran through my head: he was glad I didn't have a boyfriend, happy to be working for Daddy, but at the same time not sure what to do from here. *Fantasies, Ashlyn. You've read too many romance novels.*

"Guys are idiots," he said beneath his breath.

———— CHAPTER ELEVEN

When I came downstairs Monday morning for breakfast, Colin was already in the kitchen, sitting at the island counter top. He wore dark gray slacks and a black V-neck sweater with a blue shirt beneath it. Hot.

His crisp gaze lifted to mine. "Hey." I loved the rough cadence of his morning voice, the sound sent a buzz through me.

"Hey."

I quickly poured myself some Kashi, soy milk and stared at the empty chair next to him. He caught my appraisal of where to sit, so I couldn't go to the table at the window—I'd appear rude.

I sat next to him.

His jaw rotated with each chew, and the crackle of him eating his—Cap'n Crunch—made me giggle.

"What?" His eyes lit with teasing. "And could you chew the Cap'n and not make noise?"

I nodded.

"Oh yeah?" He held out his spoon, a pile of yellowy squares dripping with milk, poised at my lips.

His spoon. In my mouth. My cheeks warmed. Gently, he guided the spoon in and watched as I closed my lips around the cold sterling silver. "Chew."

I motioned for him to remove the spoon, trying not to spill the contents all over us both in a laugh. He tugged on the spoon, removed it and I chewed. Slowly.

"Slow is cheating."

"Is not." I swallowed.

"The Cap'n is crunchy. That's all I'm gonna say," he said.

"How'd you rate getting Cap'n Crunch in our pantry? Mother would never allow me to buy that stuff."

"She likes me better than you." He wagged his brows.

"No doubt," I snickered, and started eating.

Our chewing—his noisy, mine petite—broke the awkward yet truthful silence left behind after his comment. When we both finished, he took our bowls to the sink, rinsed them and handed them to me. I loaded them into the dishwasher.

The drive to Chatham was quiet except for the chat I'd come to expect between Colin and Eddy about the local news and Eddy's continual bad luck at lotto. With Stuart, I'd plug my earbuds in and be done with it. That was impossible with Colin. He demanded my attention simply by being. I loved the lilt of his voice, the way he moved, his confidence, strength, his surety stole into the hollowness of my life. I didn't feel as empty anymore.

We pulled up to the curb at school and Eddy opened the door. Colin slipped on his dark glasses, waited while I hoisted on my book bag, then escorted me up the stairs through the hive of uniformed girls streaming into the building.

After the weekend, I was at ease with his protective gestures. In fact, I relished the stares and glances from my schoolmates, lifting my chin, hoping to send a message—*he's mine*.

Danicka and her model friends stood just inside the doors. Had they been waiting for us? I looked at Colin, who spared the designer bunch a quick glance before his gaze returned to me.

"See ya," he said.

"See ya." I didn't want to go. I wanted to hang with him all day. Do anything. Everything. Just be with him.

I started toward the main hall, passing Danicka who stepped out from the circle of her friends and eyed me. "What happened Saturday?"

"I wasn't able to stay," I said. Then added, "Colin had other plans for us." With a smile of satisfaction on my lips, I swiveled and headed to my locker leaving Danicka with her eyes bulging.

What do you think of that, Danicka? I swung open my locker door and stuffed what books I didn't need for my first class inside. My reflection in the mirror hanging on the locker door was too pale for my liking. I quickly brushed on some MAC blush then jumped. Felicity's face popped up behind me.

"What? What? I've been in suspense mode all weekend. Tortured. You've GOT to tell me! Did you go to Danicka's party?"

"It was amazing. Not her. Ninety-Nine was super crowded and, kind of pathetic with all these older men. But what *happened* was amazing. You'll never believe it, Fel, never."

Felicity hopped up and down, squeeing. "What? And why did your Dad answer your phone?"

"He took it. But forget that. Saturday was like a scene out of a romance novel. Seriously."

"O.M.G." Felicity fanned her hands at her face. "I knew it. I knew it."

"We danced."

Felicity flattened herself against my locker in a dramatic gesture of a half-faint.

"But that wasn't all. I can't tell you every… thing…. not now. I'll tell you at lunch."

The bell shrilled.

"Cruel." Felicity backed away from me, heading down the hall in the direction of her first class. "You're cruel, you know that."

I laughed, nodded.

Cruelty, like snobbery, was in my genes.

Was it wrong of me to want to eat lunch with Colin? After all, it was because of me he was at Chatham. I toyed with this idea from first period until the lunch bell rang. Classes blurred. Teachers once again inquired if I was ill.

Felicity met me at our usual corner at the top of the main stairs, fifth floor then we took the steps down. We passed the main foyer, and I didn't see Colin. I borrowed Felicity's cell phone.

"You just spent a dream weekend with him." Felicity said, craning her neck searching for him. "That whole self defense thing was so hot and sexy, I started to sweat just hearing about it. He's going to dig you texting him."

"A dream for me. Work for him." As fun as the weekend escape had been, even with the chastisement from my parents, he probably didn't see Ninety-Nine—or our dance—like I did. But we *had* had a blast at the Spectacular. Hadn't we?

"Invite him to eat with us. Maybe he's one of those odd people who loves cafeteria food. My mom does. That and Chinese. Ugh."

I gnawed on my lower lip. Fear of rejection finally convinced me to not text him about lunch or anything else. I dragged through the cafeteria line with my tray, plucking a mandarin chicken salad and Vitamin Water. Felicity stuck with her vegetarian panini, chips, and Pepsi.

We sat at a table next to the large windows that overlooked the cement courtyard of the front of Chatham. Danicka, for how skinny she was, easy to spot—her and her pack surrounded—Colin. My heart sunk. His tall form, encircled by blue-blazers, plaid skirts and bare, never-ending legs caused me to nearly lose the first three bites of mandarin chicken.

"The skank." Felicity, seeing my fixed gaze outside, gasped. "She's making a move on him."

What if Danicka asked Colin his version of what had happened Saturday? A sickening black sludge filled my insides. Danicka stood close to Colin, who had his dark sunglasses on, so I couldn't see where his eyes were. But then, neither could Danicka. She flipped her ruler-straight blonde hair over her shoulders every five seconds, like she was in a shampoo commercial.

Colin's dimples charmed, flashing coyly. What were they talking about?

"She's done this millions of times and knows what to do and how to do it," Felicity said. The weight of my romantic inexperience crushed me a little.

I slid my book bag over my shoulder, took my tray to the conveyor belt, and left the cafeteria. Felicity tagged along beside me, her panini in one hand, Pepsi in the other, chips tucked under her arm.

"Woohoo," she squealed. "Boss is comin' down on her man."

"I'm not his boss, Fel." Even though, technically, Colin did work for me. "And he's not my man." But I was working on it.

A large floor-to-ceiling mirror donned one end of the main hall. I checked myself out as we passed by. I looked just as good as Danicka in this uniform. I may not drip Juicy jewelry, but the uniform flattered my shape and my skin was clear.

Outside, the frosty air hurt with every breath. Why was Colin out here? I found him in the courtyard, still surrounded by Danicka and her friends.

"I'm so cold," Danicka was saying, hugging herself as Felicity and I approached. "Can I wear your coat?"

Colin saw me. I broke through the circle of girls and hooked my arm in his. "Come on, we're going out for lunch."

He dipped his head near mine as we walked away. "Thanks. I owe you."

"Have you eaten?" I asked. Over his shoulder, I saw Danicka and her friends waiting. *Vultures.*

He glanced at his watch. "Do we have time?"

"Fifteen minutes," Felicity piped with a grin.

"Joe's Deli is close." I tugged his arm and the three of us started down the sidewalk in the direction of the restaurant.

"I could eat." His lips curved up.

Since he owed me, I had him take me to the bookstore again that evening. In my heart, I hoped we would spend more time sipping lattes and talking than skimming book shelves, but I didn't want him to think I had an agenda.

"Charles wants me to stay with you," he said after we entered the building. He shook away a light dusting of snow covering his pea coat.

Babysitting again? "I'm not going to take off," I said. "I promise."

He yanked off his knit hat and bunched it between his two hands while he tried to decipher whether or not I was telling him the truth.

"You believe me, right?"

"Yeah, I believe you. You're not the partying type. And you're not missing anything, trust me."

"Are you the partying type?"

"Nope."

"But you're twenty-one."

"Like I said, places like that—the people who hang there— overrated."

I liked imagining him as a person with class who knew better. If I didn't go to another club again, with its sweaty bald gyrating men, I wouldn't miss it.

No way was I going to browse romances with him standing over my shoulder. I opted for the young adult section instead. After a few minutes of trailing me, he started picking books from the shelves and thumbing through them.

I moved from one aisle to the next and continued browsing.

"Hey Ashlyn." I froze. The voice belonged to Stuart. I turned around. He'd lost some weight in the weeks since I'd last seen him. Thumbprints the color of bruises tattooed beneath his eyes spoke of lack of sleep. Grey shadowed his cheeks.

I shot a glance at Colin, a row over, his head down.

"You look… beautiful." Stuart's green eyes inched from my face down my body like a starved man.

"Did you… follow me here?" I asked, my gaze flicking from Stuart to Colin, his head still cast down—reading.

"Of course not," he said. "We live in the same city, we were bound to run into each other."

Stuart and I had come here often enough. I couldn't rid myself of the edginess creeping over my skin. Still, he'd been my bodyguard for three years—I could talk to him and be cordial.

But the desperation in his eyes was difficult to see.

"Are… you okay?" I asked.

His hands moved in the depths of his overcoat. He blinked heavily. "Yeah. Thanks… for asking. Still reading romances?" He gestured to a row of books with a trembling hand.

"Remember how I'd smuggle them in for you? Does the new guy do that?"

My throat wouldn't relax. I shook my head.

"Do you know what I used to do when we'd come here?" he asked. He stepped closer. "I'd stand over there." He nodded toward somewhere at my left. I didn't look. "And watch you. I couldn't take my eyes off you, even to look at books. You're so beautiful, Ashlyn."

I swallowed. I'd caught him watching me on more than one occasion, and had been creeped out by it.

"Have you heard back from any schools?" he asked with urgency. "You're still planning on going to college, right?"

"Yes, I am. Look, I have to go." I left Stuart, rounded the corner of the aisle and joined Colin, engrossed in reading.

He looked up. The relaxed look on his face stretched tight. "What happened?" He slipped the book back on the shelf and stepped close to me, touching my arm. I couldn't believe he could tell—with just a look—that something was wrong.

"I—uh—ran into someone from school. Someone I don't like very much."

His pointed gaze skipped around the store for a second. "Did something happen?"

"No. Why?"

"You look a little pale. Want to get something to drink?"

The smile working its way onto my lips helped me to temporarily forget my run in with Stuart. I nodded.

We took the escalator up, his arm brushing mine when he stepped aside so a bookseller could hurry past us. Worries about running into Stuart invaded me. I'd grown up on the rightwing of suspicion. Daddy had told me statistically, you're in danger if you see the same stranger more than three times.

Stuart wasn't a stranger, but he wasn't a friend either. Mother and Daddy would flip out if they knew I'd seen him. They'd never let me come to the bookstore again.

The escalator continued up, and I scanned the second floor. My heart rattled. Stuart stood near the exit, eyes locked on me as he walked out the door.

YOUR PRESENCE IS REQUESTED
AT THE ANNUAL
HOLIDAY SEASON CELEBRATION OF
CHARLES AND FIONA ADAIR

THE RESIDENCE:
2029 PARK AVENUE, NEW YORK, NY

BLACK TIE.

R.S.V.P.
212.555.4935

————— CHAPTER TWELVE

The townhouse bustled with caterers and decorators preparing for the Christmas party. Two white trucks were parked out front, causing traffic on Park Avenue to slow, drivers peering at the mansion. Loads of delicacies and Christmas decor for the party were carried inside. Colin remained stationed at the front door to thwart any security disruptions.

Workers unloaded dozens of shrink-wrapped pine trees in all shapes and sizes. Each tree was then unwrapped, colored with white lights, bows, bulbs, and ornaments, each with its own theme.

Fresh evergreen swags, rich with the scent of pine and nutty cones, were hung over doors, strewn along three-stories of banisters, and dripped from sconces throughout the halls. Every year, the decorating teams worked faster than the last. By the end of the day, the house was ready for Mother's final inspection before the decorators were released.

Since lunch had passed, I took Colin an apple. He had an iPad in one hand, the other held the front door open so workers had the freedom to come and go.

"Hey, thanks." Colin's smile swept my heart up and around. I smiled. Hands occupied, he grinned. I lifted the apple to his mouth and his teeth sunk in. We shared a laugh. Then, his gaze lit on something behind me. He stopped chewing.

I glanced over my shoulder. Daddy stood under the archway, his eyes latched on us. Darkness shadowed his face, and panic lanced through me.

"Daddy." I crossed to him. His hard gaze remained fixed on Colin. I lifted to my toes and kissed his cheek. His sharp focus on Colin broke, like he finally realized I was there, and he looked at me.

"Princess."

"The house is almost done."

"That will make your mother happy," he murmured.

"It looks fantastic," I said. He kept glancing at Colin, who remained posted at the door.

Finally, he nodded, turned and disappeared into his office. I followed him, closing the doors with a soft clip.

"Something wrong?" I crossed to him at his desk where he stood reaching for a cigar.

"What makes you think something's wrong?"

"You look... troubled. Is it Colin?"

His gaze pierced me. "You two seem to be getting along better." He didn't move a muscle, waiting for my response. Still unsure about his motives where Colin was concerned, I shrugged indifferently. "Have your feelings for him changed?" His eyes brightened, irises opening wide, exposing mysterious black depths.

"I've gotten over it, just like you've asked me to."

His lawyer-sharp gaze quartered me: heart, head, body, and soul, searching each part for discrepancies. He drew in a deep breath.

"He's your employee, Daddy."

His shoulders relaxed when I called Colin an employee. He crossed to me. "I don't want Stuart happening again."

I shuddered for his benefit. "Me either. May I invite Felicity to the party?"

"I guess it's only right that you have a chum."

I threw my arms around his neck. "Thank you."

His finger brushed my cheek. "Warn your mother."

I nodded.

"I suppose you'll need your cell phone to call her."

"It wasn't Felicity who invited me to Ninety-Nine, Daddy. It was Danicka Fiore."

"Yes, well, stay away from Miss Fiore." Daddy rounded the corner of his desk and unlocked one of the drawers. I glanced at the roaring lion head carved into the wood at the top of one of the legs. I'd often wondered why Daddy surrounded himself with frightening images. Like the paintings of lions on the African plains, tearing into prey.

He produced my cell phone and extended it to me. "That's mostly for my piece of mind. And so Colin can be in constant communication with you, if necessary."

Constant communication with Colin? An absolute necessity.

Mother allowed Felicity to attend as my guest on one condition: that Mother pick what Felicity wore. Felicity was a good sport about Mother's snobbery, and she didn't have a problem with Mother borrowing a dress from a designer friend.

"I think I like your mom." Felicity examined herself in my bathroom mirror. For the party, I slicked her short brown hair back and fastened the unruly ends in a blingy hair lock. The hairstyle worked well with the strapless black gown Mother had found for her. I was amazed how well the dress fit, seeing that Felicity hadn't gone in for any adjustments. Mother really did know bodies and clothes.

She'd chosen a retro-looking strapless, ivory dress for me, the bodice overlaid in delicate lace and beads. A transparent sun-bleached, shell-colored shrug draped over my shoulders. The hanging edges of the shrug looked like they'd been dripped in delicate beads that flashed and fired with each movement.

"You look like an angel." Mother had said during my first fitting.

"Isn't this the wrong color for a Christmas party?"

"It's perfect."

"Do I look okay?" Felicity asked now, brushing more blush on her cheeks. She had enough color to make her look like she'd spent the day at the circus, so I covertly took the container from her before any more damage was done, and set it aside.

"You look gorgeous."

"I'm so excited." Felicity bounced like a toddler on a trampoline.

"I get to dress up and eat something other than Chinese food."

I hadn't seen Colin yet, but I'd imagined him in a tailored tuxedo. Prada had designed their latest look in the cleaner cut, tapered design of the sixties. Colin would look hot in that style. He'd look hot in any style.

The string quartet mother had hired for the party played, and their classical renditions of Christmas carols started wafting through the house like holiday perfume on the air.

The party had been in swing for about an hour and the temptation to make an entrance was strong—only to see how Colin reacted to seeing me dressed up. Mother and Daddy were far too busy entertaining their guests to notice where Felicity and I spent our time.

I counted on that.

I took one last look in the mirror. My blonde hair hung in loose ribbons to my shoulders, a hint of sparkles randomly glittering from the pale vanilla depths. Around my neck was a black ribbon choker with a single stone in the center.

"Wow, Ash," Felicity whispered. "He's not going to be able to help himself."

I turned in the mirror, making sure every angle was perfect. "Let's hope, right?"

We hooked arms and took the stairs down. The entry was packed with black tuxes and a tapestry of glittering designer gowns. An overload of colognes and perfumes, mixing with hundreds of evergreen scented candles around the house, wafted upward, scenting the thickening air.

Colin had hired three extra security guys for the night. All of them looked to be older than him, one even had gray temples. The gray-templed man stood at the front door checking off guests from a roster on Colin's iPad. I'd seen the other guys posted at exits: one in the kitchen, at the back door. Another was on the upstairs patio— which made me laugh because who would come or go from three floors up in a tuxedo or pricey designer gown?

Colin was nowhere to be found.

"I was hoping Colin would see my grand entrance," I whispered with a laugh to Felicity as our heels hit the main floor.

"Men are never where you need them when you need them." She craned her head for a look around. "Except for my dad on Tuesday and Thursday nights. Chinese food takes precedence over everything else. Then, he's reliable."

I squeezed against her, giggling. I was so glad she was with me. These yearly parties usually meant I wandered alone, like a perfectly manicured pet. Sometimes I got the feeling Mother wanted me there to show me off, and not much more.

And Daddy always insisted that I play the piano.

I cringed. That moment would come soon enough, I didn't need to ruin the party by dwelling on the performance and making myself unduly nervous.

The air swelled with music from the string quartet. I wanted to lay eyes on Colin.

The high pitch of gossip and laughter pierced the air with the sharpness of arrows, shot from socially tight bows. Eyes watched me with fascinated interest. Mother and Daddy may think no one wondered why their only child was so elusive, but I saw curiosity and criticism in their friends' eyes.

Year after year.

Arm-in-arm, Felicity and I made a sweep of the main floor like curious kittens. We found Daddy in his office. The hazy scent of cologne and men filled the walnut paneled room. Soft plumes of cigar and cigarette smoke twirled into the atmosphere like wispy ghosts.

The moment I stepped into the room, Daddy looked at me. His grin widened. Conversation and laughter stopped. Every head in the room turned my direction.

"Awkward," Felicity whispered under her breath.

"I know, right?" I whispered back.

Daddy waved me over. "There's my beautiful girl." He reached out and lightly embraced me, careful of the delicate dress. "Princess, you look breathtaking."

I introduced Felicity who garnered a smile and nod from Daddy and a round of obligatory, semi-bored greetings from Daddy's associates.

"Ashlyn's going to play one of her pieces for us later, aren't you, Princess?"

"Of course." I clasped my hands and nodded, like the perfect Princess I'd been taught to be: accommodating, cordial, interested, and refined.

"You two have fun, now." Daddy's tone spoke of dismissal for business reasons, so I took the hint and linked arms in Felicity's and we continued our search for Colin.

Mother had hired a DJ to play age-appropriate music for those guests who cared to dance off some of the liquor served at the bar in Daddy's office. I planned to dance with Colin if I could sneak it in without Mother or Daddy seeing us.

Mother's laughter fluttered on the air upstairs like falling flakes of snow. We dodged a server dressed in white uniform, and headed to the music room where Michael Buble's voice floated from the speakers. In one corner, the DJ had set up his tables and accoutrements. In the center of the room, surrounded by a pack of women, Mother had her arm in Colin's.

I stopped inside the door.

"What the?" Felicity's tone echoed my shock.

Mother's hand wandered Colin's arm like a boa constrictor. Colin's back was toward me, but the two of them stood in a small gathering of other women—Mother's friends—each one lit up like a red light district.

Mother's cougar display with Colin proved to be more exciting than my entrance. Within seconds, heads turned back to Mother.

A smoldering flame of anger stoked beneath my skin. I broke free of Felicity and crossed to Mother.

Her ruby dress was beaded and sequined from head to toe, firing her eyes to electric emeralds. She kept one hand possessively on Colin's arm while the other reached out to her lady friends.

"Ashlyn, darling."

Colin's eyes flashed to mine with the hope of rescue.

Mother's friends cooed their plastic hellos, but clearly they were more interested in drooling over Mother's arm candy than me. I didn't care what they thought of me, I cared about the fool Mother was making of herself showing off Colin like he was her latest purchase.

"You're needed on the roof," I said to Colin.

He immediately slipped his arm from Mother's and touched his earpiece, ready to check with the man posted up on the patio.

I tilted my head in the direction of the music room doors.

"Big trouble on the roof," Felicity added, nodding.

Mother's gleaming smile waned into a flash of panic. "Should I be worried?"

"No," I said, escorting Colin away, "Colin knows what he's doing. Enjoy your guests, Mother."

"Hurry back, Colin," Mother gushed.

"He's working," I reminded her. Her laughing cadence vanished, as if I'd pinched her in front of her friends. She flashed narrowed eyes at me, and opened her mouth to speak but I turned my back on her, and guided Colin through curious guests to the door.

He glanced at me. "I didn't get a report of any problem on—"

"There isn't any," I said, halting once we were in the hallway. "I'm sorry about Mother. That was… embarrassing in there."

His cheeks flushed a little. He took in a deep breath and blew it out. "Thanks. I owe you again. You look… amazing," he murmured. I tingled under his sweeping appraisal.

"So do you." Just as my fertile imagination had conjured, the fitted black tuxedo enhanced perfection to the point of jaw-dropping. My tingling blood danced through my veins searching for a way to burst from the confines of my body.

"Just to be safe, you oughta take a look upstairs," Felicity suggested good-naturedly.

I nodded. "Good idea."

Colin smirked.

Gentleman that he was, Colin allowed Felicity and I to climb the stairs first. Up on the roof the wintry air blew with more force than the breeze off the street. The suit in the corner stood alone, looking out over the sparkling city view of encroaching steel buildings left and right.

Mother had adorned the roof with twinkle lights and trees. Music piped in from the music room played through speakers strategically hidden behind the evergreens decorating the area.

"Hey." Colin nodded at the security guy.

The man gave a nod back. "I doubt anyone will spend too much time out here. It's pretty nippy."

"Take five. I'll keep an eye out until you get back."

The man nodded, passed us, and the door shut behind him. Felicity went to the iron railing and gazed over. "There's like paparazzi outside," she swooned.

Colin crossed to the edge, so I did too, and we shared a moment looking down at the busy sidewalk below. The street was lined with dozens of black limos and idling cars, waiting for their owners to return. "This is insane," Colin said. "I had no idea it'd be this… epic."

"It's epic all right." I laughed at his amazement at what I found commonplace. A cold breeze ruffled his hair. The tingling in my body swam now—with want. His lips looked soft—a nicely etched extension of his carved jaw and cheekbones. A fantasy danced in my head of my exploration of his hair. Then more discovery: his mouth.

"Um. I'm gonna visit the ladies," Felicity said. A few seconds later the door to the roof shut.

An awkward silence was filled by an occasion horn, honking.

"It's not Christmas in Palos Verdes, that's for sure," I said. "You miss home?"

He lifted a shoulder. "Sure I miss it."

"Remember that year we strung real popcorn?"

"Yeah." He smiled, shook his head. "Mom kept that for years."

"My mom threw it out, it got so smelly."

He laughed. "I remember that it did. Mom couldn't bring herself to get rid of it—she's kind of like that."

"That's sweet," I said. "Better than having everything new every year. Nothing means anything because you don't have it long enough for it to be a part of you."

Was that admiration I saw as he studied me? His gaze swept me. "You're going to freeze out here in that."

"You don't like my dress?"

"It's stunning." He slipped off his jacket and placed it over my shoulders. His heat. His scent. I took in a deep breath then realized how ridiculous I must look. Colin's eyes simmered with interest.

Music piped up to the patio through speakers slowed to a romantic ballad. We were alone. I extended my hand. "Would you dance with me?"

Hesitation was obvious on his face, causing the corners of his mouth to inch downward. "Ash, I'm working."

The moon's winter white light cast him in an irresistible, angelic hue. I stepped closer, and the white plume of his breath fanned my face. The erratic rhythm taunted. I slowly placed my hands on the front of his shirt, my fingers spreading out to feel as much of him as I could.

"You'll be cold without your jacket," I said.

"Ash…" His voice was hoarse.

I peered up at him through lowered lashes. "One dance."

He seemed to struggle with words. Whatever he was feeling inside kept him from moving even an inch. He remained close—did he like to tempt himself too?

I'd read in my romance novels that women's hands often traveled up their hero's chest. Would he like that? I allowed my hands to inch upward. Beneath my palms, the silky fabric of the white shirt was slick over his warm skin.

He snatched my wrists. "We can't," he said.

Smiles we'd shared suddenly froze in the icy air, leaving me to wonder if they'd ever happened. Where had he stowed our moments?

The pressure of his fingers hurt, but alongside the pain searing through my arms a delectable enjoyment wound my blood tight. We stood silent. Seconds turned to minutes.

"So, yeah," Felicity's unnaturally loud voice—as if she was alerting us—sounded on the other side of the door. The door swung open. A path of light beamed from the opening and onto the two of us.

Colin released me.

"So, like, yeah, the Chinese food is pretty good at Chan's, but…" Felicity came to a halt, and the security guy bumped into her back. An apology scrunched her face.

Shame lashed through me. *He's rejecting you, Ashlyn. Keep your pride and go drown your bruised ego in some spiked punch.* I crossed to the door, passing the security guy and nearly tripped down the steep flight of stairs.

"Oh, man." Felicity stayed at my heels. "I tried to keep him from going out there, but he wasn't buying my conversation skills. Sorry. What happened?"

"I feel like an idiot."

"Oh, jeez," Felicity said. "Details?"

"Ash." Colin.

I stalled outside my bedroom door, turned and found him two feet away. *Oh, no. Had he heard me?*

"We need to talk," he said. "After the party."

I swallowed a lump in my throat, panicked that he'd overheard Felicity and me, but I managed to nod.

The warmth from his jacket was gone now, and I slipped the garment off my shoulders and held it out for him. He hesitated a moment, then took it, holding me in a pointed gaze for a second more before he hurried down the stairs, slipping it back on.

I went to my bedroom and Felicity followed, shutting the door at her back. I was ready to buckle in a sob, but I drew in a deep breath instead. "I… asked him to dance with me and he… refused."

"Oh, yikes. That's harsh."

"I made a fool out of myself," I said. "He sees me a job. That's it."

"Not necessarily. If he didn't care, he wouldn't have stopped you and told you he wanted to talk later."

"What if he heard us?" I fell onto the bed. "How humiliating. My life since he got here has been one humiliation after another."

"Your life has always been humiliating. Nothing's changed except that he's here, witnessing it."

"Thanks."

"Get up." She pulled me upright. "You need to be dazzling. You can't hide up here, moping. Like they say, 'nothing's more irresistible to a man that a woman he can't have.'"

"But he can have me. I *want* him to have me."

"I'm talking about right here and now. Go down there and have fun. Be irresistible."

She had a point. "But they're all way old."

"Maybe some new meat has arrived. Come on." Felicity urged me to my feet.

"Aged meat."

"Beef jerky," Felicity snorted.

We shared a laugh. "I swear Mother and Daddy don't invite anyone young into the house just to make sure I never get a chance to meet anybody."

"That has a sort of twisted logic where your Dad is concerned," Felicity commented. "Doesn't matter. Colin's here."

He's who I want.

Felicity and I ventured to the music room. Daddy was on one end, Mother on the other, entertaining guests. When we entered, Daddy looked over. I often wondered if he had a sixth sense about me; his ability to feel my presence had always been keen. Uncanny.

He excused himself from his guests and crossed the wood floor with the confident grace of a man in complete control. "Princess, where have you been? I want you to play now."

I left Felicity and accompanied Daddy to the shiny black grand piano. He waved a hand at the DJ and the room went quiet.

"Attention everyone," Daddy's voice silenced the room. "Ashlyn is going to share one of her compositions with us."

Whispers wound their way to where I sat, ready. I forced a smile, barely noticing the hovering quiet—my thoughts on Colin. Was he in the room somewhere?

My hands trembled. I pinched my eyes closed, forcing disappointment to disappear. Once my fingertips touched the cool ivory keys, I sighed and began to play Colin's song. The sweet melody filled the corners of the room, silencing whispers. In my mind, I saw him leaning over the piano, watching me, his smile alight with admiration. The way his lips moved when he said my name. That night after Ninety-Nine, when his arms had wrapped around me—I felt his embrace afresh, strong and warm as if it had just happened. The tune flowed from my head and filled the room. Haunting, powerful, leaving its echo to ebb off the walls.

Shrilling applause ripped through the air. I looked up from the keys and into the faces around me. The crowd smiled graciously. I searched for Colin—saw his dark head of hair near the back, where he stood—his expression indecipherable. He wasn't smiling. Just watching. His serious expression sent a shiver of the unknown through me.

I stood and bowed.

Daddy hugged me—claiming ownership of everything I was. Guests clamored to us. "Marvelous."

"How talented she is, Charles!"

"She's blossomed since last year."

Daddy's look at me held then, like he was contemplating the 'blossomed' comment, searching for himself what his colleague had noticed. My face warmed. Had I changed? The thought that someone had noticed thrilled me.

"So proud of you, darling." Mother kissed my cheek and embraced me. I loved seeing her genuinely pleased and proud of me. After she bragged with shameless adoration to the guests standing nearby, she took my hand. "Are you and Felicity having a good time?"

I nodded. "It's a beautiful party, Mother."

"Do you think?" She glanced around, her gaze lighting on Colin. "Excuse me, darling." Then she was gone, weaving through her friends to Colin.

The DJ started up again, and Mother took Colin onto the dance floor. A tight awkwardness jilted the atmosphere from party to floor show. Next to me, Daddy stiffened, his steely gaze locked on Mother, coaxing an obviously reluctant and very red Colin to dance with her.

"Come now, dance with me," Mother cooed over the music.

No one dared step onto the center spot—which had cleared—making way for them, or was it keeping away from them? I wasn't sure. But Daddy's face squared with displeasure.

Colin glanced over at Daddy, then me, and his discomfort was so squirmy, I ached. I laid my hand on Daddy's arm and was shocked to find his bicep rock hard.

Felicity stole to my other side and leaned close. "Um. What is your mother doing?"

"I… don't know," I whispered.

"Maybe you should do something."

Did I dare with my earlier rejection? Yet it was clear that Mother was completely clueless her actions were causing eyebrows to raise and gossip to be traded in shady whispers around the room. Either that or she adored flaunting Colin so much that she didn't care about how inane she looked or how her behavior reflected on Daddy.

I took in a breath, and crossed the empty floor to where Mother swayed with a very stiff Colin. Mother's smiling radiance dimmed when she saw me.

The moment I was close, Colin released her.

"Mother, Daddy wants a dance," I said. Mother caught sight of Daddy's tense demeanor and quickly excused herself with the graciousness honed from years of practice.

"You can dance with Mother and not me?" I whispered.

"About that," Colin said. "I'm sorry. I didn't think I'd be dancing at all tonight."

Colin took me in the traditional dance stance: one arm extended, the other around my back. Sweat beaded in a light film on his tense jaw. His hand was cold and clammy.

Discomfort evaporated from the room and the dance floor filled in with chattering guests. The DJ played an upbeat tune. I didn't dare look at Mother, but Daddy's marble demeanor was still wintry, his attention on her as they whispered back and forth.

Colin's fingers tightened at my waist and around my hand. "And, it's not that I didn't want to dance with you. I work for your father. Never mix business with pleasure."

So we would never be anything as long as he worked for Daddy? Is that what I was forced to accept? A sting burrowed into my heart. We continued to sway, but he pulled me closer, his body against me from breast to knee. I tried to read what I thought I saw: a silent message that seemed to say this move, this moment, meant more than words could verbalize.

The townhouse was like the inside of a shaken snow globe: littered with the confetti of leftovers from a successful party.

Daddy paid a cab driver to take Felicity home. She left after the last of the guests. I changed out of my dress, hung it on the back of my closet door, and then I dipped into the bath, too wound up to luxuriate in bubbles, heat, and fragrance. I couldn't get Colin's face out of my mind, or the way he'd pulled me against him. Had he really been trying to say something to me? Something real?

I hated that my repertoire of experience was fictional and could be found between the paperback flaps of romance fiction.

I laughed. Right. He worked for Daddy. We'd never be lovers, or anything else if he followed that 'no mixing business with pleasure' rule. I was pleased he chose to live a standard I wasn't even sure my own father kept. Mother, clearly, didn't care.

I dressed in my pajamas and decided to seek Colin and feel out how he felt about what had happened tonight.

I slipped my robe over my pajamas. In the hall, I heard the snapping of my parents' voices from the main floor. I took the stairs down. They were arguing in Daddy's office, the doors cracked. I stopped near the bottom stair.

"Don't *ever* do that to me again." Daddy.

"You're hurting me," Mother whimpered.

"Good."

Good? Dad's cold comment stabbed an icicle into my heart.

A clattering followed a thud. I took the stairs back up, and was about to cross the hall into the safety of my bedroom to digest the argument, but I saw Colin standing at the top of the third flight of stairs. His sober expression indicated he, too, had overheard Mother and Daddy. The compassion on his face seemed to invite me toward him, so I took the final flight up. Mother's sniffling, and her heels on the marble stairs caused both Colin and I to duck into the shadows of the third floor hall. My heart pattered. What if Mother didn't go directly to her room? What if I was discovered with Colin?

Daddy's office doors slammed. A tense silence burrowed into the townhouse. Colin turned and his eyes carried a slant of sadness. "Are you okay?"

I nodded. This may have been the first time he'd heard them argue, but their marriage had been fraught with ugly fights— escalating recently—like a body consumed with cancer cells.

The doors to Daddy's office clamored open and I scampered with nowhere to go. Daddy's heavy footfalls sounded on the stairs. Colin snatched me into his bedroom. He pointed at the closet. I darted over, crouched down beneath the hanging clothes and closed the door.

"Charles."

"Can I have a word?" Daddy's agitated tone ground to a slow growl.

"Yes, of course."

I could tell they'd moved into Colin's room. The proximity of their voices neared. Nerves skittered beneath my skin. I reached up and grabbed hold of the sleeve of Colin's coat so I wouldn't lose my balance.

"I apologize for Fiona's behavior tonight. She had too much to drink. I realize her actions put you in a compromising position. I wouldn't blame you if you found my employ no longer acceptable."

"No. It's fine."

A pause followed. Colin's response calmed me.

"Do you want some time to consider this?"

"Charles, no harm was done."

"I'm going out of town for a few days. You have my cell phone."

"Yes, sir."

The door closed and I realized I'd been holding my breath. I let it out, and with a deep breath took in Colin's scent worn into the fabric of his clothes surrounding me. Colin opened the closet door and extended his hand. I took it and he gently pulled me to my feet.

My nerves ticked. "Are you sure you don't want to quit?" I asked. I wanted to see his eyes when he gave me his answer.

"I'm not quitting, Ash." He looked at me for a long moment, with something grave that caused my stomach to turn over as if I needed to vomit.

"Is something wrong?" I asked.

He bowed his head a moment and I couldn't see his face. When his eyes met mine, his brows cinched. "It's late. You should get some sleep."

I wasn't tired. Not when I was with him. He, on the other hand, had wilted. Dark smudges surfaced beneath his gaze. Something— perhaps the bizarre event on the dance floor with Mother— weighed him down. I wanted to touch his sore eyes, kiss them.

I stepped closer, reached up, and his gaze suddenly became brighter. My arms slipped around him and I hugged him. "Good night."

One of his arms wove around my waist. I waited to feel his muscles pull away with the message *I'm done*, but the firmness in his core didn't shift at all. He held me close. I closed my eyes. I could sleep in his arms. I could wake in his arms. His embrace was not threatening, but assuring. Not caging, but empowering.

When his body finally moved, I gripped him harder for an impulsive instant. His hands remained on my shoulders for two seconds before he drew back. He stepped away, as if finally realizing he was touching me.

"Goodnight," he whispered.

──── CHAPTER THIRTEEN

A thick haze hung inside the townhouse the next day, as if the previous night's nasty gossip still slinked the halls and rooms like ghouls. Even daylight streaming through the windows couldn't break through the miasma.

A cleaning crew came in early to take care of the aftermath. I heard a vacuum somewhere. I dressed in jeans and a shirt before venturing down stairs to the kitchen, sure I'd find the house filled with strangers.

Colin stood in the entry. My heart lifted a few octaves in my chest. He was speaking Spanish to a worker, but his calming voice stopped when his gaze found me. Then he finished his instructions to the nodding maid and she went on her way.

He met me at the bottom stair. His jeans and a long sleeved tee shirt accentuated his casual stride.

"Hey," I said.

"Morning."

"You're up early," I observed.

"Early?" He glanced at his watch. "It's eleven. Taking care of the cleaning crew."

"Where's Mother?"

"I haven't seen her yet. Charles called me early this morning and gave me instructions for the cleaning staff." He waved a hand, indicating the sparkling townhouse. The scent of orange spritzed the air.

Mother was probably holing up in her room, or sleeping off her yearly post-Christmas party hangover. "I'm sorry."

"What for?"

"Last night. Today."

"Aren't they done yet?" Mother's voice sounded like an old car engine barely able to shift into first gear. She navigated down the stairs with the care of the blind through a mine field. Usually, she slept off her post-party hangover. She wore black from head to toe—silk sweats and running jacket. Her auburn hair poked up on end. Her bug-eye black sunglasses covered her eyes.

"Ashlyn. Rockstar," Mother snapped.

I bristled, but didn't move. Mother continued her cautious decline. "*Ash-lyn.*"

Blowing out a silent breath, I crossed to the kitchen. I could still hear their conversation.

"Ashlyn, get one for Colin!" Mother shouted.

"No," Colin called. Then louder, "No thank you."

I grabbed a Rockstar from Mother's stash and hurried back into the entry.

"No vices, dear boy?" Mother tilted her head at him.

I shoved the cold can at Mother. "Quit coming onto him like a cougar."

"How dare you speak to me in that vulgar manner," Mother hissed.

"Since when was the truth vulgar?"

"Your father is going to hear about this, young lady." Mother wagged her finger in my face. I batted it back like it was an annoying gnat. She lifted her arm to strike me. I ducked.

Colin's hand caught her wrist in mid-swing. "Fiona."

Mother wobbled. Her expression was flat, emotionless, but her body shook. Her mouth opened, like she wanted to protest Colin stopping her with physical force, but she seemed speechless, and astounded by the strength in his grip.

When her anger appeared to have subsided, Colin let her go. Her arm sagged like a dead member to her side. She pointed a finger at Colin. "You work for me, remember that."

Then she turned and stalked back and forth a few feet away, chugging the drink.

"I am so sorry," I said. Erasing the awkwardness that had just happened was impossible.

He brought himself close, his gaze filled with concern. "Has she hit you before?"

"I've taken my share of her slaps," I muttered. Colin shifted with obvious discomfort. Had he ever been slapped? Imagining Barb, Phil, the kind patience I remembered them having when I was a child, I doubted Colin had ever been hit.

One of the cleaning team quietly appeared. Had the guy been waiting for the fireworks to stop? I couldn't help but wonder if the worker's image of the family on Park Avenue was now one of disgust that people like us fight over such stupid things.

He spoke to Colin in Spanish. Colin nodded, shook his hand and the young man pulled out a cell phone and made a call. Within minutes, three other maids appeared and the group of them left.

"Good as new." Colin's gaze swept the entry.

Mother would be the judge of that and in her mood, I wouldn't put it past her to slip on a white glove and don her bi-focals for inspection. Of course, it wasn't Colin's job to see that the house was put back together.

"Is it like this every year?" he asked with a glance at Mother, still prowling a few feet away.

"Like what? Mom hung-over, Dad gone?"

He hesitated, but nodded.

"Merry Christmas, right? I don't blame you for wanting to go home for the holidays. It's not very… there's not a lot of Christmas spirit here."

Mother sauntered over. She stopped close. Her breath was sour and rancid, mixing with stale perfume applied the night before. "Haven't Barb and Phil ever argued?" Her tone cut with sarcasm. "Or are they still blissfully married?"

"Don't attack Colin's family, Mother."

"It's true. They were always so happy," she said with a tinge of envy.

"Fiona, I don't want to be the reason for an argument."

"You're not the reason, darling," Mother said. "Charles and I have been like this for years. I'm sure Ashlyn was going to fill you in on every dirty little Adair secret, weren't you, Ash-lyn? I'll save her the breath. Separate bedrooms make for more than geographical troubles. I'll bet Barb and Phil still sleep in the same bed, am I right?"

"Mother!"

"Am I?" Mother glared at Colin.

Colin's jaw twitched. "The house is clean. I excused the temps. I'm going to take Ashlyn out for something to eat." He took my elbow in his fingers and turned me toward the door.

"Oh, lovely. How. Lovely." Mother's tone balanced on a tightrope of frustration and jealousy. Colin grabbed our jackets from the coat closet, entered the security code into the keypad, and the door unlocked. He reached around me, opened the door and ushered me out into the bright, cold afternoon.

The door slammed at our backs.

Colin eyed me for a moment, unsure of how to respond. I wasn't afraid, not angry even. This was my life. I stood surrounded by everything, but in reality, had very little. Dad and Mother barely tolerated each other and I bounced somewhere in between.

He wrapped an arm around my shoulders and held me at his side for a few seconds. One glance over his shoulder at the townhouse and he released me, probably because he wasn't sure whether or not Mother was watching.

He hailed a cab and within seconds one zoomed to a stop and we slid into the stuffy backseat.

Middle Eastern music twanged from speakers. The driver's black eyes held on Colin through the rearview mirror as if silently expecting the next command.

"Rendezvous on 8th and Broadway."

The driver pulled into traffic.

Colin watched me across the cab, then his fingers reached out and touched my cheek again.

"I'm so sorry," I said.

"Quit apologizing for your parents."

"How are you going to deal with Mother? Why would you want to?" Stuart had been right when he'd told me to get far away. I kept hiding behind the every-family-has-problems, routine answer. But that hiding place was exposed now. Vulnerable.

"I can take care of myself," he said, softly. His arm stretched out along the backseat, near my shoulder.

"Now you know," I murmured. Relief tried to soothe me, but at the same time I was overcome with fear that he'd leave.

"All families have problems."

Dare I further twist open the can? Would the wretchedness of Daddy's obsession be the unbearable stench that finally drove Colin to quit?

"I'm not sure I'm qualified to have an opinion. But I can listen, if you want to talk."

I kept my gaze on my hands, clutched in my lap. Daddy would not approve of me sharing my feelings with anyone outside of the family. He had to know I'd talked to Felicity, but he trusted me so implicitly, it hurt down deep even considering sharing my woes about my life with Colin.

Yet, in Colin's gaze I saw invitation and trust.

We arrived at Rendezvous and Colin paid the driver. He got out and held his hand extended so I could slide across the backseat and out to the safety of the sidewalk rather than exit on the other side, in the busy street.

Exotic bouquets of spices mingled and filled my head when we entered the small, colorfully decorated place. Giant sheers hung from the ceiling, rippling softly from a current created by gemstone crusted fans.

We were escorted to the back, where we sat on fluffy pillows around a table decorated with vanilla candles and beaded placemats.

A round-bellied man with a turban and thick beard left us two menus before attending to other customers.

"How did you find this place?"

"One day when I was lost." He laughed and the relaxing sound rippled through my blood.

My appetite slowly returned as time passed. I'd never enjoyed looking at someone so much. His eyelashes—the way they almost brushed his cheekbones when his eyes were downcast, like now as he looked at the menu. The flirtatious dance of his dimples when he spoke, ate, laughed.

"There's that smile again," he said. I frowned and he grinned. "You never told me what inspires you."

"You mean when I write music?"

He nodded, setting his menu aside.

"Events, mostly—things that happen in my life, people I know."

"That song you played last night. I've heard it a lot since I've been at the house. What's it called?"

I reached for my water glass, hiding a cringe. *Do I dare?* "I don't have a name for it yet. It's new."

"I like it."

"You should," I said, then sipped. He tilted his head, curious.

"Why do you say that?"

"It's your song." I couldn't believe the words left my mouth, but the relief I felt was empowering. His brown eyes lowered to my mouth and held for half a second, before he looked into my eyes again.

"My song?" he croaked.

I set down my glass and clasped my hands on the table, pinning him with a look I'd read about in my romance novels: one meant to communicate something. What, I wasn't sure—I had a windmill of emotions going round in my head.

"Wow. That's...flattering."

"I started writing it that first night you came to the townhouse."

"Really?" His dimples deepened. "I thought you hated me that night. I was sure of it."

"I did."

His smile slowly disappeared. We stared at each other. I'd never had a conversation where I drove the subject matter through rough terrain before.

"Why?" he asked.

"It doesn't matter anymore."

"If you hated me, why is the song so...beautiful?"

My fortitude faltered. Deep in my belly, resilience caved, trembled, and turned soft as I gazed into his curious eyes. "Because..."

"May I take your order?" The turban-headed man returned, smiling.

The tension building between Colin and I snapped like a cinnamon stick. Colin aimed a teasing, knowing grin at me, which I mirrored. "This conversation is not over," he said.

I bit my lower lip.

We ordered, and the waiter took our menus and left. Colin sat forward, as if he couldn't remain in his seat a second longer. His dark eyes sparkled with light. "Because?"

"Because my feelings for you... changed." I stunned myself with my words, yet as each layer of the thick protection covering my feelings was peeled back, I felt lighter, stronger, and more capable than I ever had.

His cheeks colored a deep fuschia shade, like the scarves hanging from the ceiling. "I'm honored," he said.

"You've never been the muse?" I teased.

He shook his head, boyishly cute. "Not that I know of."

"Well, I'm happy to be a first for you."

His smile slowly crept away, and a look of depth and wonder replaced it. Long seconds drifted by. "You really are very...unique, Ashlyn," he said. "You are a first for me. I can't remember the last time a came across a someone so...genuinely innocent."

"I hate being innocent," I grumbled.

"Don't. I like it."

Though I would rather be refreshing and special some other way, I smiled. "Thank you, I think."

"That was you I ran into on the street that day, wasn't it?"

"Yes."

"So how come the story? Wait, you were alone, weren't you?"

I nodded. "And late. One of many attempts at freedom, foiled."

His brows knit over piercing eyes. "Tell me about that."

A knot lodged in my throat. I picked up my glass, drank, but the knot remained. "I told you, I don't get out much."

"I'm getting that. Why? I mean, Charles' concern for your safety runs so deep. Is it tied to what happened years ago?"

"You remember?"

"Are you kidding? My parents talked about it for weeks. I was only eight but I remember it like I remember the day Princess Diana died. Is it okay to talk about or would you rather not—"

"No, honestly, I was five years old. My memory is fragmented, at best."

"Still, it must have been traumatic."

"For Mother and Daddy. They insisted I go to therapy. But, honestly, the only thing I remember is the afternoon, how it was sunset. I was running toward the street, and there were all these police cars, lights flashing and millions of people."

"The day they found you." Colin nodded. "Mom and Dad were with your parents non-stop until you were found."

"Melissa didn't hurt me. She was always kind to me."

"Do you ever hear about her?"

"Daddy…doesn't like bringing up any of that." Daddy had been mortified and disturbed about the ramifications of the young nanny's obsessive infatuation with him. So much so that he'd up and relocated from California to New York in attempt to be as far away from the nightmare as possible. "You know, I never thought of it before now, but it isn't that unusual that she'd become lovesick with Daddy. I can see how it could happen." I'd often wondered if there were other women in Daddy's life besides Mother. Felicity had been the first to bring the suggestion to my attention when she'd found out my parents slept in different bedrooms. *"Your dad's like a movie star,"* she'd said after meeting him. *"No wonder women stare."*

I'd never noticed because whenever Daddy and I were together, his attention had always been wholly focused on me.

"As I remember," Colin began, "she kidnapped you and threatened to kill you unless he left your mother for her."

"But she never hurt me. Not that that mattered to Daddy. The very idea of it haunted him. Changed his life forever." *And mine.*

He sat back against the stucco wall. "I guess I understand why he's concerned for your safety."

Obsessed was a more accurate word. "Still, that was years ago. I wish he'd relax about it now."

"When he hired me I asked him if there had been any threats recently. He was evasive about it."

I shrugged. "He's told me that there are people out there who want to hurt him, and they'll use me to do that."

"Interesting."

Our food came, steaming and aromatic, to our table. My stomach moaned in response to the heavenly scents. We started eating the lamb and vegetables in spicy sauce over confetti rice.

After a few moments, Colin said, "I'm glad you talked to me about it."

"Daddy refuses to elaborate about the incident. But technology made finding out about it, easy. All I had to do was get online and read old news reports. It was weird because, like I said, I only have that one memory. And I'm not even sure that memory hasn't been tainted by the news footage I used to watch over and over."

"It was pretty big news."

"But it's over," I reiterated. And I wanted to talk about him. "Do you miss your parents?" I asked.

He wiped his mouth with his napkin, set it on his lap. "I do. I love New York, school." His gaze held mine for a long moment. "But I like what I'm doing now, here…with you."

I bit my lip. Warmth flushed my face. Could he see it? Pleased that he was happy, my fears about him leaving began to lessen. I cleared my throat.

"I remember going to Redondo Beach pier and eating cracked crab with your family."

He laughed. "Every Sunday."

"One time you chased me with a live crab."

"I did?"

I nodded, remembering how terrified I'd been. How silly it seemed now. He'd been maybe eleven at the time. "I was…" My throat locked. I swallowed. Colin stopped chewing, waiting for me to continue. "I was afraid of you."

Whatever was in his mouth went down in a gulp. With a shadow of grave reality he looked away for a moment, then back at me. He shook his head, put his napkin aside. "Back then, I wasn't very nice to you. Especially in light of what happened. I'm sorry."

I was shocked that he added his memory to the truth, validating feelings I'd often questioned. But I'd put all of that behind me. "I don't know why I mentioned it, I—"

"I'm glad you did. It was wrong. Forgive me?"

"I already have."

After lunch, we stood outside of Rendezvous both of us looking up and down 8th Avenue like we weren't sure where to go next.

"What now?" I asked.

Storm clouds filled the sky. I rarely looked up, rarely took note of the weather because I was either shuttled in our car wherever I had to go, or inside buildings.

"How long…" Colin scratched the back of his head. I could tell he wasn't sure how to proceed, and I was also sure what he was going to say.

"Will Mother be in her current state?"

"Yeah."

"It varies. I stay in my bedroom or in the music room until things settle down."

Colin's cell phone rang and he retrieved it from his front pocket. "Speaking of." Our gazes remained attached as he clicked on the phone. "Fiona?"

Mother's sobbing transcended the plastic device and city noise. "Where are you? I need you here."

"What's wrong?" Colin's brows knit tight.

"I don't like being here alone." Click.

With urgency in his grip, Colin guided me to the curb, his scan searching for a cab.

"Is Mother okay?" I asked.

"I don't know." His jaw knotted. "We should get back."

What if Mother was manipulating him—us, to get us back to the townhouse. How wrong that would be, how twisted. How could Colin stand one more day of her behavior?

A very real fear rooted deep inside of me. I was falling for him. I'd opened my heart and was leaving it open—hoping that by some miracle he'd see me as more than a job someday.

A cab finally pulled to the curb. Once inside, I stared at him, watching the way his leg jittered. His gaze aimed pensively out the window. After a few minutes, he looked over. The moment his eyes met mine, his leg went still.

At home, the front door echoed at our backs when Colin shut it and the bolt slid in place. We remained in the entry. Seconds flashed by.

"Mother?" I started up the stairs.

Colin headed toward the kitchen. "Fiona?"

A crashing of glass rang through the main floor. I took the stairs down. Colin jogged out from the hall and stopped, listened. Mother's sobs seeped beneath the closed doors of Daddy's office.

My pulse sped through my veins.

Reaching for a gun that wasn't on him, a look of frustration flashed over Colin's face. He muttered a curse and cautiously opened the doors, peering inside.

His eyes widened and he darted through the open doors. I crept closer, fear lancing my heart.

Mother stood at Daddy's gun case, her arm mangled in one of the glass doors. Splattered blood, like red wine spewed from a broken bottle, drenched her. My heart plummeted to my feet.

"Get me a sheet," Colin said. "Fast."

I ran upstairs to the linen closet, grabbed a sheet and tore back down the stairs. Colin was finishing up a call to 911. I shoved the sheet at him and he ripped it into smaller scarves, tossing excess to the floor. He moved behind Mother, wrapped his arms around her and her howls scorched the air. "Careful," he said.

He wrapped a tourniquet around her arm, just above the elbow. Mother tried to rip her arm out of the glass' jagged teeth.

"Keep still," Colin commanded. "The EMTs will be here any second."

Shaking, I stood with my hands covering my mouth. Every inch of her skin was the color of cement, dead and flat. Her eyes were glazed over. Head bobbling, her heavy-lidded gaze swooped from me to Colin. In the distance, the far off wail of emergency sirens spun in the outside air.

"I can't feel my fingers," Mother mumbled, her head falling forward.

"Easy now." Colin held her perfectly still against his frame.

Mother moaned. "You're hurting me."

"I'm sorry," Colin whispered. "But you've got to stay still."

"You always hurt me," she muttered. "You don't care anymore."

Colin's eyes shifted to mine.

I rode in the ambulance with Mother. I remained pressed against the singular passenger seat, strapped in, watching two EMTs monitor Mother's blood pressure. They replaced Colin's makeshift tourniquet with a heavy duty one. Blood covered Mother like an abstract painting of gore. I stared at her with my insides scraped by the recurring question: *why?* My mind remained an empty cavern—no logical answer fit the raw, skewed edge of the puzzle.

Colin rode behind us in a police car. Had he called Daddy? I hadn't thought about it until now. I dug out my cell phone. My hands shook so violently, I couldn't read the words on my screen. I had messages but couldn't decipher who they were from.

Mother moaned and whimpered. I bit my lip. Another round of *why* sprang through my head.

At the hospital, Mother was ushered inside and I was led with her to a curtained slot in the emergency room. Colin appeared seconds later, his face drawn with concern. His gaze latched briefly on Mother, surrounded by a team of doctors and nurses dressed in pale green and other pastel-colored scrubs. Then he looked at me. A sob rose up in my throat.

In two fast strides he was by my side and wrapped around me. The gentle stroke of his hand against my head sent comfort oozing into every fearful place inside me.

"Daddy?" I asked.

I felt him nod. "I called him."

Relieved, I closed my eyes. Voices blurred around me. I wasn't sure if I lost consciousness temporarily or what, but the next thing I knew, the powerful timbre of Daddy's commanding voice rolled into the area.

Colin's arms fell away, leaving the cool air to chase my skin. Daddy's presence filled the curtained area with absolute authority. His eyes were glued to Mother, but he conversed with the doctor.

Finally, my own head sharpened enough that I was able to hear Daddy's exchanges with the doctor.

"That's good news, then." Daddy's tone was artificial, prematurely upbeat.

"I'll speak with you after surgery." With that, the surgeon left. Daddy's controlled demeanor shifted like a black curtain, closing the stage after a performance. His blue eyes remained on Mother in an unblinking stare that sent a strange shiver down my spine. Did he still love Mother—at all?

Mother was now hooked up to an IV and unconscious. Nurses scuttled around her, preparing to wheel her away.

Dad's stony gaze followed Mother until she was out of sight, and then he slid a look at Colin. A few nurses still lingered in earshot, so he stepped closer, hands fisted. "What the hell happened?"

"I found her in your office. She'd put her fist through the glass of your gun cabinet."

Dad's composure remained even, so controlled, the only visible difference was that his chest rose and fell with more exigency beneath his casual shirt, sweater, and jacket. He ticked his head to the right, indicating to Colin he wanted to speak with him away from me, which hurt my feelings. She was my mother, after all.

Colin followed Dad a dozen steps to a private corner of the curtained area, and I trailed them until Dad caught me behind him and turned.

"Princess, I need to speak with Colin alone." He placed his hands on my shoulders and I shrugged them off.

"She's my mother. I was there, Dad."

White shock blanched his skin. At first, I didn't register his reaction as anything significant, but later I would realize that my calling him Dad had measured a momentous change in the way I saw our relationship.

He seemed cornered by the reality of my statement and directed his now steely gaze at Colin. "What provoked the incident?" he demanded.

"I think it's obvious," I said.

A gleam of warning shone in his eyes. "Ashlyn, I can see this unfortunate incident has upset you. You should rest in the waiting room."

Anger sizzled beneath the surface of my skin. Out the corner of my eye, I noticed a couple of nurses glancing over. Dad's practiced demeanor tightened. He stepped closer to me.

"I'm not tired," I snapped. "Mother wants your attention. That's why she—"

"Enough." He took my elbow in his strong grip and turned me so that my voice and my face were off limits to anyone nearby.

I tried to break free, but his fingers dug into my arm. Colin moved closer, standing next to me, his hard gaze fixing on Dad's, his hands up ready to restrain Daddy. "Charles."

Dad released my arm. "I will not discuss this here," Dad finally whispered. "Take Ashlyn home."

"I want to know what's going on with Mother," I protested.

"She's going to be fine, but the doctors have to repair the damage," he said.

As if the damage could be 'fixed' with one surgery. "I want to stay until I know she's okay."

"That's not an option."

"Why?" I hissed. "It's too late for this to be anonymous."

"Take Ashlyn back to the townhouse," he said to Colin. Then he turned and crossed out of the ER.

"Did he really just leave?" I muttered, disbelief rode the rising tone of my voice. Colin turned me to face him. "He left. Left!" I nearly shouted.

Colin's hands cupped my shoulders in tight assurance. "Let him deal with this, Ashlyn. He's in shock."

"He's a lawyer. He's never in shock." I paced. "Always in control. He's afraid this will get out, that his friends will find out his wife did something desperate just for his attention. That's what he's afraid of." Or maybe it was all an act.

Colin leaned down so he was at my eye level. His warm palms framed my cheeks. "Maybe that's true, but she's his wife first, your mother second."

He was right. Still, how could Dad ask me to leave?

Colin and I took a cab back to the townhouse. Neither of us spoke. He'd seen so much of our family now, each layer peeled back exposed an uglier, more rotted heart of the fruit. I closed my eyes and leaned my head back.

When the cab stopped, I opened my eyes. Colin watched me from across the seat.

Inside, I shivered at the tomb-like silence within the townhouse. Gavin wasn't here. Colin and I were alone. He stood next to me—and I became acutely aware of his humanness against the cold marble on the floor, up the stairs, all around us—Mother's décor pristine and frozen as a museum.

Mother. I would not have guessed she would resort to such a

desperate act.

The cold look in Dad's eye assaulted my sense of family decency. *Who was that man?* Questions clogged my head in a black, indecipherable muck. My shoulders buckled under a sob. I covered my face and wept into the protection my hands provided. Colin's strong embrace encircled me instantly and then I was against his chest, his utterance of *hush* softly whispering over my hair.

What was happening to my family? How had things gotten so distant? So fragile?

My hands fisted around his back, clinging to his shirt. I wept until my head ached. My eyes numbed. My body weakened. Slumping further against him, I felt his strength hold me upright until the next thing I knew, I was cradled in his arms.

I pressed tears into the crook of his neck, infused with the smell of his skin, the gentle sway of his body as he carried me so carefully, the movement coaxing the mourning from my soul.

He didn't walk very far, and I figured we were in the living room. He laid me on the couch and sat next to me, one arm poised on the back of the furniture, while the other continued to stroke my hair.

"I'm sorry," I muttered. "I don't mean to be so out of control."

"It's okay."

I wiped the tears away. The weakness tiring my body after the emotional purge created a torn opening in my soul I couldn't close. I was vulnerable, unable to hide truth. "Mother and her… problems. Dad and his issues. Why would you stay?"

"I'm not going anywhere."

A dense silence fell. Cocooned. I wanted him to hold me. Hurt vanished in the feel of him. I wanted that addicting anesthetic. His expression shifted from soft kindness to something unidentifiable to my inexperienced heart, but not unnatural. In fact, curious invitation spread through my soul in beckoning fingers.

My heart patted against my ribs. I inched toward Colin. He seemed unable to move. I intended to simply wrap my arms around him, but my mouth was drawn to his. The tips of my mouth fluttered against his. My eyes closed. His fingers poised at my cheek, gripped my chin and jaw, and he stopped my advance.

I opened my eyes. His were unmoving. Black. His heart pounded against mine. He licked his lips. "Ash…"

"Please."

He closed his eyes, as if in pain, and shook his head.

"Why?"

He swallowed, and his eyes looked into mine as if what I asked of him was too much to bear. "Your mother's in the hospital. You're in shock."

"That doesn't mean you can't kiss me."

"I work for your father," came his hoarse reply. His countenance was taut as a paper kite in a hurricane.

His fingers traced my cheek, and his gaze followed their path, lingering on my mouth, so close to his I breathed in his breath. He placed his hand on the side of my brow and pressed my head against his chest, his arms wrapping around me.

My dreams scattered through reality and fantasy:

Blood.

Dad's cold eyes.

Shattering glass.

Colin pressing me against my bedroom door, kissing me.

I woke on the living room couch. Colin sat near the room entrance in one of Mother's Louis XV brocade chairs. Elbows on his knees, fingers clasped at his pensive mouth, dark eyes on me. At first I thought I was dreaming.

I glanced around, sat upright. "Is Dad home yet?" My voice grated from rough sleep.

"Not yet. He called, said the surgery went well."

Relief poured over my nerves like water over parched grass. "Oh. Good. Did he say anything else?"

Colin blinked heavily, and sat back, for the first time I noticed dark slashes of exhaustion beneath his eyes. "No."

I pulled my cell phone from my pocket, but it was dead, so I slid it back. "What time is it?"

"Six a.m."

"Did you sleep at all?"

Had he spent the night watching over me? I brought my legs up to my chest—he'd taken off my shoes—they were next to the couch, and my stocking feet sunk into the softness of the cushion.

"No," he said. He rubbed his face.

"You should have slept," I protested.

"I couldn't." He leveled me with a look that ended the conversation. I touched my cheeks, felt the heat rush to my cheeks.

I stood, stretched, and when my gaze swung back to his, his eyes hadn't left me. "I'm going to get some breakfast." I crossed to him, his shadowed gaze tracking me like a hawk. "Want some?"

He nodded.

I left the living room with his gaze tickling my back. Would he follow me? I was too embarrassed to check over my shoulder. I didn't need to, his presence now familiar to me and close as my shadow.

"Gavin will freak," I said upon entering the kitchen. "He and Mother are like Regis and Kelly."

"Charles asked me to call him last night. He was pretty flustered. How long has he worked for you?"

"Since we moved here." I opened the refrigerator. Every stainless steel surface shined. Items were lined up, stacked and organized in alphabetical perfection. I brought out milk.

"You cook?" Colin pulled out a bar stool and plopped onto it, obvious weariness spreading through his limbs.

"I do cereal." I smiled. Inexpressible relief resided in my system that Mother's arm was going to heal. "Mine or yours?" I brought out two boxes: Kashi and Capn' Crunch. I bit my lower lip, thinking about Mother making sure he had his favorite items stocked in our pantry.

He yawned. "No question. The Capn' gets it hands down."

I grabbed two bowls, soy milk and dairy milk, and set everything on the counter. All the while Colin's attention never left me. Pleasure scrambled beneath my skin. Why was he so intently following my every move?

"Did I tell you I caught Charles eating a bowl of Capn' the other day?" he grinned.

"Seriously?" It had been years since I'd seen Dad eat anything but something healthy before walking out the door in the morning.

Colin nodded. "He swore me to secrecy."

I smiled. "Who knew? Dad and junk food. I guess it's not all that surprising, considering how he loves his Cuban cigars." I asked. Being domestic for Colin felt amazingly good. I had a ridiculous fantasy of myself, donned in a flirty apron, making him meals—as his wife.

"So." I dismissed the image from my head. "The Brennens eat everything? That's cool. It's hard living with picky parents."

He didn't respond, and my eyes met his. The focused attention he'd had on me since I'd awakened hadn't lessened. I wondered if I had smeared eye makeup on my face? Drool?

I sat next to him and reached for the box of Kashi, covertly smoothing a hand over my cheeks in hopes I'd remove anything offensive.

"I guess it's all in what you're used to." Colin poured Capn' into a bowl. "But the whole rigidity you live with, man, that would have driven me nuts. Have they always been this strict?"

"Yes."

"Makes sense after what happened, I guess," Colin observed. He wanted to say more, I could tell a million thoughts tossed in his mind, like clothes in a dryer. In his mind, the wrinkles in family shouldn't be difficult to iron out.

"Why do you think your mother put her hand through your dad's gun chest?"

Silence thudded in the air between us. I was relieved and surprised he'd asked the unspoken question. I poured Kashi into my bowl. His eyes held mine without breaking, waiting for my answer.

I swallowed. "I'd rather know what you think made her do it," I said.

His study of me deepened, lengthened, widened until the moments stretched unbearably long and taut. "I think you were right. She wants your dad's attention."

"You see that?"

He hesitated, then nodded. His gaze lowered to his food but he didn't pick up his spoon. For a long time he just stared at the bowl of cereal. I doubted he was thinking about eating.

Finally he picked up his spoon, but he only poked at his breakfast. A sliver of concern dug into me.

"What's wrong?" I asked. But I knew. He was getting closer to the cave, and the dark abyss was disconcerting.

A smattering of sound came from the front of the townhouse. My parents were home.

——— CHAPTER FOURTEEN

I quickly headed toward the entry, the sound of Colin's barstool scraping and his footfalls behind me offering me relief that he was following me, I wasn't alone.

Dad had his arm around Mother, who was wilted as a dying rose. They headed up the stairs. I raced over. Mother's head bobbed, her eyes half open. "Ashlyn, dar-ling."

Dad glanced at me and Colin briefly, before turning his attention to Mother and maneuvering her up the stairs. His courtroom perfect appearance had faded like a theatrical poster that had seen too much sun.

"Do you need any help?" Colin asked.

"I can manage, thank you," Daddy snapped.

"Is she okay?" I asked. Colin and I trailed after their near-crawl up the cold marble staircase.

"She needs to sleep," Dad stated with finality. His movements were robotic, emotionless. I was shocked that I saw little, if any, marital or even loyal devotion in his actions. The reality of my parents' dead marriage sliced into me with the gravity of a layer of my heart being shorn away. I stopped. Colin came to a halt next to me, and I felt his curious eyes search my face.

Dad didn't notice, though I half expected him to turn and ask me what was wrong. He'd spent each day of my life picking up on everything from a flunked lie to an earned A. The numbness spreading through me prevented me from feeling anything at all, even the truth about the state of my parents' marriage.

Colin's brief touch at my shoulder was assuring. What did he know of the counterfeit life of which I'd been no more than currency, an ivory pawn? His life had been authentic, with parents who didn't care if he wore ragged jeans and mismatched tops, who let him choose his friends, trusted him to fall and pick himself up, shake off the dirt and keep going.

Mother and Dad disappeared into her bedroom, and the door shut. I stayed fixed on the stairs. Numbness remained. I wondered what I'd feel next.

I dragged to my bedroom, afraid I'd crumble in front of Colin, and shut the door with a single swing of my hand. But I heard Colin's palm thud against it.

Crossing to my bed, I stopped myself from plunging onto it, ready to dissolve into the comforter in a river of emotion I couldn't hold back. Crying about it wouldn't change anything.

"Ashlyn?" His tone was caring, tentative. I'd spoken to Stuart enough times from the distance of the door that I knew Colin had kept Dad's rule and remained in the threshold.

I shook my head. Wasn't sure I could speak. I understood the stage in New York City didn't simply exist on Broadway, with actors playing out parts. The most dramatic, unforgettable and horrifying theatrical experiences happened within the walls of homes.

"Ash." Colin's soft tone reached across the room for me. I turned and met his compassionate gaze.

He hemmed in the door. I longed for him to break Dad's rule, to prove to me that I mattered more than Dad, the job, and the rule.

Colin swallowed. As if he gripped the doorframe for his very stability, his fingers tensed against the wood. A sudden movement behind him caught my eye. Dad.

Seeing my gaze shift, Colin glanced over his shoulder. When he saw Dad, he cleared the doorway. "Charles."

Dad's drained countenance sharpened on Colin. He eyed him a moment, then peered past him at me. "Everything all right, Princess?"

"Yes, of course." I crossed to him, wiping tears from my eyes. "How is she? What did the doctor say?"

Dad stepped into the room and came to me, his arms extended. His embrace wound around me, and I hugged him back, accustomed to the rote response. Beneath my lashes, my gaze remained with Colin standing in the doorway. His brows drew together over an expression I couldn't decipher.

"She's going to be fine, Princess."

I had to press myself against the lock of his arms to ease back, and the resistance I felt sent a flash of annoyance through me. "What did the doctor say?"

Dad cupped my cheeks, his usual modus operandi, and a practiced smile filled his lips. "Don't you worry about any of this, she's—"

"She's my mother. Don't tell me not to worry about her. Are you embarrassed? Ashamed?"

His hands iced on my cheeks. The adept grin on his lips evaporated like water under flame. Dad's hands slowly lowered to his sides. "Colin, would you mind closing the door as you leave?"

Colin nodded, reached in and brought the door to a close. "I realize you're in shock about what happened to your mother, but I will not allow you to speak to me disrespectfully."

"You'd rather I not speak about this at all, wouldn't you?" I snapped. "Mother slamming her hand into your gun case isn't going to go away. It happened, and everyone we know will know about it."

Dad's jaw twitched. "Your mother had an unfortunate accident as the result of inebriation."

"Inebriation to drown her issues with you."

"You think your mother hurt herself on purpose?" His arrogant tone slapped my sense of intelligence.

"I know it."

Neither of us said anything. Dad was expert in creating, holding and orchestrating silence, time, and other tools of manipulation for his benefit. Up until that moment he hadn't given me credit for understanding his expertise. Could he really have thought nearly eighteen years of living with such proficiency wouldn't create a student?

"Your mother would never do anything so damaging to her persona. She's too vain."

"She's desperate."

"You're blaming me for her stupidity?"

"This is *your* vanity talking. I don't believe for one second you don't know what's going on between you and Mother. *That* would be stupidity."

Dad's eyes bulged. The skin on his face stretched over his jaws. "Is this behavior the influence of your friends? If so, I'll suggest that Colin follow your every move at Chatham if I have to, to ensure your associations remain lady-like."

I blew out a breath, exasperated. Dad stood more erect. "Ashlyn?"

"This is me, grown up." I lifted my chin. "Seeing things. Understanding reality."

"Reality is that your mother got drunk." His tone was smooth and slick as oil. "She lost control, like all intoxicated people do, and she acted without thinking."

"No, Dad. Reality is that you and Mother ignore each other. You pretend. Your relationship sucks."

He slapped me. The force of the blow ripped my head right, fiery pain splintering through my jaw and skull. I reached up to touch the stinging burn and his hand cuffed my wrist.

"Don't use that street talk with me, Ashlyn."

My mind went blank. Stunned, I was paralyzed. His eyes widened, and I thought I witnessed sorrow flashing through his countenance. His shoulders drooped slightly and he averted his face.

He'd never hit me before.

I forced my body to turn and head for the bedroom door, my head a storm of burgeoning emotion.

"Ashlyn?" Dad demanded.

I crossed over the threshold and was out in the hall. Rain beat against the brick exterior of the townhouse, the sound like the glass of Dad's cabinet, shattering. Would he follow me? Insist I formally ask to be excused? Ask me to apologize to him? I didn't look back. Numbness spread from my bones to my trembling muscles. The slap still reverberated from my cheek, like a hit cymbal. Only one place could soothe the tumultuous storm raging inside of me.

I slammed the doors of the music room closed. A hive of angry black bees was loose in my blood. Muscles eased and stretched the instant my fingers touched the piano keys. The first melody my brain released was Dad's. The tune had once been a joy to play, but now, new chords in low, commanding octaves bombarded the piano keys, violent—tearing the air with raging noise.

I closed my eyes. Tears raced for escape down my cheeks. Dad's melody pushed the walls endeavoring to hold the raging flames of hurt in. There was nowhere for the captured melody to run but back to my wounded heart, and there it burned with the hostility of a brush fire.

He hit me.

The sting penetrated my cheek and jaw afresh.

A presence. My hands stilled on the keys. The tune leapt off the empty walls in enraged flames.

Colin sat next to me.

Concern drew his features into an apprehensive expression. When the last remnant of the song burned out, he spoke. "Are you okay?"

"My father…" I shook my head, bowed it over the quiet piano keys where my fingers rested.

His arm slid around my shoulders and he drew me against him. "Ash."

Tears flowed, dragging remnants of anger, fear, sadness, and mourning for my family out of my heart and into the open. I collapsed into Colin's side, my hands pressing into the ivory keys in a tumultuous chord that sounded like the final notes of a dying song, hanging by the noose of a lone note.

"It'll be okay." His comforting whisper tried to soothe and reassure. I'd lived with my parents' mock marriage long enough, even if some of those years of living had been lived in innocent bliss, to know not that the end was inevitable, but that the charade would surely, and sadly, continue.

With me forever caught in the middle.

"I'm tired," I mumbled against him. "Tired of the whole thing. The fakeness of it all. I can't believe he doesn't take some responsibility for this." I eased back, my weeping gaze on his. "Can you believe it?"

Colin's eyes darkened. "I'm sorry."

"That's more than he said." Fresh anger boiled through my veins. "He hit me," I murmured.

Colin's body turned stony and hard.

"He's never hit me," I whispered. "People who love each other don't hit each other." Colin seemed to fill like a balloon overflowing with boiling water.

"Wait here." His tone struggled with control.

He jerked to his feet, his stride long and fast across the hard wood toward the doors. Minutes later, I heard Dad's voice, and Colin's, the two jabbing like swords.

I quickly went to the door, stepped into the dark hall. Their sharp voices sliced the air up from the main floor.

"I will not have my employee overstepping boundaries." Dad's tone was courtroom.

"You hit her, Charles."

"She's my child, and she needed to be reprimanded."

"Open your eyes. She's not a child, she's a woman, an adult. It won't be long before you won't be able to keep her here like a—"

"That's enough," Dad's command boomed, causing the sconces to tremble. "This conversation is over."

The doors to Dad's study slammed. My heart thrummed. Colin marched up the stairs. I stepped into the shadows thinking he wouldn't see me, but his fierce gaze latched on mine as though he sensed me. At the landing he paused, looking barely able to contain rage. Then he continued up to the third floor, and closed the door of his bedroom.

———— CHAPTER FIFTEEN

Mother lay propped on her bed in the bloodied, stiff clothes she'd worn when she'd left the townhouse. Dad hadn't had the decency to help her change?

I crossed to her bed and stared at her pallid, sleeping form. She looked like the branch of a fallen aspen. Sadness cloaked me. I sat on the bed, and the depression on the mattress caused her to stir.

Her eyes blinked heavily. "Darling." She reached for me with her good arm, and winced.

I took her cold hand in mine. "How are you feeling?"

Mother's consciousness labored for clarity, like she was blinking through mud to see. She focused on me and seemed to remember everything that had happened, her eyes latching on mine as though last night's events played behind her irises and into her awareness.

She sighed and closed her eyes, her head rolling to the side. Then she peered through cracked lids at her bandaged arm, in a sling, tight to her chest. A tear escaped the corner of her eye and raced down her cheek.

I squeezed her hand.

"Is my hand—is—am I—"

"Yes, you're okay. Don't worry about it now. Sleep."

Pity gouged my heart. I eased next to her and she stirred, cracked open her eyes and they held mine for a moment. She turned her face from my view.

I cuddled closer, like I had when I'd been little—on the occasions Dad had been gone and she'd let me sleep in their bed with her— when they'd shared a bed.

My mind sogged with sadness. For Mother. For Dad. For our

crumbling family. *Where do we go from here?*

I closed my eyes.

Mother's weeping awakened me. I wasn't sure how long I'd lain there next to her, but the light outside the windows was like a black and purple bruise.

I sat up, touched the side of my face Dad had slapped, but the burning was gone. The outrage over the assault remained, and I closed my eyes against a wave of tears. *No tears. Not for him. Not for that.*

"Ashlyn?" Mother's voice was groggy.

"I'm here."

She nodded. "I know. Darling, you didn't have to stay with me. Hand me a tissue, will you?"

I plucked a white sheet from a box sitting on the table next to her bedside and handed it to her. With her free hand, she dabbed at her eyes. "I must look dreadful."

"Mother, you just got back from the hospital."

"Help me sit up, please."

I slid off the bed and rounded the foot of the mattress. Once at Mother's side, I propped four feathery pillows behind her back and neck and helped her sit erect.

"Much better." She adjusted the blankets and sheets around her waist, wincing from movement that compromised her arm.

I crossed to her bathroom, wet a washcloth until it steamed and brought it to her.

A weary smile quivered on her lips. "Thank you. That's just what I need." She took the cloth with her free hand and gently padded it over her face. Then she held it out to me and I took it back to the bathroom sink.

"Want some water or anything?" I asked, noticing the crystal goblet she kept permanently in the bathroom. A tiny drop of red wine sat at the bottom, like blood.

"I'd take a Rockstar," she said.

I grinned and crossed back to the bed. Her smile was a little stronger and genuine then: with tears glistening in her eyes. Not the synthetic smile I'd become accustomed to, the one she put on in the morning along with her Christian Dior makeup.

"Be back in a second," I said. "Are you hungry?"

She blinked, swallowed, like she couldn't speak. She shook her head. Then she dabbed the tissue to her eyes, and waved me away.

I left with a smile. Years ago, Mother's emotions had been juggled along with cotillion, mommy love, play group, and visits to the park. As time had passed and her friends and social life had stepped out from behind the curtain and closer to center stage, displays of emotion had slowly turned into drama for the sake of performance rather than emotion drawn to the surface by love.

I, for one, was pleased to see this quality hadn't died completely in Mother. Maybe it would come back.

Raised voices drew my attention to Dad's office. The doors were ajar, and I recognized the smooth cadence of Colin's voice twisting with the sharp bite of Dad's.

"Is this a value judgment I'm hearing?" Dad asked. "You work for me. You do as I say. That's the end of your responsibility."

"I was speaking as a friend, Charles."

"I don't need a twenty-one year old telling me how to raise my daughter. You're excused," Dad said.

A bomb of silence deafened the area. I continued to the kitchen, grabbed a Rockstar for Mother and hurried toward the stairs.

I passed Dad's office on my way in, and the door swung open and Colin, eyes feral, body jumpy, stepped out into the hall. He came to a halt when he saw me.

Injustice smoldered inside of me. "He doesn't have the right. Don't let him—"

"It's fine." He shut the door at his back. "How is she?" His frustrated expression softened. He took my elbow in his fingers and led me to the kitchen.

"She wants a Rockstar, so she must be feeling better, right?" I forced a smile on my lips. "But seriously, don't take his courtroom crap."

He placed his hands on my shoulders. "I can take care of myself." A faint smile tried to form on his mouth, barely creasing his dimples.

I grabbed the Rockstar. "Let me get this to Mother and then… I need to get out of here. Want to?"

He nodded. "Sure."

Upstairs, I slipped into Mother's dark bedroom. Her weeping sliced the black, chilly air. Mother hated overhead lighting, so I felt my way to the nearest lamp which was on a bureau and I flicked it on. Pinkish, gold light spilled over the floor, the surface of furnishings. Mother's crying stopped.

"I'm here," I said, crawling up next to her on the bed. I held out the can but she kept her face half buried in the mountain of pillows supporting her. "Mother?" She didn't respond for a few long minutes. She didn't even move. Finally, she extended her good hand for the drink. I carefully placed the Rockstar in her grip.

The can shook.

I took it back.

She wept again.

Setting the drink on the round table next to the bed, I gently wrapped my arms around her shoulders. Her body was cold, so I got off the bed and endeavored to pull sheets and blankets up higher so she'd be warm, but she shook her head.

"I need to bathe," she choked out. "Look at me. I'm a mess."

"Let me help." I pulled back the covers and helped her stand.

"I can do this," she muttered. "I'm not crippled. It's just my arm."

She walked by herself—me at her elbow—to her bathroom.

I started a bath because she couldn't shower, as the arm dressing would get wet. She kept a variety of bath scents, and I chose a pretty floral and poured a capful under the hot stream. She labored slowly out of her the stiff, blood-soaked running suit.

When she couldn't free herself of the top, she bit back a curse. Her emotion-bludgeoned face contorted in anger. "Dammit. Get pair of scissors, will you? In the top drawer. There!"

I snatched a pair of pearl-handled scissors and began cutting away the garment. Strips and chunks of velour dropped to the tile floor. Mother eyed the carnage, her face bunched.

They'd taken her bra off at the hospital. She slipped out of her panties and climbed into the Jacuzzi-tub.

I turned off the running water.

Resting her head back on the soft pillow, Mother immersed herself as far as she could into the white, popping bubbles, her arm up over her head. I grabbed a towel, rolled it and placed it on the edge of the tub so she could rest on it.

A long silence dripped between us. Her face was puffy and drawn, distorted from emotional havoc. She was coherent and I wanted some answers.

"Why did you do it?"

She sighed. "I don't want to talk about this right now."

"To get Dad's attention?"

Mother's eyes widened for a second when I used the term Dad. The corner of her lip lifted. "I said, I don't want to talk about this." But her usual strength wasn't in the command.

"Too bad. You and Dad need to talk about what happened. Maybe go to therapy."

A weak laugh hissed out. "Your father wouldn't be caught dead in therapy. Thank you for your concern, darling, but I'm done talk—"

"Well I'm not." I stepped closer to the tub. She opened her eyes and looked at me. "Were you trying to grab a gun? Were you going to kill yourself?"

"Of course not."

"Then why did you do it?" The frustration and anger in my voice accelerated. "I want to know. I want the truth."

"Ashlyn." Dad's voice severed the conversation. He stood in the bedroom, just outside of the bathroom door, in the darkness. How long had he been there?

———— CHAPTER SIXTEEN

Dad stepped into the light. Mother tossed him an irritated glance and lowered herself under the blanket of bubbles.

He moved into the bathroom. "Your mother doesn't want to talk about this now."

"It's about time you showed up," I snapped. "You're coming to her defense? Why, so you can prep the witness?"

Dad's shoulders stiffened.

"What?" I egged. "Going to hit me again?"

Mother gasped. Her eyes widened with horror and flicked from Dad to me. "You hit her?"

"Yes," Dad spoke with the confidence of justification. "Her behavior warranted severe action."

"My behavior?" I spat. "I told you the truth. That Mother cut herself to get your attention."

"I did not cut myself." Mother reached for a towel and labored to stand, but her balance was off and she teetered. Dad and I both lunged for her, but I stopped. How far would he go to help her?

Dad steadied Mother with one hand and ripped the towel off the bar with the other, slinging it around her. He wrapped his arms around her soapy wet form. Mother froze. Looked up into his eyes. He looked into hers. Awkwardness thickened the muggy air.

All I could think was this moment could have been unifying. Instead, their discomfited embrace was like strangers bumping into each other on a street corner. Disgusted, I shifted.

"Don't go beyond what's absolutely necessary, Dad. I can take over from here." I stepped forward, excusing his pathetic attempt at being a husband.

"Ashlyn," Mother whispered.

Dad glared at me for a few seconds, then his calm and practiced demeanor returned. He eased back, keeping the towel wrapped around mother. "Ashlyn's right," he said. The words shocked me, but I braced for a continued performance. "I apologize for shirking my responsibility." Dad's persuasive gaze held Mother's. Was she buying his apology?

The sting of his betrayal fresh on my cheek, I doubted his sincerity so soon. I stepped close, looking at his eyes the way he'd looked at mine so many times: like I held a knife, and I was ready to dig as deep as I had to for truth.

Dad blinked. The brightness of being unnerved that I saw in his eyes empowered me. He never allowed any weakness to linger, and any intimidation I witnessed vanished with his next blink.

I leveled him with an I'm-not-buying-this glare, then turned to Mother. "What do you want, Mother?"

Mother paled, but on her lips, and in her eyes, a smile flickered. "Your father can help me, darling. Thank you."

"Where do you think you're going?" Dad demanded.

"Wherever I damn well please," I tossed over my shoulder.

"You're not leaving this house without—"

"Colin," I bit out, interrupting him. "I know, I know." I couldn't look at him, the very sight of his arrogance grating me.

I'm not taking this anymore, Dad.

I grabbed a coat, hat, and gloves and took the stairs two-at-a time up to Colin's room. I pounded on the door. His surprised expression vanished when he opened the door and realized it was me knocking. He glanced both ways down the hall. "You okay?"

"Yeah." My body jittered. "Let's go."

He nodded, reached for his coat and shut the bedroom door at his back.

I was ready to explode. Leading the way, I skipped down the

stairs. The events of the last twenty-four hours pushed me toward the front door.

"Ashlyn!" Dad's voice cannon-balled from the second floor balcony. I waited until my feet hit the cold marble floor in the entry before I forced myself to turn around. Colin, still on the stairs, slowed, volleying his attention between me and Dad.

"Come here," Dad commanded.

I should have known he wouldn't put up with any attitude. I locked my knees. "I'm going out."

Dad's hands wrapped around the black wrought iron railing, his knuckles glaring white.

"Yes, you've made that clear. Before you go out, I intend to talk to you."

I ground my teeth. He wanted to talk? "Fine." I didn't move.

The corner of Dad's jaw squared. His fingers loosened from the railing and he glided down the curved stairs as if he was on his way to greet the President of the United States, not lecture his daughter. Colin joined me, standing close enough that our shoulders brushed. I glanced at him, but his locked gazed remained on Dad.

Dad crossed to us, so cool and arrogant that the anger swirling through my system flared hotter.

"Colin, wait outside." Dad's smooth tone sent my heart into a frightened pound.

Colin didn't move. Dad's head pivoted toward Colin. Outrage pinched his brows and lips. "Did you hear me?"

"Yes, sir." Colin's tone was firm.

"Then what part of my instruction did you not understand?"

"I'm here to protect Ashlyn, Charles."

My heart leapt to my throat. Dad's glare sent a shiver of fear through me.

"He's doing what you hired him to do," I said. *I need protection from you.*

The faintest slit in Dad's eyes was the only clue that I was ruffling his perfectly groomed feathers. I felt stripped bare beneath his gaze, and silently lashed with each second his eyes bore into mine.

I forced fear out of my bloodstream and focused on the blue rim around his irises, a trick he'd taught me, telling me I could stare anyone down if I picked one color fleck within the eyes to concentrate on.

Dad leaned close. I jerked back. Colin stepped between us. Dad stood chest-to-chest with Colin, palpable fight bouncing between them.

"I'm going to kiss my daughter goodbye," he hissed.

Colin held his position for two, four, seven seconds. Heart stammering, I put my hand on his arm. "It's okay," I said.

Colin stepped aside but his warning gaze never left Dad's.

Once my hand fell left Colin's arm and fell to my side, Dad's eyes moved to mine. He kissed my cheek. "Have a good walk, Princess."

Not even the frigid air could cool my skin. The temperature had plunged, turning the rain into swirling snowflakes. Twenty feet down the street from the townhouse, Colin hailed a cab.

We got in, and a blast of heat melted the snow covering us both from head to toe. Colin rubbed his bare hands back and forth. I felt bad that I hadn't given him time to grab a pair of gloves.

"Where to?" the dark-skinned, turban-head-dressed driver queried us through the reflection of the rear-view mirror.

Colin looked at me.

"Just drive," I said. Being spontaneous wasn't something I'd been allowed to do. Dad insisted he know my whereabouts 24/7.

Colin pulled his ringing cell phone out of his pocket. The name on the screen: Charles. Colin clicked on the phone. "Yes, Charles... we're in a cab, heading west. I'm not sure. Yes. Yes. Of course. I'll let you know. Yes, sir." He shut the phone and his leg started tapping. "He wants to know where we're going." Colin's gaze skimmed the street, buildings and what few people we passed as we drove.

My skin prickled. "Let him wonder."

His dark eyes met mine across the den of the back seat. "You're justified in feeling angry right now. But I have to keep him abreast of where we go, that's my job."

His delivery was kind, the tone softened me. I couldn't bring myself to say anything, so I gazed out the window.

"Where do you want to go?" he asked. His cell phone vibrated again.

"Europe. Paris. California. Let's get on a plane and go to the beach." Impossible as the idea was, thrill raced along my blood for the opportunity to up and leave. "We could visit the old neighborhood. I'd love to see our house."

Colin smiled. His phone buzzed and he pulled it out. This time, he kept the screen angled in such a way that I couldn't see it. "Where do you want to go that won't get me thrown in jail?"

I crossed my arms over my chest and scrunched down into the worn seat. "That's exactly what Dad would do," I grumbled. "Some stupid kidnapping charge even though it's my idea. Ugh."

He stuffed his cell phone back in the pocket of his coat and reached out, and his fingers skimmed my shoulder in a gesture meant to comfort. Thrill rolled through my body like a dozen runaway balls downhill. His hand slowly went still. He swallowed, and withdrew.

"Central Park," I said.

The driver stopped at the corner of 59th and 5th Avenue. I reached to open the door and Colin's hand cuffed my wrist.

"Don't forget to pay the driver." I grinned, thrust open the door and jumped out. Colin, still in the back seat, scrambled for cash, tossed some bills over the partition and jumped out after me.

He remained next to me, his gaze jumpy. Snow fluttered from billowing gray clouds overhead. I started toward an opening in the low rock wall skirting this section of the park. I took three steps into the park before Colin took my arm in a firm grip that stopped me. "You're not going in."

"Yes, I am." I pulled free and started into the park. He kept pace with me, his head in constant motion, eyes darting, arms anxious at this sides.

"Ash, the park is dangerous after dark, everyone knows that."

"I don't care."

He grabbed my upper arms and swung me around. His dark eyes flashed. "I do."

"You're with me," I said, wiggling to free myself. Clearly uncomfortable holding me prisoner, he released me, but jittered like his blood itched.

He rammed a hand through his hair. "You *want* to put yourself in danger?"

I started to run. "I won't be in danger with you," I called to him.

Without effort, he stayed at my side, matching my pace. I'd read scenes like this: the hero chasing the heroine, the two of them ending up in a tumble followed by a hot kiss. But love-chases usually happened in daylight, without snow, and in warm, tropic environments.

I laughed and picked up my speed.

Walkways were slippery, iced over in spots. What few lamps lit the near-black area were covered in a veil of white, and the pale illumination through glass didn't do much to melt the ice. Paths were empty. Darkness appeared from the collection of shrubs, giant rocks, trees, and the occasional bridge that popped up.

My lungs started to ache with each breath. Frosty plumes blew out in front of my face, leaving a trail behind me. An umbrella of trees kept wet flakes from soaking us. Colin stayed a foot behind, his alert gaze like a searchlight.

"Ash," he said. "We've got to go back."

The innards of the park grew more dense, twisted, and black. No one smart ventured this deep into the park at night. The lights came fewer and far between. Colin's aura was tense, aware, and feral.

I slowed, catching my breath then reached skyward, my eyes closed, savoring freedom. Dad didn't know where we were. No one knew, except Colin and me. We were alone. *Alone.* I whirled, laughed, and stuck my tongue out, tasting the slushy falling flakes.

We may not have been on a beach in the tropics, and we may not have ended up in a rolling kiss, but we were alone.

I looked at him. Chest rising. Eyes latched on mine, so endlessly dark, impossible to read. I stepped toward him, heart pounding in my throat, and brought myself close enough that my chest brushed the rise and fall of his. I slid my arms up around his neck and his tight lips parted—shock? Wonder?

I would taste him and find out for myself.

Hands locked behind his neck, I held his gaze until my lips pressed against his. I closed my eyes. A dreamy rush streamed from my mouth to the tips of my fingers and toes. My lips moved of their own desire exploring the mouth I'd been fascinated by, tormented by, seduced by since I remembered the first heartbeat that told me, this heartbeat—this feeling he evoked, was different.

I waited for his lips to respond, the open bud of my mouth yearning. He remained still. Was he breathing? His chest had stopped moving. The dreamy rush flooding me evaporated. I opened my eyes. His were closed, dark lashes fluttering tight against his cheeks as if he was using every last ounce of strength he had to resist.

My arms slipped back to my sides.

I flushed with embarrassment. His eyes flashed open with a predatory look that forced me back a step. Ashamed that he'd rejected me, I couldn't bear the silence. The aloneness. I darted around him and ran back the way we'd come.

Colin snatched my arm. I wrenched free, stumbled. He reached out to steady me and we fell to the slick, snow-crisped grass and mud, and slid to a stop.

"Leave me alone," I said.

"Ashlyn."

I tried to writhe free, horrified that I'd kissed him. He didn't want me, and that realization stung as much as Dad's slap. Trying to keep my face from his view, I scrambled away, but he was longer, stronger, and his body covered mine, pinning me to the wet, frosty ground.

He snatched my flailing hands in his, holding me in place beneath him.

"I'm sorry. Please let me go." I turned my head as far right as I could, the humiliation unbearable.

Colin levered himself up, his hands still linked to mine, and he gently pulled me to my feet. My legs, back, and sides were chilled from being rammed in slushy grass. Hands on my shoulders, he held me firmly in front of him but I kept my gaze downward, refusing to meet his.

"Look at me."

I shook my head. My downcast gaze caught the mud smeared all over the front of him as if he'd just emerged from a mud fight. "We should get back," I muttered.

"Not till you look at me." His finger touched my chin, urged my face up.

My heart trembled. Too many shadows crossed his face for me to read what he was thinking.

"I've never done anything like that," I said. "I don't know what— I'm so embarrassed."

His hands slid up along my shoulder blades, to my neck, finally cupping my cheeks. The air around us seemed unseasonably hot, but that was impossible. Our breaths plumed in unison. His brows drew tight over determined, fierce eyes.

He shook his head. Eyes closed, he turned his face. His hands pressed my cheeks like he might crush my bones. Fear fought with curiosity, weaving my blood into a spin of desire.

What struggle took place inside of him? "Colin?"

A slow, controlled breath eased from his chest. He swallowed. "Say my name again."

"Colin."

He lowered his head. The crown of his dark hair reflected a remnant of moonlight, reminding me of that first day I'd seen him on the street. I'd known, with just a glance, that it was him.

He lifted his confused gaze to mine. He stepped back. "You know I can't…"

I reached out. He shook his head. The snap of a branch crackled somewhere behind him and he whirled around, blocking me with his body. His back faced me and beneath his peacoat his muscles locked in place. His head jerked right, then left.

I listened to his pounding breath. My heart rate notched up. Who or what had made that sound? Bushes and trees rustled, and a dark shape emerged. Colin stepped back, his arms out at his sides to shield me. Panic froze my blood.

"You got a dollar?" a craggy voice asked.

I peered around Colin's shoulder. A homeless man dressed in layers of shredded black and gray clothing emerged. He started toward us, a stuffed backpack flung over his shoulder. "I'll take anything," he begged.

"Sorry." Colin took me by the arm and we started at a brisk jog toward the entrance.

The stranger followed us. "I need money!" He stumbled to a stop.

Colin ignored the man, and his alert gaze swept the dark areas we passed. Guilt punched my conscience. If I hadn't brought us into the park, this wouldn't have happened.

Once the light from the street seeped into the park, and we were near the entrance, nervousness began to leave me. We didn't speak, and the rush of cars passing, the occasional pack of tourists chatting as they strolled helped fill the uncomfortable awkwardness my behavior had thrust between us.

His cell phone vibrated over and over, the repetitive buzz audible over the city noise. No doubt Dad.

I couldn't keep up with his furious, long stride and he took a two-foot lead, dropping hold of my arm. Part of me was relieved to have him not dragging me along like a parent drags a slow child. Another part of me enjoyed any physical contact we had—invited or forced.

He crossed the sidewalk and stood on the edge, his gaze on traffic. He waved at each cab that passed. *What are you doing, Ashlyn? You've really turned him off with tonight's drama.*

Finally, a cab pulled over. Colin opened the back door and we both got in. His cell phone continued to vibrate, the sound a soft buzz in the stuffy back of the cab.

Dad. Impatient, furious, demanding Dad.

How would we explain our filthy clothing? Shivers ravaged my skin, the wet cold sinking to my bones. Worse, I imagined Dad taking one look at me and firing Colin without listening to an explanation.

Colin retrieved his cell phone. From where I sat, I could see the screen: Charles.

—— CHAPTER SEVENTEEN

The townhouse was silent when Colin and I walked in a few minutes later. I took the stairs up hoping to change my clothes before Dad saw me and avoid any questions. Colin followed. Was he thinking what I was thinking?

My foot hit the second floor landing and I felt Colin's presence draw closer, like I'd just moved into the protective shade of a tree. "Ashlyn."

I faced him.

Dad cleared his throat. Colin turned. Dad stood a dozen feet away, just outside of Mother's bedroom door. I stepped around Colin so Dad was in my line of vision. Dad's wide-eyed gaze scraped us both from head to toe.

He crossed to us. "What happened?"

Colin and I looked like cats that'd been playing in the sewer. Dad's carefully controlled face contorted in concern, sharp eyes examining my clothing. "Are you all right?"

"Dad, yes. Nothing happened. We got caught in the storm, that's all."

"You didn't have the smarts to keep her dry?" Dad's question pierced the air when he jerked his head at Colin.

"It was my fault." I stepped in front of Colin, forcing Dad to look at me. "I wanted to take a walk."

"And see where that got you." Dad's brow arched.

"We're wet, so what?" I said.

Dad's jaw twitched. "Ashlyn, excuse us."

Panic grabbed my heart. I'd heard that tone before, when Dad had fired Stuart. "This isn't his fault. This was my idea."

"And your clothes? Explain that," Dad demanded.

"I fell. Colin tried to help me when a lame cab sped by, splashing snow and mud all over us."

Dad's eyes narrowed, then shifted to Colin whose face was stretched taut as a body on a torture rack. On a deep breath, the muscles in Dad's jaw slackened. "Get cleaned up, Princess. You must be cold."

"You're not firing him because of me, this isn't his fault."

More silence ticked by. Dad's gaze slid to Colin.

"Go get dry, Ashlyn," Dad directed.

I was afraid to leave Colin, not because he couldn't handle Dad on his own—he could—but because my legs turned to noodles beneath me even thinking about Colin not being here. But I'd said what I could to patch up the mess I'd made—and I had made a mess.

I bit my lower lip, not sure what else I could do to convince Dad that nothing illicit had happened between Colin and me.

"Colin," Dad slid a hand into one of the pockets of his slacks. "Take the rest of the night off."

What is Dad planning?

Shock was plain on Colin's face. "Yes sir."

With a quick glance at me, Colin excused himself. Where would he go? What would he do? My gaze followed him up the stairs until he disappeared. I found Dad watching me, his eyes narrowed.

Turning, I went into my bedroom and shut the door.

Usually, I took a long, hot soak in a bath full of cherry blossom scented bubbles. Not tonight. I took a quick, tepid shower, dressed in pjs, stuck my hair in a pony tail and headed for the music room. On my way, my gaze shifted to the third floor.

The soft hiss of liquid through pipes answered my question. I shook off the image of his flesh under an onslaught of water. *You've done nothing but cause trouble for him. You're only a job. He's probably going to go to some club and...* But he'd told me he didn't like clubbing. Where would he go?

A door shut upstairs. The soft pad of feet passed overhead. I inched to the stairwell, covertly leaned over the banister and snuck a peek at the third floor just in time to catch the firm muscles of his back. A white towel was slung low around his hips. His hair was a muss of dark, wet tips and spikes. He vanished into his bedroom and shut the door.

I swallowed, trying to moisten my dry throat. **Music. Music. Music.** Between the image of Colin's beautiful, carved back, and the movement of his body beneath the towel and his long legs, his song sprung into my head with a pulsing need for release.

I didn't close the doors to the music room, too anxious for my fingers to liberate the tune inside of me. I sat, and the instant my fingertips made contact with the piano keys every sensation burst and raced through my arms.

The music room filled with Colin's aura, as if his soul was in the room with me. Pounding his melody into the piano only served to create more building frustration, filling me with a want I'd never known. The one thing I did know was that I wanted him all to myself.

Dad entered, but I didn't stop—couldn't—so irresistible was my craving, and unsatisfied. He stopped next to the piano and waited for me to finish.

"I've heard that song a lot lately, who does it belong to?"

My nerves frayed. I met his gaze, and saw challenge there. "It belongs to me," I said. His brow arched ever so slightly, but the rest of his face remained curious.

Dad leaned and kissed the top of my head. "Feeling better?"

"I feel fine," I snapped. Was he going to apologize to me? "Why would you ask that?"

"You were cold and wet."

My fingers remained poised to play. I *needed* to play.

"Charles." Colin's voice wove into me from where he stood in the open doors. Dressed in designer black from head to toe, it was obvious he was going somewhere. My heart plummeted to my stomach.

Dad turned. "Yes?"

"I'm taking off now." Colin's brown eyes flicked to mine for a second and held, then he was all business back to Dad.

Dad nodded. "Very good. Thank you for letting me know."

I tore hurt, angry eyes from Colin and stared at the piano keys, now blurring through my tears.

Silent seconds skipped by. "He needed a night off," Dad said.

I closed my eyes. Need it? I could relate to that need. Feeling like you were going to explode, you wanted freedom so badly. *But you had freedom, and you lost it.*

"He is a red-blooded man," Dad's tone was amused. "I'm sure he has a number of women he sees."

I opened my eyes but kept my gaze downcast to hide welling tears. "Play my song for me, Princess. I haven't heard it in a long time."

His was the last song I wanted to play. But when he leaned his frame against the piano, I understood he was going to plant himself next to me until I'd played the song. The melody wrung out every last ounce of self control I had. My twisted feelings about Dad at the moment made it difficult for me to play with grace. I fought pounding the keys. As anger built, my breath heaved in and out, and my hands demanded truth. I thrashed the keyboard. The tune raked against the empty walls, shattering in upper octaves until I forced my hands down to lower registers where the song finally emptied.

I gasped. Sweat beaded on my face. I looked at Dad, face tight with pale shock. He studied me as if I was a witness who'd just dropped a bomb in court. Without a word, he turned and left the room.

My hands crumpled on the keys, sending a distorted mix of chords echoing into the air. I stood, went to the window and gazed out. Colin was out there somewhere. I didn't want to think about what he was doing.

I locked myself in my bedroom. Even my favorite books couldn't keep my mind engaged. The only thoughts raging through my head were fleshy pictures of Colin and some Barbie, making out. An image Dad's suggestion had planted in my head.

Hours crawled by. I remained alone. Mother and Dad's arguing jabbed out from behind Mother's bedroom, or Dad's—I wasn't sure which. Consumed by where Colin was and what he was doing, I ignored their bickering.

A door slammed, startling me. Dad's angry footfalls tore through the house. I stared at my closed door. Was I next?

My cell phone buzzed, and I felt my first wave of relief in hours seeing Felicity's home phone number.

"Hey," I said. "What happened to your cell phone?"

"I can't find it. I've looked everywhere. Ugh. Where've you been? I've tried to call you for hours."

I realized that with Mother's accident, I hadn't even checked my phone for messages, much less thought about calling her. "I'm sorry. You won't believe what happened." I told her about Mother. About Dad slapping me. About Colin coming to my defense, and our detour in the park.

"OMG! Wow, Ash. Talk about drama. Is your mom okay?"

"I think so. I just wish they'd stop fighting. I don't understand why they can't discuss things and move on."

"They've been like this forever," Felicity said, then quickly added, "I mean—I didn't mean to say that, Ash, I—"

"No… you're right." Still, knowing that Felicity had seen beyond my parents' *Town & Country* performance surprised me, though it shouldn't have. But if she'd seen it, there was no hope their friends hadn't. If they knew the farce was transparent, why did they keep it up?

"I can't believe it," Felicity muttered. "Was she trying to reach the guns?"

"She says she wasn't." Tears filled my eyes. Mother, so desperate for Dad that she'd hurt herself. The idea disintegrated my fantasies and dreams of our family ever being happy. I wept.

"Oh, sweetie." Felicity's tone softened. "I'm so sorry. I wish I could come over."

Like Dad would allow that now. "Yeah, me too."

"You'll never guess who I ran into today."

I was glad she was changing the subject. "Who?"

"Stuart."

"Really?" New York was, in miles, a small place, but a creepy scratch still trickled down my spine at the coincidence.

"Outside my apartment building. He said he lives around the corner from me now."

On the Upper West Side? How could he afford that? "Seriously?"

"Yeah. He looked terrible—like he's just gotten back from a month in Guantanamo."

"So he talked to you?"

"I was getting back from the store, and he was walking by the building. We stopped for a second. I was shocked he didn't ask about you."

"I'm glad he didn't. Did I tell you I ran into him at the bookstore a while back? He said he'd followed me there, he knew my routine."

"Ew! I bet your Dad flipped out."

"He doesn't know."

The sound of Dad's footsteps shook the walls of my bedroom like an earthquake. The door flew open and crashed into the wall. He filled the frame, fury squaring his face. My hand, holding the cell phone, inched away from my ear in stunned trepidation.

Felicity's voice trickled into the air. "Ash? Are you okay? Ash?"

I hung up on her. Mother's voice screeched from behind Dad. "Yes, go to her, Charles. Lie to her."

"Ashlyn," Dad's voice throttled the air. "Pack. You and I are leaving."

"What?"

By this time, Mother had finally made it to Dad, but she remained a few feet behind him. "You can't take her from me!"

Mother reached out and weakly yanked at his sleeve. Dad shoved her hand away, causing her to stumble back. Her eyes flared with fury. Dad whirled and towered over her. Breath locked in my throat.

No one moved. I stood, knees shaking. "I'm not going."

"Do as I say," he ground out.

I crossed to them. "My life is here and I'm not leaving." I wove my arms over my chest.

Dad pivoted my direction. He snagged my upper arms and yanked me against him. Pain cut through my shoulders and fired down to my wrists. "You're going to slap me again?" I snapped.

"Pack." He threw me with such power, I tripped to the foot of my bed in a heap.

———— CHAPTER EIGHTEEN

It was midnight and Eddy was off duty, so Dad arranged for a cab. With shaky hands I threw some clothes in an overnight suitcase. Mother and Dad continued arguing, Mother's threats like arrows, Dad's fired back like cannonballs.

Tears streamed down my cheeks.

Would Colin be told about this? What would he do?

Dad escorted me down the stairs, passing Mother who remained poised next to the pencil Christmas tree she'd had decorated with imported French cloisonné bulbs. Her shoulders trembled, her eyes were red.

Dad pulled open the front door and the wreath hanging on the inside fell to the floor, rolled a foot and tipped, breaking the glass ornaments nestled inside of it. My arm in his fist, Dad took me to the curb where the cab waited for us.

He opened the door and I got in. The front door to the townhouse was left wide open, and I could see Mother at the tree, her good hand over her lips, eyes slit in tears.

"The Ritz Carlton," Dad said. He sat back and sighed.

"I hate you," I hissed.

His dazed eyes remained out the front window like he didn't hear me.

We were ushered into the Central Park Ritz Carlton by a bevy of uniformed doormen. Dad spoke to them as if he knew them, and I realized then that he probably came here with whomever he spent time with when he wasn't at home.

Revulsion turned my stomach, and I stepped ahead of him, not wanting to be anywhere near him.

Dad bypassed the check in, striding directly to me as two bell boys loaded our luggage onto a brass luggage trolley. The dazed look I'd seen in his eyes during the drive over was gone. He was alert now.

"Is this where you bring your mistresses?" I bit out, staring up at the floor indicators above the closed elevator doors.

Dad glanced around to make sure I hadn't been overheard. His fingers pinched my elbow. The elevator doors slid silently open and he guided me inside. I pulled free and stepped away from him.

He pinned me with one of his cutthroat lawyer gazes. "Yes."

The doors shut. Part of me was shocked he'd admit the truth, another part was disappointed that he'd admitted to something I'd suspected, but had hoped wasn't true.

I swallowed a lump. Knowing should have empowered me, but he was too smart to admit something to me if he didn't want it getting out in the open or back to Mother, which slapped me with the realization that I was the last to know.

The car stopped on the thirtieth floor, and the doors opened. He led me to a suite, and I gasped when I stepped into the luxury of white on white, every surface pristine, clean and elegant in neutral colors.

Like he'd entered home, Dad tossed his keys on a waiting side table. He strolled into the living area and went directly to the mini bar. I remained in the entry.

He poured himself a scotch—no ice—and drank it down with one sharp tilt of his head. The glass landed on the bar with a clunk, and he poured another. My eyes widened. He repeated his first downing, and then leaned heavily on his arms, staring into the racks of liquor.

A knock at the door caused me to shake.

Dad crossed to the door and peered through the peep hole, then opened the door. The bellman nodded at him, smiled flirtatiously at me and wheeled in our suitcases. Dad handed him a bill and the young guy shot me one last glance before saying, "Thank you, Mr. Adair."

Familiarity hung in the air like tacky cologne. "He probably thinks I'm one of your mistresses," I sneered. I rolled my eyes when Dad swung around and looked at me.

"Your room is through there." With a nod, he gestured behind me.

I took the opportunity to check out the place. Just as elegant and five star as the living area with every accessory a wealthy traveler could want: phones on every table, forty inch plasma TVs everywhere you turned, wet bars, fridges, giant fresh flower arrangements pouring out of crystal vases.

Dad plopped my suitcase on the bed, turned and left, closing the door behind him. I was overcome with exhaustion and shock. I dropped to the mattress, blowing out a sigh. My phone vibrated and I pulled it out. Mother.

Are you all right?

So Dad wouldn't hear me and blow a gasket, I texted her back.

Yeah, u?

Miss you

Miss u what is going 2 happen?

Not to worry darling, dad and I will figure this out

I hoped so.

Are you at the Ritz?

How did u k now?

A few moments passed, and she didn't respond. How long had she known about Dad and the hotel? Sickened, I hoped she wasn't crying. I bruised inside for her. She never replied, so I placed my phone on one of the tables next to the bed. I heard Dad's voice, but also another. Colin?

I rose and went to the door, cracking it open just enough that as I peered out I caught sight of Colin. He wore the same outfit he'd had on when I'd seen him leave for his night out. A small suitcase sat at his side. My heart swooped.

"I've got to be at the office first thing in the morning, so I'm going to retire," Dad was saying. Though his back faced me, Colin's body language looked like he was uncomfortable and at odds with the situation.

"You can take the couch." Dad made no excuses for the accommodations he offered, and no apology for changing our address. "Carry on as usual. School. Then here. You are not to return to the townhouse. If Ashlyn needs her things brought over, you can hire someone to retrieve them. Understood?"

Colin hesitated. "Yes, sir," his voice was quiet.

Dad turned and vanished into his room, shutting the door with a final thud.

Colin's gaze swept his surroundings, and I opened the door of my room so that when his quizzical gaze came round, he saw me. His eyes fastened to mine and a myriad of questions flashed over his face. "Ash, what happened?" He started toward me.

I swallowed. He looked so sincerely interested—in me. "They had a fight."

He continued my direction. Was he still angry about the park? I couldn't read his face, and the day's events bore down on me. I backed into my bedroom, even as he closed in on me, and I slipped inside, shut the door, and pressed my forehead against it. My heart hammered. I had the fleeting fantasy of him bursting through, pinning me and kissing me. Ridiculous.

I took a long, hot bath, dressed in my white pjs and picked up one of a dozen magazines left for my pleasure, but none grabbed me. A handful of suspense paperbacks lined the built in bookshelf, but I couldn't think about reading. Not with Colin just outside the door. I paced. Almost texted Felicity, but it was way too late for that. Knowing Colin was closer than he'd been at the townhouse filled my blood with the familiar fluttering of curiosity and wonder his nearness always induced.

I took a deep breath and opened the door. Complete darkness. My eyes blinked, trying to adjust. Any exhaustion must have swirled down the drain along with my bathwater, because I was amazingly alert at four a.m.

I crept out into the living room area, my distorted vision trained on one of two couches. A light flashed on.

I blinked, covered my eyes while they settled.

Colin lay, half-sitting on one of the couches. White sheets and a fuzzy blanket tucked loosely around his waist, his naked shoulders and upper body framed against large, puckered white pillows.

His face scrunched in the light. "Are you okay?" he whispered.

I nodded, and hesitated before tiptoeing to him. His smooth skin looked like velvet against the white bedding.

"I'm sorry I woke you." I kept my voice just above a whisper, my gaze flicking to Dad's room, an ominous black space between the carpet and the bottom of the closed door.

"You didn't." Colin scratched his mussed hair. I wanted to touch it. "What happened?" he asked around a yawn.

"Dad demanded he and I leave the townhouse." I searched for a place to sit. Colin pulled back the coverings on the opposite end of the couch, making room for me. I squeezed into the space, but my thigh still touched his toes.

"I gathered that much when I went to pick up my things," Colin said.

"Did you see Mother?"

He nodded. "She was a wreck." He studied me through caring eyes. "Jeez, I'm sorry Ash." He shook his head.

"It's okay." I lied and the look of compassion on his face told me he saw through it. A fresh round of tears veiled my eyes. I buried my face in my hands, ashamed I was crying again.

The couch shifted beneath me, then his warm skin surrounded me. I burrowed my face into his neck. My arms wrapped around his back. He absorbed my tears, my weeping lost in his flesh.

He kissed the top of my head and the feeling of his mouth there drew my face up. His dark eyes penetrated me, sending want through my cells, need through my blood.

He swallowed. Against my chest, the taut planes of his bare torso lifted in an erratic rhythm. His head bent close, and my heart nearly burst waiting to feel his lips.

His mouth met mine in soft, sweet pressure. His skin, beneath my fingers was firm. Smooth. My hands spread out to feel the ridges of rib and muscle in his back, the strong curve of his spine. Moving toward me, he eased me into the cushions of the couch.

Sheets and blankets fell away, baring more long lean velvet, covered only by a pair of black boxers. He crouched toward me, as if he wanted to cover and consume me.

Pressed into the cushion, I felt like a delicate eggshell on a downy pillow. Colin's hand skimmed down my neck, anchored to the side of my head, his other and mirrored the action. He stayed poised above me, his arms roped into strong shoulders, his head hovered over mine, eyes black.

Seconds sizzled into hot minutes. He seemed to decide what to do next. My body lifted toward his, magnetized. Lightly, the tips of my fingers drew over his shoulders, behind his neck and clasped.

He closed his eyes as if in excruciating pain. Then his dark eyes opened. "Ash." his voice was hoarse.

"Kiss me again."

He lowered toward me, the muscles in his arms shifting in the soft lamplight until his mouth met mine. This kiss was like the petals of one flower gently coaxing another to open and bloom.

After, he sat back and touched my face. "I'm going to hate myself for doing that."

"I won't. I wanted you to kiss me. I've wanted you to for a long time. Who cares if you work for Dad? He's lied to me. He's lied to Mom. He doesn't deserve your loyalty."

"I shouldn't have kissed you, not here, not when you're vulnerable."

"Didn't you want to kiss me?"

"Yes." His hands broke free of mine and he fell back into the downy cushions, his hands shoved into his hair. "Yes, I wanted to."

"I wanted it, too."

The struggle he wrestled with became as apparent as if he suffered with a consuming fever, and I felt the first layer of weight for my part in making him go against something he'd held important. "I'm sorry." I could barely whisper, submerged with culpability.

I stood. He reached and took hold of my hand. "Ashlyn." The

gentle way he said my name melted as it seeped into my soul. I would never be able to numb the want I had for him, and seeing his body tangled in the sheets and blankets, his face turned up to me, urgency in his gaze, was an image I would never forget. I wanted him all to myself.

I woke hours later to a darkened room. Light peered through the solitary crack in the seam where blackout drapes came together over the window. The unfamiliar generic scent of the sheets I lay on reminded me that I wasn't home in the townhouse, I was in a hotel.

Coffee scented the air. I found the clock, it was ten. I jerked upright. Why hadn't Dad awakened me for school?

I tore back the sheets and stood. The night before, I'd overheard Dad tell Colin he had to be at the office early, so Dad was gone. That meant Colin and I were alone.

The thought liquefied my bones.

I wanted to see him, but would he want to see me after last night? *Dress, Ashlyn. Dress for school.* But I'd forgotten to pack my uniform.

I tore through my open suitcase, even though I knew the uniform wasn't there. I'd been so distracted by Mother and Daddy's fight, school hadn't entered my thought process in the slightest.

I washed my face, brushed my hair, and pinched my cheeks before opening the door. The aroma of coffee soothed, but I hesitated facing Colin. Is this what the morning after is like? I wondered. A stifled laugh sent goose bumps over my skin. *As if.*

Movement in the kitchen drew my attention, so I crossed through the living room and entered the white and blue area. Colin wore jeans and a light gray, V-neck sweater, the sleeves pushed halfway up his forearms. He stood over the sink, washing out a glass coffee pot. When I entered, he turned.

His hands went still. "Hey."

The usual sparkle in his eyes wasn't there, and my heart sunk. I stayed in the doorframe. "Hey."

"Coffee?" He nodded to a steaming cup he'd put aside.

"Thanks." I stepped into the room and took the cup into my hands. "Why didn't Dad wake me? I'm late for school."

"Charles said not to. I guess he figured you'd need the sleep."

"Can't say I'm not glad." I sipped the hot liquid. "I forgot my uniform."

Colin rinsed the coffee pot and set it on a towel to dry. Then he turned, crossed his arms and leaned his hip against the sink. "I'll have your things brought over."

I frowned. How long did Dad plan on us being here? My gut hollowed. Mother had said they'd work this out.

Colin stepped toward me, and his hands covered mine. It was then I noticed my hands were shaking, the coffee in the cup sloshing like the tide of the ocean. His touch stilled the trembling on contact.

The connective fuse we'd woven last night sparked again. The flicker of desire I'd seen in his eyes before was there.

"What's going to happen?"

He took a deep breath, shook his head. "I don't know."

"I can't *not* see Mother."

"I'm sorry."

"It's not your fault. But thank you for listening. And being here. I'm sorry about last night. I would never make you do something you—"

"Ash, you didn't *make* me do anything. This isn't easy for me."

"It's not easy for me, either."

He stepped close. "How am I going to resist you?"

Nothing came to my head. The fire racing through me had gone full circle and burned words into oblivion.

Colin. And me. Alone.

"If I'm not going to school today, then what?" I rasped. The stark image of him on the couch made me think of returning to the scene of last night's kiss.

The kitchen walls suddenly seemed to close us in. The temperature spiked. He swallowed.

"We should get out of here," he said.

I swallowed, nodded. "Let me get dressed."

I showered, put on underwear and slipped into the cloudy, soft robe hanging in the bathroom. Fingering my hair back, I reached for the blow dryer but froze when the raised voices of Dad and Colin struck the air like a bolt of lightning.

I knotted the sash at my waist and opened the bedroom door. Dad and Colin stood nose-to-nose in the living room. Dad wore one of his pristine suits, his skin the color of his scarlet tie. He stopped mid-sentence when I entered.

I folded my arms over my chest. "What's going on?"

We stood in starched silence.

Dad glided over to me, glossing over the moment. "How did you sleep?"

"You need to talk to Mother," I said.

"I'm on my lunch hour, and wanted to check on you. Colin's going to arrange to have your things brought—"

"Wait. You're really moving us here? For how long, Dad? We can't live here. We have a home."

"I'm not going to discuss this with you." Dad placed his hands on my shoulders and I jerked out of his hold.

"When are you going to stop treating me like a child? Go home and talk to Mother. Work this out."

The corner of Dad's jaw knotted. "What's happened between your mother and I isn't your concern. That's final." He burned me with one, long glare and then turned and walked out the door.

I let out a growl. "He's so infuriating."

"You've made your feelings clear, Ash. This is their problem to solve, not yours."

"I know that," I paced. And that was what frustrated me—that I couldn't force them to care about each other enough to work through it.

———— CHAPTER NINETEEN

Dad's unwillingness to try and work things out with Mother clawed at me the rest of the day, leaving me emotionally shredded. I had a hard time even bringing myself out of the mire to enjoy being with Colin. I should have been elated.

As we walked without aim, he kept a watchful eye on me. When we crossed a street, I felt the gentle pressure of his hand at my back. Inside, my anxiety for my parents built, the pressure causing my heart to burn.

We stopped at a corner and Colin did his usually sweep of the crowds surrounding us when his head paused a moment, his gaze behind his black glasses aimed at something to our right.

I followed his keen attention but saw nothing in the busy, five-o-clock pedestrian traffic. It always got darker faster in the city, the mammoth buildings and their shadows adding deeper abyss to the falling twilight.

"What?" I asked.

"Nothing."

The streetlight changed and he guided me along with the crowd of people. My cell phone vibrated in my pocket. I hoped it was Mother, I hadn't heard from her since earlier, and I wondered how she was holding up.

Felicity's mother's phone number appeared. "Hello?"

"Where were you today?" Felicity asked. "You sick?"

"Still haven't found your phone?"

"No. I've looked everywhere."

"Oh, no."

"I know. Sucks. So, what's up?"

I relayed what had happened. Felicity gasped. "Oh, no. I'm sorry, Ash. That sucks big time."

"Yeah."

"Are they gonna try to make up? Or what?"

"I don't know. What did I miss?" I asked. The sound of cars honking and city noise filtered into the phone on Felicity's end.

"Danicka asked where you were. I told her you and Colin were taking a long lunch *eating*—something she and her friends might want to take up since—clearly—Colin is a man, and men like meat, dogs like bones. He's there, right? Are you having a fabu time?"

I glanced at Colin, hoping he couldn't hear Felicity. "Well, kind of."

"I shouldn't have asked. You're worried about your mom and dad. Sorry. I miss you."

"Miss you, too."

"We're heading to Chows. Surprise. Ugh. I expect you to do some serious damage to that boy while I'm dining on chop suey. Got it? I want a full report later."

I laughed and glanced at Colin, hoping he hadn't overheard. "Oh sure, right. Bye."

"Felicity?" Colin asked.

I nodded.

"How did you meet?"

"At Chatham. She makes that place bearable."

He nodded. "Gotta have friends like that."

The Ritz was on the next block. Colin whipped his ringing phone out of the pocket of his coat. "Yes, sir? We're outside the building, actually. Yes. We can do that." The lightness in his expression vanished.

"Something wrong?"

"Charles wants us to meet him for dinner at Solange in ten."

"Where's that?"

"In the hotel."

We approached the hotel with its gold and red striped awnings and massive planters filled with holiday Christmas trees decorated in jewel-bright bulbs.

Colin whisked me past doormen who held the giant brass doors open for us.

"I need to wash my hands," I said. Walking through the city demanded a thorough scrubbing before eating, something Mother had taught me. Colin stood outside the bathroom door and waited for me.

The bathrooms were Italian marble from floor to ceiling. I washed my hands and made sure my hair wasn't windblown, my makeup was fresh and I spritzed a spray of one of five complimentary perfumes sitting on an ornate glass tray.

"Ready?" he asked when I came out of the ladies room.

I nodded. He escorted me down a hall and back through the large lobby, bustling with travelers, bellmen, and other hotel employees. Guests lounged in comfortable tuxedo-style couches. Some guests read, others chatted.

We crossed the lobby to another wide hall and ventured down the long, mirrored vestal until the scent of garlic, onions, and fragrant herbs filled the air. Solange was packed with men in suits and ties, a handful of women dressed in dresses, suits, or sleek designer wear.

Colin and I exchanged glances, both of us seeming to think the same thing: we were out of place in jeans and casual sweaters.

The maître d' escorted us to the back of Solange, where we found Dad still in his suit, his cell phone at his ear. He grinned and waved us over. Dad brought me against him in a side-hug and my spine stiffened.

Both Colin and Dad reached to pull out my chair. A half-second of sticky heat held Dad's and Colin's gazes together. It was Colin who finished the gentlemanly gesture, and I sat, cheeks warm.

"I'll call you back," Dad said. Conversation ended, and he slipped his phone into the front pocket of his suit jacket. He sat across from me, Colin next to me. A low, lemon light glowed from a miniature lamp centered on the gold table cloth.

"Hungry, Princess?"

I sighed. "I've asked you not to call me that."

He opened his menu, but his gray eyes held mine. "I apologize."

Dad rambled about the dinner choices but all I could think was his familiarity with the menu was directly linked to his familiarity with the hotel because of his infidelity to my mother.

To our family.

My appetite died.

"That sounds good." Colin closed his menu when I tuned back into the conversation.

"How about you, Ashlyn?" Dad didn't blink when he said my name.

"Whatever." I dropped the menu on the table and propped my elbows on the table edge—a dining faux pas Mother would have punished me for if I'd been a younger. Dad's lips curved up, slight amusement flickering in his eyes.

"So, you missed school today," Dad said. "What did you do?"

"I spent a lot of time wondering what the hell you're doing," I said.

Dad stiffened. Next to me, Colin shifted. Dad's fake cheery demeanor hardened to marble. He clasped his hands on the table, but didn't take his gaze from mine. "I understand your confusion."

"Try contempt." I tossed my napkin down.

"Let's order before we discuss the matter and thereby begin the process of indigestion," Dad said with a forced smile. I didn't appreciate his attempt at humor, and crossed my arms over my chest. Colin sent me a glance. Handle this like an adult, I thought and I uncrossed my arms and set them in my lap like I'd been taught.

The waiter returned to our table with a nod at Dad. "Drinks, sir?"

"Bring me a scotch—straight."

The waiter turned to Colin. "And for you, sir?"

Colin shook his head. "Water, thanks."

"Miss?"

Dad piped, "She's not—"

"I'll take a virgin strawberry daiquiri, please." I flashed a smile.

With a nod, the waiter disappeared.

"Now, to answer your question," Dad began. "Your mother and I are separating."

The muddled sound of dozens of nearby conversations, and the far-off clank of dishes filled the silence now sitting between us.

"Would you like me to let you two talk alone?" Colin asked.

Dad waved a hand, then loosened his tie a notch. "You're fine. I'm sorry this has come out like this, Ashlyn." Dad's voice was soft. His eyes seemed sincerely remorseful and stayed hooked to mine. "Sometimes, relationships are irreparable."

My heart sunk. "I see."

"I don't know what your mother has told you, or what she *will* tell you, but there are always two sides to a story."

Left wordless, I nodded.

He reached a hand out and laid it over mine for a brief moment, the contact shooting countless memories of him holding me, soothing me, caring for me through the years. Disappointment surged with sadness and I swallowed a surge of emotion rushing up my throat.

"Are you sure you can't work things out?" I asked, my voice barely a whisper.

Dad squeezed my hands. "Positive."

Sadness veiled his face for the first time since the topic was opened, but I wasn't sure if he was sad because of the failure or because I knew about it.

"You really don't love her anymore?" I asked.

In my peripheral vision, Colin shifted and lowered his head.

Dad held my gaze without a blink. "Like I said, there's a point where a relationship is beyond repair."

Empty inside, my appetite had vanished along with every other emotion except gouging shock. It wouldn't matter what I said, this disintegration had begun long before my voice carried enough weight to sway the outcome.

Dad laid a hand meant to comfort on my shoulder. "This is for the best, you'll see."

"Why didn't you try to work things out before it was too late?"

The waiter, carrying a tray, arrived at the table and delivered Dad's scotch and my daiquiri. Dad thanked him and tipped back the entire drink. Glass empty, he set it on the table, staring at it. "We waited too long."

Emotions threatened to flood my throat and eyes. "May I be excused?" I set down my napkin.

Colin stood.

"I'm just going to the ladies room," I said.

Colin's gaze held on Dad's for instruction. Dad's attention flicked from me, to Colin, back to me. He nodded. Slowly, Colin lowered back into the chair.

Sorrow echoed deep down in my heart for Dad. For Mother. For us.

Alone, I wove through the dining room. For the first time I was by myself in public—with Dad's blessing, and I couldn't enjoy it, not with my parents' marriage crumbling. Realistically, I figured they would be happier going different directions, rather than continuing to live a farce together. Still, deep down I hoped they could live happily ever after.

Happily ever after was the farce.

Though I figured Dad would send Colin to trail after me, I meant to take a deep breath and return to the table in a timely manner so Dad could see that he could allow me freedom and believe that everything was going to be okay.

Once I entered the lobby, my cell phone vibrated. I half expected it to be Dad. But it was a text from Felicity.

U found u r phone, yay

Why was she texting me in caps?

WHERE R U I NEED TO TALK NOW

What happened?

STUFF. CAN I SEE U?

k. I'm at the Ritz.

MEET ME IN THE LOBBY IN 5

I shot a glance around the room, didn't see her in the bodies coming and going.

On my way

LET ME KNO WHEN U R HERE

I headed for the same bathroom I'd used on my way in. I really hadn't needed to use the bathroom, I just wanted to take a breath. Now, I looked at my reflection, pleased that I'd stuck to my guns.

Venturing back to the lobby, I stood against a wall, inconspicuously, so I could watch the front entrance for Felicity. What had happened? Just short of an hour ago she'd been on her way to dinner with her parents. Felicity was bright and bouncy as a balloon, loose in the sky. I hoped whatever was going on wasn't that bad.

I gnawed on my lower lip, my nerves ticking the time I'd been away from the table. Dad or Colin would come after me any second. My hands were clammy. I was nervous for no reason. I was inside the hotel. Dad and Colin were only a few feet away. There were lots of people around. *Relax.*

My cell phone vibrated again.

CAN'T COME IN

why not?

I LOOK LIKE CRAP MEET ME OUTSIDE K

My nerves ratcheted up a notch. *where r u?*

SIDE ENTRANCE NORTH.

I looked north in the lobby and saw a hall. Figuring that must be the area she spoke of, I crossed to it, smiling at the steward who'd brought our luggage up to our rooms the day before. The hall was large, long and had a few chairs scattered along the walls for reading or waiting.

The hall ended in a T formation: one direction heading back into the hotel, the other an exit that let out to a side street.

No doormen were stationed at this entrance because you had to have a room card in order to enter. Heart skipping, I opened the door. Twilight had submitted to completed darkness, and the only light in the immediate area were those beneath the striped canopy hanging over head.

I poked my head out and looked left. Cars lined the street. The nearest had its parking lights on at eerie glow. "Fel?"

I held the door open, because I didn't have my purse—I'd left it on the chair, back in the dining room—when my phone vibrated again.

Felicity. *WHERE R U*
at the entrance where r u?

I stepped onto the sidewalk, hand still on the door and a gloved palm wrapped around my mouth, the scent of leather filled my nose. Another hand snatched and locked me against a solid, strong male body. A soggy cloth with a sickly stench was shoved over my nose and mouth. Everything went black.

My lids dragged open to near darkness. The pounding through my head felt like a jackhammer. I tried to move but my hands and feet wouldn't budge. Panic stuttered through my limbs.

I blinked and stretched my eyes as wide as I could. Wood paneled walls. A musty smell. Mushroom-colored lamp light.

Stuart.

My heart jerked. He sat on a chair, next to the bed I was tied to—arms over my head, legs spread, bound to the iron footboard. His eyes were fierce. His gaunt face twisted with concern and terror.

I opened my mouth but the only sound was a gravelly rasp. He reached out slowly to touch me. I tried to yank away but couldn't. Binding my hands was yards of fat pink, satin ribbon looped and knotted around each wrist. Ankles: same. My hands were cold, fingertips tingling from loss of circulation. I lay on a stiff mattress covered with a soft quilt, and it smelled thickly of body odor. Panic rushed through my veins. I was sure my heart would explode from my chest.

"You kidnapped me?" I finally managed to ask.

"I rescued you." Stuart jumped to his feet, and paced. His restless hands scrubbed his face over and over. "I'm not a kidnapper."

Why did he do this? What is he planning on doing to me? The thought of what he wanted sucked breath from my lungs. *Calm down, calm down. You have your clothes on. Maybe he won't hurt you.* I closed my eyes. Tears streamed down the sides of my face. Dad had told me if I ever found myself in a situation like this to keep calm. So had

Colin. Fear killed common sense and capability. Think. Act.

I hated that I was helpless. I screamed. Pushing every last ounce of air from my lungs, I bellowed as loud as I could.

Stuart lunged, clamping both hands over my mouth. Our gazes gripped each other. "Stop screaming," he growled.

If there was any way in this world anyone anywhere would hear me, I had to give it a shot. Screaming shredded my voice into wispy sobs. My stomach muscles bunched and cramped.

"You going to be quiet?" he demanded. I nodded. He removed his palms from my mouth.

"Let me go."

He jerked to his feet, antsy.

"Let me go, Stuart."

His feral gaze didn't blink. "Quiet." He paced again, muttering words I couldn't understand under his breath.

Convince him you're on his side. You can do this. You can.

He stopped, stared like he still couldn't believe I was there. "I saw Charles take you to the hotel and—I couldn't let him keep you in that filthy place."

"You knew about that?"

"Everybody knows, except you." His breath started to skip. His face flushed scarlet. "What kind of man locks away his daughter? You would have fallen in love with me if he hadn't hired me to work for you."

Never.

He stepped to the edge of the bed.

Heart racing, fists clenched, I endured him stroking my head. I closed my eyes, worked to stop the sob creeping into my chest. Tears continued to rush down the sides of my face, but my breath slowly turned from a race to a pant.

Stuart's hand left my head and my eyes flashed open. He headed for the open door. He wore khaki slacks, and a navy sweater— clothes I recognized from when he'd lived with us.

I stole the moment to look around. I was in a bedroom. One window, half covered with white, eyelet curtains, pulled closed.

Paneling—the cheap kind people threw up to cover old walls. Photos hung too-high on the wood, a decorating faux-pas Mother detested. I almost laughed that I'd notice such a thing when I was tied to a bed, my future uncertain.

My hands were beginning to turn purple and cold. Same with my feet. *Someone help me*. My eyes closed against a fresh round of tears. *There's no one to help you. You have to get yourself out of this.*

Stuart returned with a moist washcloth. He held it out, gesturing that he was going to use it on my face. He waited for my approval. I finally nodded.

He sat and gently patted the warm cloth over my cheeks, forehead, chin. "Don't cry. I won't hurt you. I love you."

My chin started to tremble. More tears threatened to burst from my eyes, but I blinked hard, fast, and steadied my emotions. *Love?*

"If we'd met like normal people, you'd have fallen in love with me."

He withdrew the cool cloth and sat back, studying me. I wouldn't have ever found him attractive. I hated hairy, big men. Dad knew that.

Dad. Knew.

A lump grew in my throat.

"I don't blame you for hating your bodyguards, you couldn't see past it."

Dad. Knew.

Urgency leapt from his voice and eyes. He leaned close. "Being together, away from that hell-hole, you'll see your real feelings for me." Stuart's eyes watched me with a dreamy haze. His gaze intensified on my mouth, fingertips like feathers fluttering over the outer ridges of my upper lip, then along my bottom lip. Sweat seeped from my pores. "You're so beautiful. I want to kiss you." His throaty desire sent a shiver of revulsion across my skin.

Oh no. No. But if denied him, he'd do what he wanted anyway. I couldn't stop him. "I don't like being tied up, Stuart."

His fingers stilled on my lips. "I've wanted you for so long." He continued to move his fingers over my lips, then over my head, through my hair, skimming the base of my neck. Panic trembled through me. "Don't be afraid," he murmured. His face neared, breath smelling of onions and the nearness caused my body to shake. His teeth took my earlobe and gently nibbled. I turned my head, swallowing the vomit surging up my throat.

Paralyzing fear gripped my every muscle. I focused on steadying my breath, on relaxing so as to not give ravaging fear any chance to reveal itself.

"Beautiful, beautiful Ash." His palms now made a slow ascent up my arms to my bound wrists.

"Untie me," my voice cracked. My body shook so violently, I was sure he'd read the reaction for the disgust that it was. Too distracted by his own desire, he was deaf to my plea. I pinched my eyes closed. The slick, stickiness of his mouth covered mine, slobbery, starved, like a hound devouring a meal.

I writhed and bucked.

———— CHAPTER TWENTY

And threw up.

Stuart jumped to his feet, stunned. He stared down at his clothes, at me, at the bed—now covered with my vomit.

"What the hell?" he spit barf out. His gag reflex kicked in and he darted from the room. My skin blanched in sweat. What would he do now?

He returned, muttering curses and wiping himself off with a towel. "Why did you do that?"

"I didn't do it on purpose." My throat stung from bile. I wanted to clean up.

"You barfed in my mouth." His skin reddened. He unbuttoned his shirt, ripped it off, squeezed it between his fists, biceps bulging. The sight of his rock-hard body sent panic racing through me. He was so big, stronger than me. He eyed me a moment, then turned and left the room. I lay there, fighting the aftershock effect to continue vomiting, the stench so wretched.

A few minutes later he returned in fresh clothes. He stopped in the door, seemed to ponder his next move, then crossed to the bed and stared down at me. "I should leave you in your puke."

"I need to clean up," I said. "Untie me."

His eyes swept me from chest to toes, then scanned the bedspread and floor. Finally, he came to the bed and leaned over me. His untucked shirt hung in my face, and from where I lay, I saw his belly button and the path of blonde curly hair that led below the waist of his jeans. Another round of bile rolled up my throat, but I swallowed.

Hands free, he carefully brought my arms down to rest on my

chest. His eyes never leaving mine, he moved to the foot of the bed, his hands working to loosen the thick pink ribbons.

When my feet were free, he snatched my ankles into his fists and held my legs. My heart screamed in my chest.

"Don't run."

Frozen with fear, I couldn't respond. He held my legs long enough to prove his point, then lowered them to the bed. Coming to the side, he barely blinked, so intent on following my every move. "Get up. The bathroom's this way."

It took effort to stand. I wobbled. His hands supported my shoulders. "Why did you bring me here if you're going to be mean?" I sneered.

His tight grip on my shoulders softened a little. "You hucked all over me."

We exited the bedroom and entered a living room—a small area painted light blue with seascape paintings and old family portraits scattered on the walls. Curtains were drawn, so I couldn't see outside. Lamplight kept the space in a grey haze. The front door had a deadbolt and a chain.

My gaze skipped over every surface, into every corner, in search of anything that could aid me in escaping. Choosing the right moment proved harder than I thought. What if I tried and failed? He'd hurt me for sure. He guided me through a short hall where his school photos hung—from kindergarten to high school. So normal. What had driven him to take me?

His life would never be normal again now.

But mine could.

My mind flashed the handful of self-defense techniques Colin had taught me. All I needed was the right moment.

Stuart gestured to an open door. We stopped in the jamb and he flicked on the light. He room was a small bath tiled in yellow and white with lemon-colored curtains.

I stepped in, and a powder scent filled my head.

Stuart planted himself in the door, crossing his arms over his chest. My eyes widened.

"Take a shower."

"With you standing there?"

"I'm not letting you out of my sight."

"Then I'm not showering."

He unfolded his arms and moved his bulk into the small space with me. My heart banged. "Take off your clothes."

Fear squashed my voice. I shook my head.

His eyes flashed with malice. "Then I'll strip you myself."

I jumped into the tub and turned on the shower water. Icy pellets hit my skin and I shuddered, adjusting the knob to hot.

"Going to shower with your clothes on?" he snickered.

"You're not touching me."

Anger boiled in his muscles, tensing and bunching beneath his clothes. He lunged, and ripped at my sopping clothes.

I shoved at his chest. He was like grappling with a grizzly. I twisted. My backside was against him. He continued to rip my clothes. Hot water spray burned through the fabric of my clothes. I thrust my head back in a head-butt and felt the impact of his nose vibrate through my skull. He swore. His grip bruised my ribs.

I caught sight of a bar of soap in the caddy. I head butted him again. He jerked his head aside. His palm wrapped around my jaw, locking my face in a tight hold. I shoved my elbow into his gut. He winced but didn't move. He had my head captured between his neck and jaw. I bit down his ear. He groaned. His arms released enough for me to break free. I grabbed the soap, coated my fingers with suds, whirled and gouged his eyes with my fingers.

He screamed. His hands slapped over his eyes.

I pushed past him, and ran, sloshing and sliding out of the bathroom. I flew through the living room to the front door. Behind me, Stuart's shrieks increased. Hands shaking, I unlatched the chain, yanked open door and leapt out into the darkness.

My eyes took forever to adjust—or seemed to. I darted across a small front yard, the frigid air freezing my drenched clothes. A street—lined with houses and cars. I fled down the middle, saw two guys up ahead—one on a bike, another hurrying alongside him, both coming my direction.

I shouted, waving my arms. The street seemed to stretch before me. Safety was so far away. Finally, I was there. I couldn't speak. No breath. Behind me—no sound.

"Are you okay?" The older man's gaze swept me from soaking feet to head.

The teenager's eyes widened. "Hey, it's that girl on the news."

Sirens sliced the air like samurai swords in full swing. It seemed I blinked and was surrounded by police cars, swirling red and white light, and black uniformed officers. I mumbled my name, adrenaline drowning my senses. A blanket was wrapped around me. The additional weight only added to the strange suffocation my soaked, cold clothing was imposing on me. I was tucked in the back seat of one of the cars and whisked away.

I stared out the window. We sped past houses. Slummy neighborhoods.

Two officers sat in the front seat, a woman sat in the back with me. She introduced herself, but her name slipped off my numb brain.

"You warm enough? I've got more blankets where that came from," the female officer asked. Her badge read Ahearn.

I shook my head. I wished the shakes erupting through me would settle.

"Want some water?" she asked.

"No thanks."

"Coffee?"

Eyes out the window, I shook my head. My stomach was restless.

"You take it easy," she said. "We'll get you into some dry clothes at the hospital."

Weariness cloaked me and I leaned my head back. The adrenaline surging through me was slowly draining, and my muscles, eyelids, became heavy.

The squad car drove into a yellow lit tunnel. The inside of the vehicle vibrated with the sound of speeding wheels and churning engines all racing through the cylinder. I closed my eyes. My brain blanked out—I don't know for how long, but when I opened my eyes it was black night. We were on the island. The grating pitch of the police radio scratched the air.

"A male, six foot two inches, two hundred forty pounds, blond hair and green eyes has been apprehended and is in police custody."

I swallowed.

"Looks like they got Reed." Detective Ahearn drew my attention, her voice soft and calm as she eyed me across the darkness.

"How did you know about him?" I asked.

"When we questioned your father, Stuart was at the top of the list of suspects."

Dad. Mother. I closed my eyes, suppressing tears. Colin.

"How did you find me so fast?" I asked, looking at her again.

"The tracking device told us you were in the area."

"Excuse me?"

"The tracking device inside of you."

My empty stomach rolled. Her expression faltered. She must have realized from my stunned silence that I had no idea that I had a tracking device inside of me. *Tracking device.* When? I'd never been in the hospital, never been put under except for minor dental work. I touched the small white line in my arm—was that it? The supposed "mole scar"? I was both shocked and relieved at the depths Dad had gone to ensure my safety.

I was safe, after all. Or was I?

None of this would have happened if Dad hadn't hired Stuart.

We pulled into St. Mary's Hospital, and wound underground through a parking maze of cement. The patrol car stopped at an open elevator.

The elevator smelled stale, like yesterday's cigarettes. Stuffy, Close. At the eleventh floor, the doors slid open to a long, antiseptic hall.

Detective Ahearn escorted me into a small examination room where a female doctor in a long, white medical coat smiled and extended her hand to me. She introduced herself, but it seemed that every word floated through my consciousness.

Detective Ahearn left and the doctor's silky voice calmed me into lying down on the examination table while she checked my blood pressure, felt for broken bones and asked me what had happened.

Exhausted, answers dropped from my mouth in one-word replies.

She crossed the room to a closet and brought out a pair of dark blue scrubs. "Change into these. They need your clothes and undergarments to do some tests. I'll wait outside the door."

I sat a moment, holding the light-weight, neatly folded garments in my hands, my gaze on them, but my eyes out of focus.

I was taken into a large private room—white walls, white lights, white bed. Colin stood in the center. My heart lodged in my throat. He whirled when the door opened, and our eyes met. His black slacks and sweater were stark against the whiteness.

I bolted from the wheelchair and flew into his arms. Those in the room fell silent. His embrace crushed me. I wept against him. He stroked my head, whispered my name. Squeezed me so ferociously, I thought my ribs would break. We stood fastened until my sobs dissipated.

His hand stroked my cheek. I was vaguely aware of the female officer chatting in hushed tones to someone. Then, she ushered everyone from the room and the door shut behind her.

"Ashlyn?" Mother whispered.

Colin gently urged me to turn so I could see her.

Mother's ashen face sagged, eye sockets like canyons, as if she'd taken two fists in the face. I crossed to her. Her free arm slipped around my back and clung to my moist clothes. She wept on my shoulder.

"Where's Dad?" I asked

She drew back, her tear-ravaged face blotchy. "Before we talk about him, I want to know what happened. Are you all right?"

"Yes, Mother, I'm all right."

The sight of Colin and Mother caused reassurance to wrap around me. This ordeal was over. My muscles went slack. I had to fight not submitting to the overpowering desire to collapse into sleep.

I began from when I left the dinner table. Sweat clung to my skin as I neared the moment I woke, and found myself bound to a bed.

Mother gasped.

Colin's chest rose beneath his arms, tightly crossed.

"He had me tied with pink ribbon," I said.

Mother sucked in air.

"And?" Colin's sharp tone cut through Mother's hysteria, silencing her. Her hand fluttered at her breastbone like she'd just swallowed something and might choke.

"He kept saying he wasn't a kidnapper, that he didn't mean to take me—"

"That's ridiculous," Mother injected. "He is obviously psychotic—"

"Fiona," Colin snapped. Mother's eyes bulged at him, but she pinched her lips. "What happened next?" he asked.

I swallowed. "He told me he kidnapped me because Dad had taken me to the hotel where he took his mistress." I glanced at Mother's rapidly paling face. "Stuart didn't like that."

"Well," Mother's brow cocked. "He's not the only one."

"Fiona, please." Colin slid her a glare meant to silence. "Then?" he urged.

"He…" I swallowed. "Kissed me."

"How awful." Mother covered her mouth with her hands.

"I threw up all over him. He was a mess, so he untied me and took me to the shower. I head-butted him, shoved soap in his eyes and got away."

Mother wrapped around me again. "Darling. You're safe now." She released me.

Colin remained unmoved by my admission, deciphering, but an edge of emotion caused his steady demeanor to twitch. Mother wiped her teary eyes with a tissue she plucked from a pocket.

"When did you and Dad have the tracking chip implanted inside of me?" I asked.

Mother blinked, but didn't respond for a few long moments. Colin's eyes deepened with—what? Had he known about the chip?

"The minute your father was able to get his hands on one," Mother explained. "You were eight. He was out of his mind with worry that anything like *this* would ever happen. I disagreed with it, but he does what he wants." She tilted her head, and reached out her good arm her hand covering mine. "I'm sorry—I'm sure you were—"

"I am shocked. And disgusted. Outraged. How come you never told me?"

"It worked, that's the important thing."

"Yes." A flame burned inside of me. "But he did it without my consent."

"You were too young."

"I should have been told."

"You were kidnapped, Ashlyn. Neither one of us wanted that happening again."

"But it did happen again!" Frustration burned in my voice.

Colin's body tensed like a rabbit in a cage. Mother's gaze flicked to him, then back to me.

"Did you know?" I asked him.

"Not until a few hours ago."

"You must think we're depraved," I said under my breath, sure he was at the end of endurance rope now.

"He thinks no such thing!" Mother's skin flushed red. "We had every right to take whatever precautions we saw necessary for your safety. A few months living under the same roof doesn't give anyone the right to judge—"

"Mother, calm down."

Mother steamed, and stood.

"I'm not judging," Colin boomed. Silence echoed in the room. Mother's tight shoulders erected.

"It's been a long day for everyone," Colin said, voice gentle.

"I need a drink." Mother crossed to the door. She hemmed a moment, then relented. "Do you want anything, darling?"

I shook my head.

She turned a raised brow to Colin. "Colin?"

"No, thank you," he said.

"They'd better have a Rockstar in this damned place." The moment Mother left, the empty quiet suddenly tensed.

Colin crossed to me. "What really happened with Stuart?"

"I told you—"

"I've studied victims of violent crime, they suppress things, it's the first—"

"I'm not suppressing anything," I said. "I told you what happened, exactly like it happened."

"Ninety-eight percent of kidnap victims are sexually assaulted by their abductors. You need to be examined, to make sure you're healthy and that he didn't—"

"He didn't touch me. He kissed me, that was all."

Colin's dark eyes slipped to my mouth and held a moment. Jaw twitching, he shoved a hand into his hair. He took one step and his face was inches from mine. "You're telling me he tied you to a bed and didn't take advantage of that?"

My mouth hung open for a few long moments of disbelief. "I wasn't raped." The very thought of Stuart kissing me shot goose bumps all over my flesh and bile surging up my throat.

I'd never seen Colin angry. Even knowing he was angry at Stuart—not me, grafted panic to my nerves and bones in a trembling that wouldn't stop.

The news channel was on the television, and the announcement of my name caused us to watch the screen. A photo of me flashed.

"Ashlyn Adair was reportedly found shortly after midnight in a suburb of New Jersey, at the home of her ex-bodyguard, Stuart Reed."

The report ended with the promise of more news as it broke. Seeing my face on the screen caused a shiver of discomfort down my spine. My life had been so anonymous, to have my picture splayed for the world to see—the only reason Dad must have agreed to allow the exhibit was to aid in finding me.

"Where is Dad, anyway?" I didn't disguise the lividness roaring through my veins. I wanted to talk to him. Now. "Is he *hiding*?"

Colin shifted. Swallowed. A pit opened in my stomach. "Did something happen to him?"

"Your mother should talk to you."

The pit in my gut gaped wide. "Where is he?"

Mother entered with a silver and gold can. "I can't believe they didn't have a Rockstar." The weariness in her expression had perked some, like a flower after rain. A brief smile lit her lips. "But the nicest young man offered to run down the street to the deli and pick one up for me."

"Mother," I started in her direction. "Where's Dad?"

Her stride slowed at my question, but she continued until she joined Colin and me in the center of the room. "He's having a stint put in, darling. Nothing serious." Then she held the can out to Colin with her good hand. "Would you mind, dear boy?"

Colin opened the can and handed it to her. Mother offered me the first sip.

I waved the can away. "Nothing serious? Sounds serious to me."

"He had a heart attack." Mother stated the words matter-of-factly, sipping the Rockstar like the illness was commonplace.

"Oh, no." I hugged myself, and then felt the warm comfort of Colin's arm slide in place around my shoulders.

Mother shrugged. "He's going to be fine."

"When did it happen?"

"About an hour after you were taken," she said.

"Was it me?" I asked. "Because of what happened?"

"His heart attack is not your fault," Mother's tone was sharp.

Colin took a deep breath. "The doctors only said that he needed to go in for surgery immediately."

I closed my eyes. "He doesn't know they found me yet."

"He doesn't." Mother strolled across the floor to the couch, and sat. "But that's a good thing. Wanting to make sure you're okay will give him the will to live. That, and his woman."

When it was determined that I was ok, I was discharged. Mother, Colin and I were escorted to a waiting room.

Mother laid down on the couch. Colin crossed to the floor-to-ceiling windows and stared out over the city.

My gazed remained fixed on the clock: 1:30

3:15

3:47

"Mrs. Adair?" A soft voice startled us.

A doctor stood in the door, waiting for our attention. Countenance edgy with anticipation, Mother rose from the couch. I joined her, and wrapped my arm around her waist. Colin came away from the window where he'd been staring out at the city lights, twinkling as if they adorned steel Christmas trees.

Dad lay in a bed, his still form dressed in a blue and white hospital gown. His eyes were closed. The sight was like a punch in the gut, knocking my breath out. The nurse attending him was adjusting his IV.

Mother let go of me and moved to the side of Dad's bed. Her drawn features didn't perk any, not with the murky remnants of their marriage lingering in her gaze.

"He'll be tired when he wakes up," the nurse said. "Should be in about an hour." She turned and left.

My legs moved to Dad's bed like they were cast in cement. With the news of an hour's wait before he came out of the anesthesia, my body yearned for sleep. I settled for standing opposite Mother at Dad's bedside. Colin showed signs of exhaustion by taking the only chair in the room and falling into it.

Mother stared at Dad's face. What was she thinking? Somehow, I doubted her mind was brimming with happy memories at that moment, and that saddened me. Dad, powerful, never-failing Dad lay not with the easy, natural comfort of sleep but in dormant anguish.

A loud, tired, sigh of concession escaped Mother's lungs. She left Dad's side and Colin vacated the chair for her. She lowered herself into it with weary effort.

No one spoke. I gently sat on the foot of Dad's bed, my nerves stretched. Dad's condition was precarious.

My world was crumbling like Mother's soggy, used tissue.

Colin now leaned against the wall. His eyes hung on mine without a blink.

6:20 am

Mother fell asleep in the chair. Her head was tilted back, mouth gaping open, a raw snore zigzagging from her lungs. Her hand hung to the side, empty Rockstar can on the floor.

My gaze flicked to Colin's continually to see if he was watching me. Finally, I could take no more. I eased off the bed and crossed to him, stopping directly in front of him.

The concern drawing his brows together softened a little. He reached out and skimmed my cheek with the back of his fingers. "I'm so sorry, Ash."

I nodded. "I'm okay now. I took his hands in mine and held them tight. "Everyone who has ever done anything to me has been someone Dad has brought into my life—Melissa. Stuart."

Colin shook his head. "The irony."

A low groan came from Dad and his foot moved beneath the white sheet and blanket. I hurried to his side. His lids labored apart, his gaze opening directly on me. His milky-white eyes widened, then pinched closed. Tears squeezed out between his lashes and streamed down his cheeks.

"Dad, I'm here." I grasped his hand, shocked at his weakened grip.

"Did he hurt you?" he asked.

I shook my head.

Disbelief struggled to leave Dad's eyes as they searched mine. His shoulders buckled. "I'm so sorry."

My questions had to wait.

——— CHAPTER TWENTY-ONE

Hours later, Colin, Mother and I were escorted down to the parking garage and into a waiting unmarked police car. Difficult as it was to leave Dad, I felt like I clung to the branch of a tree while a tornado whirled around me.

My gaze volleyed between the buildings we passed and Colin. At one point, I caught Mother watching me and I forced aside the gnaw I had inside to continue to look at Colin and steadied my gaze out the window. "We're not going to the Ritz?" I asked, seeing that the car was headed for the townhouse.

"Of course not," Mother scoffed. "You're coming home."

I could see why Mother was exerting control, at the same time, I hated being a pawn.

In front of the townhouse, news vans, parked along the street—some double parked—opened, and reporters and camera men hopped out and jogged over. My palms moistened. Cameras flashed the moment we pulled up next to the curb. Voices shouted questions.

Colin surveyed the surroundings with hawk-like concentration.

"NYPD has officers posted outside." He looked at Mother.

"Thankfully. I couldn't deal with this alone." She, too, seemed awed and frightened of the crowd hunkered down in front of the townhouse.

"What do they want?" My voice sounded too small.

Colin's dark eyes slid to mine. "You."

He leaned forward, to address the driver. "Take us to Eighty Sixteen Charles Street."

The officer nodded and sped away from the snapping jaws of

the crowd we left behind.

"Where are we going?" Mother's free hand gripped the door handle as the car surged forward.

"My place." Colin delivered the information with authority.

Mother blinked, as if shocked he'd take the reins in his hands. "I need my toiletries. Fresh clothes. My own bed."

"Not tonight. You wouldn't sleep with that mob outside."

"The police assured me they would take care of things."

"Their presence will help, but do you honestly feel like you could nod off with a pack of wolves outside your front door?"

"No," I said. The thought caused more sweat to glaze my skin. "I don't want to be here."

Mother's rigidity relaxed as she seemed to ponder his suggestion. "All right. I want you to make a statement on behalf of the family tomorrow."

Colin nodded.

We drove through traffic toward lower Manhattan. We didn't say anything more until we reached Colin's apartment building, a brick, ten-story place with crumbling cement steps out front.

Colin unlocked the main door. A waft of musty air barraged my senses. He led us up one set of stairs to the second floor and slipped his key into a door marked 202 A. "It's a small but it's away from the media." His gaze shifted to Mother. "You two can have my bedroom. I'll sleep on the couch."

"I'm sure it will be fine," she replied.

The moment I stepped over the threshold, weariness thickened my limbs. He flicked on one overhead light and a dull, warm color of gold doused the room. Colin's place. The white walls were empty, the floor was wood but clean, and the small room was bare but for a plaid blue and black couch and a wooden crate he used as a coffee table. A picture of his parents was on the crate.

Colin held the door open and Mother followed me inside, surveying the place with alarm in her eyes. "Well."

I elbowed her gently in the ribs.

Colin shut, locked, and bolted the door. "Like I said, it's not much.

But no one knows we're here. The bedroom and bath is in the back, through the kitchen." He started toward the kitchen: about the size of one of our hallways at the townhouse, allotted with the necessities: stove, sink, and mini fridge.

Another door off the kitchen led to a bedroom just big enough for a queen-sized bed covered in a black bedspread with blue pillows. Mother stood in the door, her hand patting her breastbone.

"My." She eyed the small window the size of a card table top. "How did they get a bed in here?"

"Carefully," Colin quipped. "Bath's here." He stepped around Mother and pushed open another door. When he pulled a dangling chain, a bulb hanging from the ceiling lit the tiny, cream-color tiled room to look like the inside of an eggshell. "The sheets are clean. And I know for a fact the landlady bombed for roaches last month."

A squeaking gasp escaped Mother. She took my hand and squeezed it to her chest. I recognized the flash of panic in her eyes and patted her arm. Colin's lip lifted in amusement.

He went into the bathroom and dug two towels out of a small cabinet. He hung them over the towel bar. "Feel free to take a bath. I can bring in some dish soap if you want to—"

"I'm too exhausted to do anything but sleep." Mother's wide-eyed gaze swept the room.

"Can I get you anything else? Some sweats to sleep in?"

Mother and I exchanged glances. Her brow arched over a playful grin. "I'm fine, darling. But thank you for the offer."

"I'll take one of your shirts," I piped.

Colin's dimples flashed. "Sure." He opened his closet and pulled out a black, oversized NYU tee shirt and extended it to me. Our fingers brushed when I retrieved it.

"Good night," he said.

"Night," Mother and I replied in unison.

Colin squeezed by us and shut the bedroom door. Mother, in bug-alert mode, shuddered and tip-toed around the room, her nose crimped as her gaze searched.

"Mother, I'm sure we're going to be fine."

Distracted, she didn't respond, but lifted up the bedspread and threw it back in a flash, sure she'd expose an infestation of bedbugs. Nothing but clean, white sheets covered Colin's mattress.

She sighed and her shoulders sloped forward. She collapsed on the bed. "This has been the longest day of my life." She looked at me and her expression softened. She patted the bed next to her.

I sat, my body melting into the mattress. Colin's mattress. I would lie where he slept, breathe in his scent all night and sleep in total safety. Mother pushed the hair off my face, touched the bandages, and her eyes teared.

She snatched me against her with her free arm. "I love you, darling."

"Love you, too, Mom."

I covered myself with his sheets, his shirt against my skin. Next to me, Mother slept soundly, a soft buzzing snore slipping in and out of her lips. Moonlight sliced through plastic Levelor shades. Colin was right, the room was quiet. I wasn't afraid to sleep, not lying in Colin's bed, surrounded by his things—meager though they were. He was twelve feet away on the couch. The front door was locked and bolted.

I had nothing to be afraid of.

No one was coming after me.

I hadn't thought of Stuart once since I'd been found—except when I'd retold what had happened. Even then his face hadn't come fully into my mind, rather, in the ensuing hours his image had vaporized from my thoughts. The entire experience now faded, or maybe I was choosing to block it out somehow. I didn't care.

My safety wasn't an issue anymore. The knowledge was freeing. Each muscle stretched out, and my breathing slowed.

I closed my eyes and slept.

The scent of coffee slipping into the room from beneath the closed bedroom door awakened me the next morning. Mother stirred next to me. Faint movement on the other side of the door meant Colin was up.

I enjoyed each moment I could between his sheets, smiling at the innuendo—I was very far from doing anything more than sleeping in his bed, but I was okay with that. A dreamy image of his dark hair mussed like a porcupine inches away, the smooth curve of his back disappearing beneath the coverings sent warmth to my toes.

I didn't want to awaken Mother, so I slid out of bed as seamlessly as I could and crossed the floor into the bathroom. The scrapes and bruises on my face had bloomed to a blue-gray like a rotted eggplant. I touched them lightly and cringed. My mind flashed the moment Stuart had grappled with me in the shower. I shuddered.

Thankfully, I got away.

There was no point in dwelling on what might have happened if I hadn't taken that chance, though pictures flashed in my head of him ripping off my clothes, of him smothering breath from my lungs as he mashed his mouth over mine.

But I was here, and he was in custody.

I gingerly splashed water on my face, finger-combed my hair and frowned at my reflection.

"You look beautiful." Mother came up behind me, her short auburn hair matted and sticking up like a hedgehog. Her mouth lifted in a smile. She placed her free hand on my shoulder.

"Did you sleep all right?" she asked, smoothing my hair.

"Yes. You?"

"Like a log." Her gaze shifted to the mirror and her eyes bulged. "Now that's truly frightening."

"Mom, stop." I turned and faced her. She touched my face, the cool tips of her fingers skimming my scratches.

"You sure you're all right?" she asked.

"Yes. Don't worry about me, please."

"Nightmares?"

"No," I said.

"You might have them, Ashlyn. We might have to have you go see Dr. Schwartzman again for a while."

"Mother, I appreciate your concern." Her eyes overflowed with so much love I couldn't hurt her by disvaluing her worry for me. "I'm fine. But if you want me to see him, I will. For you."

She let out a breath. "Well, we'll talk about it. Now, I must get to work on damage control." She left me, went to her purse sitting on the floor in the corner of Colin's bedroom, and she dug out her cell phone. "I hope no little critters crawled in my bag last night. They do that you know—stow away in your purse and then infest everything they touch." She shuddered visibly.

I giggled and joined her, my gaze shifting to the unkempt bed. A vision of a shirtless Colin sprawled in the sheets suddenly snuck into my thoughts. I cleared my throat and helped Mother make the bed.

When it was box-wrap perfect, Mother took her bag in one hand, her other slipped around my waist and she guided me into the small bathroom with her. "Thank heavens I have the essentials. Want to share? Not that you need anything, young and beautiful as you are."

"Aw. Thank you. I wonder how Dad is."

She patted her fingers beneath her eyes. "I'm sure he's fine."

"Shouldn't we call the hospital and find out?"

Mother stood back and, studying her reflection in the mirror turned her face left, then right. "Be my guest."

I tilted my head at her and she sighed and extended her hand with a wave. "Fine, I'll call. Bring me my phone."

I dug her phone out of her bag and handed it to her. She dialed.

Mother held her cell phone to her ear and asked for Dad's room. "Yes, this is Fiona Adair calling. How is he this morning? Oh, very good. No, I'll speak to him later. Thank you." She clicked the device off. "Well, your father's still alive." Her smug tone lanced the air with sarcasm. She cared, but she was hurt. I understood that.

"I'm glad he got to see me last night. So he knows I'm okay," I said. "We should get uptown as soon as we can."

"I'm going to try to do something with this face of mine so I look reasonably acceptable. Would you mind bringing me a cup of that coffee Colin is brewing? Woke me from a sound sleep—it's so very *Folgers*."

"Mother!" I chuckled. "Once a snob, always a snob?"

Mother shrugged. "Meh."

____ CHAPTER TWENTY-TWO

I smoothed the FBI shirt. I still wore the hospital scrub pants. The combination was hilariously ugly, but I didn't mind. *In light of everything that's happened, who cares?*

Colin wore jeans and a white undershirt—his black sweater from the night before was draped over the single chair in the kitchen. His back faced me as he wiped the counter with a black dishcloth. My heart jumped. I loved the way the muscles in his back shifted when he reached his arm out to swipe the countertop. His straight shoulders, tapered waist. The back of his thighs pressing through his jeans.

He turned, his dimples creasing. "Hey, how'd you sleep?"

"Great, thanks." I entered the kitchen, saw two mugs of hot coffee on the counter. "Your bed is really comfortable."

His eyes deepened a shade. "Coffee?" He nodded at the mugs.

I took one. "For Mother. Be right back."

I crossed to the bedroom and found Mother in the bathroom, nose pressed to the mirror.

"Ugh," she moaned, fingers working the puffs beneath her eyes. "I wonder if he has any jasmine root juice and fresh ginger."

"Somehow I doubt it." I handed her the hot mug.

She took it and sipped. Her face contorted. "That's awful. Aren't you having any?"

"Mine's in the kitchen."

"You go… *enjoy.*" She turned back around to her reflection and groaned again.

I laughed and left her to rejoin Colin in the kitchen. He leaned his back against the counter top, legs crossed at the ankles, arms folded over his chest.

A dazzling grin later, he handed the mug to me. "I can warm it up if it's not hot enough."

It was hot enough.

He pulled his cell phone out of his front pocket and handed it to me. "Felicity. I promised her I'd have you call."

"How did Stuart get her phone?" I asked.

"Officer Ahearn said he stole it from her yesterday."

Felicity had told me she'd 'bumped' into Stuart. A creepy vibe scratched my spine. I dialed Felicity's house phone. Colin sipped from his mug, eyes on me over the rim of the cup.

"Fel?"

"Oh my gosh, Ash." She sobbed into the phone.

"I'm okay."

Her weeping shifted to sniffling. "Is there something I can do? I feel so stupid. I don't know what to say."

"It's okay, you don't have to say anything, I want to see you."

"Yeah," Felicity sniffed. "Whenever you feel ready. Don't feel pressured."

I assured her that I was all right but it took some convincing.

"I'm so glad you're okay," her voice hitched.

"I am. I'll call you later, k?"

"Okay."

I clicked the phone off and handed it to Colin. "She's a good friend," I said. He slipped the cell into his pocket, his gaze still keen on me.

I sipped the lukewarm liquid watching his eyes skim my face. "How do those feel today?" He tapped his own cheek indicating my injuries.

I shrugged, keeping the mug at my lips because just looking at him made me want to smile. His gaze slipped to my mouth, and he quickly averted his eyes.

"Thanks to you I got away from him," I said. His light expression darkened.

"What do you mean?"

"I did what you told me to do. Head butted him, gouged his eyes—with soap. It worked."

He shook his head, a smile of pride on his lips. "You're something else. You saved yourself."

"Yeah, but you taught me."

He lowered his head. "Nah. It was you. How is Fiona this morning?"

"Fine."

"I imagine she wants to get to the hospital as soon as possible."

"Probably home first, to change."

He unfolded his arms, rested his palms behind him on the counter ledge. Was he nervous?

I sipped again. The coffee was room temperature now, but the air in the small kitchen smoldered.

Colin's foot jittered. He looked ready to launch himself from his casual stance to—where? The way his eyes sparkled with black mischief reminded me of when we were kids. He'd get that same look when he'd corner me and tease me without mercy. My insides buzzed.

"Dad's okay this morning. We called."

Colin shifted his feet. "That's good." The grin playing on his lips slowly vanished. His eyes intensified like black fire, the flames leaping across the small space to me, licking the surface of my skin with tempting heat.

I swallowed.

Is this what it's like to crave? To want someone so much talking seemed irrelevant. I could barely breathe, my chest was so tight. Did he feel the same?

I was going to cross to the sink to wash out the remaining coffee, but as I began the short trek, craving took me to him. I stopped when my body was close enough to his to touch. *I want you.* The thought spun on an endless loop in my head. I hoped he saw in my eyes that I wasn't backing down.

"Thank you for everything." I embraced him. He had to understand how important he was to me. He hesitated only a second before his arms wound around my body.

His fingers opened across my back and shoulder blades. "Please, don't thank me."

"I have to. I know you're doing your job, but—"

"It's more than that." His hands moved to my shoulders, he eased me back so he could look at me. His finger lifted my chin and his gaze fixed on my mouth. A tingle raced beneath my lips. His head dipped, until our lips brushed. "I love you," he whispered the words and kissed me.

Joy spiraled through my soul. I wrapped my arms around his neck, burying tears of joy against the beat of his heart. "I love you, too."

Colin arranged for Eddy to pick us up and take us uptown. Eddy and Mother talked about Dad quietly in the front. Colin sat in the back with me. Eddy stole glances at me through the rearview mirror, like he couldn't believe I was there. He'd worked for Dad since we'd moved to New York. He'd always been friendly when he'd driven me to and from school, occasionally sharing stories about his own boy and girl, his wife, and his dreams of world travel someday.

"It's good to see you, Miss Adair," he finally said once his conversation with Mother came to an end.

"Thank you, Eddy."

His smiling eyes seemed to want to say much more to me, but he didn't.

As we approached the townhouse, my pulse skipped. News vans with satellite dishes perched on their roofs lined the street out front. A small gathering of media, dressed in dark coats, hats and scarves waited—for us.

"They're still here?" I whispered.

"Of course," Colin murmured, eyeing them through the glass. "How many people can say they've been kidnapped twice in their lifetime—by separate individuals who work for their father?" His eyes met mine.

"Here we go." Mother's gaze was latched on the crowd.

Colin leaned forward. "I'll take care of it."

He gave Eddy instructions. As we neared, I noticed two police cars. Colin whipped out his cell phone, made a call and spoke with someone on the police force.

Mother and I put on our sunglasses.

When the car stopped, two officers held back the media creating an opening from the curb to the door. Photographers and reporters turned their attention to us, hovering closer with cameras and mics.

Colin slipped on his dark glasses and opened the door. In fluid precision he helped Mother and me from the car and ushered us through the flood of shouts and camera clicks to the front door of the townhouse without incident.

Mother shook. Trepidation whitened her face. Colin tapped in the code and the door opened. He thrust us both in and brought the door to a close.

Alone in the empty silence of the townhouse, Mother and I stood together, breath speeding in and out of our chests. I heard Colin's muffled voice through the door, but I couldn't make out what he was saying, even though the roar of the media ebbed as he spoke.

The familiar scent of home mixed with some spicy scents wafting from the kitchen. Gavin came fluttering from the back of the house, his hands flapping, face twisted like a pretzel.

"Mrs. Adair. I was frantic. *Frantic.* Ashlyn! Oh heavens. How is Mr. Adair? Is he all right?" He buzzed to Mother and they embraced.

"Mr. Adair is fine, Gavin."

"But our little Ashlyn." He embraced me next, quickly—his doughy body gave when mine pressed into him—then he clapped his hands at his round chest. "It's unimaginable. Unbelievable. How are you, sweetie?"

"I'm good, thank you."

"I'm making linguini," Gavin said, breathless, his earnest gaze jumping from Mother to me. "I wasn't sure if either of you would be hungry, but it will be ready this evening if you have an appetite."

Mother touched Gavin's elbow. "It smells heavenly." Distracted, Mother glanced at the front door. "Do you think he's all right?" she asked me.

"He's fine," I said, completely confident in Colin's ability to handle anything.

"Colin?" Gavin scuttled into the front room and peered through the shutters. "They've been here all night. I tried to leave and was accosted by some photographer perched on the back wall."

Mother gasped. "The police were supposed to be here."

"They were. I had to have an escort to my car." Gavin shook his head, eyes alight with excitement. "I had paparazzi offer me money for information." His fingers covered his mouth.

"No," Mother whispered.

"Yes." Gavin nodded. "But I didn't take one penny, of course. The phone has not stopped ringing. Incessant, I tell you."

A wave of shouts and voices suddenly surged through the front door as it swung open, the questions trailing Colin like verbal baseballs as he stepped inside. He closed the door and his eyes met mine. He took a deep breath.

"Did you make the statement?" Mother's voice was tentative.

Colin came away from the door with an unaffected nod.

"Oh, thank you, dear boy." Mother reached out her free hand to him and he took it. She grasped it like a lifeline had been extended to her. Her eyes misted. "I'm going to go freshen up." Her voice cracked, and Gavin studied her.

Mother started up the stairs. Gavin excused himself and returned to the kitchen.

"Go." Colin's hand pressed with urgency into the small of my back.

"What about you?"

"Don't worry about me." The phone rang throughout the house, the sound coming from Dad's office. The kitchen. Upstairs.

"I'll take care of it," Colin said. He leaned close and kissed my cheek. His gaze seemed to say, *everything is going to work out.*

I took the stairs up and Colin's gaze remained fastened to mine with each step. He didn't move. I stopped outside my bedroom door, peering down at him.

I want you, I thought.

Be realistic. You need to shower and get dressed. You need to talk to Dad.

My reflection had changed. I didn't see the princess looking back at me in the mirror. The strong, scrolled frame still encased me, but something different was cast in my eyes now. The innocence I'd seen in myself—and had come to dislike because I had associated the quality with naiveté—wasn't quite as obvious. Not tarnished by what I'd experienced, rather matured.

Pleased, I left the mirror with a smile on my lips. I showered, dressed in jeans with jeweled back pockets, and a black t-shirt. I peered out my window at the media gathered below.

I took a deep breath. If I spoke to them, maybe they'd leave us alone.

Mother appeared at my door, looking refreshed in her soft plum slacks and charcoal sweater. "Darling." She gleamed as she crossed to me. Joining me at the window, her gaze shifted to the crowds below. Her smile faltered.

"I'm going to talk to them," I said.

"You most certainly are not."

"Yes, Mother, I am."

"I am not going to have you recounting the horror of what happened just so the world can satisfy its sick need for voyeurism," she said.

"I'm not talking to them for the world, I'm talking to them for us, so they'll leave us alone. I don't want people hanging around, wondering. Do you? If I say what I want to say, they'll be pacified."

Mother took a deep breath. She studied me, smiled. "I suppose you're right. You're brilliant my darling."

My lips curved up. "Brilliance is in my genes."

Mother and I found Colin in the kitchen with Gavin. Gavin stood over a pot of sauce, the scent of which seasoned the air with garlic and basil. Colin was on the phone. He held a sesame breadstick—half-eaten—in one hand.

"Yes. Thank you." He hung up the house phone and disconnected the cord from the wall. "I've arranged for a service to take calls for the next few days." He looked at Mother. "The inbox is full—mostly media asking for interviews. That was the *Today Show*, hoping to get Ashlyn on tomorrow morning."

Gavin rolled his eyes. "Piranhas."

"Not going to happen," I said. "But I'll make a statement. I want to be left alone. The only way they're going to do that is if they hear from me."

"Maybe the *Today Show* would be the best option." Mother tapped her chin with her finger. "At least you'd be in a safe, protected venue."

"No." I turned, a wave of audacity sweeping through my system, and headed for the front door. I heard movement behind me. "I'm not in danger."

"Ashlyn." Colin grabbed my elbow and stopped me. Mother was behind him, Gavin at her heels. "I agree. You're the one they want to hear from and it's great that you want to do this. They're going to ask questions. They're going to dig. Mercilessly. Are you ready for that?"

Fear tried to shatter my courage but I siphoned strength from the underlying reassurance in his eyes. "Will you be with me?"

His grip on my arm softened. He nodded.

The moment he opened the front door, voices and the clicking of cameras battered me like a swarm of killer bees. Two police officers quieted the crowd. Colin and I stood side-by-side. He had his arms crossed over his chest, sunglasses on, gaze surveying the commotion as if at any moment, if the need arose, he could whisk me into his protective embrace and carry me to safety.

My nerves jumbled. I took a deep breath, waited for silence. "I'm grateful to be home. I hope you'll allow my family and me the privacy we need at this time." Beside me, Colin remained stoic. "Thank you."

Questions rang in the air. "How long had Mr. Reed worked as your bodyguard?"

"Is it true your father had a heart attack after you were abducted?"

"Does your father know you're safe?"

"What are your plans now?"

"If necessary, will you testify against Mr. Reed?"

"Have there been any more threats on your life?"

Colin stepped forward. "Miss Adair is finished. Thank you." He stepped in front of me, his body creating a barrier between me and the media. The questions continued to fire into the air like bullets.

I let out a shaky breath once we were inside and the door shut. Colin pulled out his cell phone, dialed a number stepped away from me. He spoke quietly into the mouthpiece, I couldn't hear what was being said.

Mother and Gavin hurried out of the living room where they'd apparently watched me give my statement from behind the opened, shuttered windows.

"Are you all right?" she asked, brows furrowed.

"Yes." My hands were clammy, and the shaking in my limbs hadn't subsided. "We should go see Dad now."

Mother's tufted expression turned taut. "Colin can take you. I'm not going to see your father."

Gavin's mouth opened.

Silence in the air was broken only by the scraggly chatter on the other side of the front door. I held Mother's cool gaze in disbelief. Their marriage really was over.

"I respect your decision, but I don't agree with it," I said.

"So much like your father." She kissed my cheek and worked a smile onto her lips. "You're the only one he wants to see anyhow." Her eyes remained cold—not a trace of emotion in their depths.

It seemed oddly natural that Mother wasn't at the hospital and even more necessary that I talk to Dad alone. I had a lot to say and questions that demanded answers.

Colin and I rode up in the elevator, standing across from each other. "Are you okay?" he asked.

I nodded, amazed at how light I felt. I should have had knots in my stomach, anticipating seeing Dad, but I didn't. I was ready to face him.

The elevator doors slid open and a draft of medicinal air hit my face. The scent tore me back to last night, being wheeled in, surrounded, stared at, questioned. A chill screeched over my skin. Colin put his hand on my shoulder.

A nurse escorted us to Dad's room. He was still in the cardiac wing, having been moved from ICU sometime after I'd left last night. I took that as a good sign.

Dad lay under a white blanket. The sight of his weak arms—once so strong and vibrant—hooked to IVs and various monitors stopped my breath. I slowed once inside the room. Would he sense me like he always did? The war-worn exhaustion on his face shocked me. Had I not heard the heart monitor beeping, I would have thought he was dead.

He turned his head, opened his eyes. His bloodshot gaze was rimmed in red, like he'd battled an emotional infection, too.

I crossed and stopped at his bedside.

Dad's shaking hands reached out. He wanted me to hug him. I leaned over and carefully embraced him. The first buckle of his chest sent panic through me. Should he allow himself to get upset in his condition? His sobs gushed, loud, heavy—a broken reservoir. I whispered that I was okay, but the sound of my voice sent another surge of sobs wrenching from his throat.

Hands quaking, he eased me back, took my face between his hands, his feverish, frightened, horrified eyes soaking me up with an insatiable appetite.

Finally, he released me, his hands falling to his sides on the bed, head back, eyes closed as he gasped for breath. My heart jumped. Colin moved closer, clearly as alarmed as I.

"Dad?"

"Tissue," he rasped. "Please."

Colin searched, found, and plucked a tissue from a utilitarian box sitting near the sink. He handed it to me, and I tucked it in Dad's fingers. Dad lifted his head and brought the tissue to his eyes and nose.

When he was finished, I took the tissue and threw it into the trash.

His teary eyes locked on me. "You said he didn't hurt you. Is that the truth?"

I swallowed. My eyes shifted to Colin for a second. "Yes."

"I want to know what really happened."

"I don't want you upsetting yourself."

His hands knotted around the blanket and sheets. "Tell me."

I took Dad through each moment and detail knowing he would never forgive me if he found out later that I had left one thing out.

He was riveted. His eyes widened, teared. His chest lifted, fell.

"Why didn't you tell me about the tracking device?" I asked when I finished. A cold silence filled the room. His heart monitor raced. He closed his eyes, breathed deep. His fists opened and closed around the bed coverings. The monitor finally slowed.

"I did what I had to, to protect you."

Anger flurried through my system. "And look where it got me."

He looked straight ahead at nothing and said nothing.

"Colin," he finally spoke, voice gravelly.

"Yes, Charles?"

"Leave us for a few minutes please."

Colin flicked a look at me, as if making sure I was all right. I gave a small nod. He left.

Dad turned his head and looked at me. "I don't blame anyone but myself for this."

"Good."

His bloodshot eyes widened. "I won't apologize for protecting you, Ashlyn."

I was speechless that he still clung to this ridiculous notion that I was in danger. "Even after the people you hired to protect me were the ones who tried to hurt me?"

"Has Colin tried to hurt you?"

"Why do you ask?"

"I saw the way you looked at him. I know how difficult it's been for you to put his cruelties behind you."

Dad. Knew. "Isn't that why you hired him?"

The beep from the heart monitor notched up. He took a deep breath. "I hired him because he was qualified for the job."

"Qualified because I hated him, and you knew I hated him. Like I hated Stuart. So there was never any chance I'd be attracted to either one of them."

"Is that too much to ask? That my daughter not find the *help* attractive?"

"You don't want me finding anyone attractive, Dad. You want me to stay with you and never leave."

The beeping ramped at a full run. I glanced at the monitor, watched the green line jag up and down. Dad's control was remarkable. He didn't blink or react in any way to the truth. He didn't speak. Didn't defend himself. Only the beeping monitor betrayed him.

"I want what's best for you," he finally said.

My patience waned. "Define 'what's best?'"

"Your safety comes first." His eyes darkened, but the intended threat had lost its impact. He was attached to tubes and wires, his heart had nearly failed him, and his relationship with his daughter and wife was about to change radically because of his choices.

"The only harm that has ever come to me has been by people you've employed," I said.

A long moment passed, our heated gazes fastened to each other.

"An unfortunate irony I admit," he stated. "Nevertheless, I'm not prepared to give any on the subject, Ashlyn. You're far too…too…"

My blood sizzled. I leaned close to make my point. "What are you afraid of?"

For the first time since the other night at dinner, I saw honest urgency in his eyes. "It's not you I don't trust, it's the stranger I don't trust."

Dad really did think he had to spend the rest of his life protecting me. What would it take for him to see his position was wrong? I hoped it wouldn't come down to living my life without him in it.

I gazed at his hand, clasped tight around mine. "I'm going to live with Mother," I said quietly.

He pulled his hand free. His eyes flamed. "You will live with me. There will be no more discussion about it."

I stood, stared down at him. He was trapped. In bed. There was nothing he could do at this moment, or any moment in the near future until he gained back his strength.

"Goodbye, Dad. I hope you feel better."

Colin took one look at my face as I exited Dad's room and brushed past me, pushing the door open. He disappeared inside. Muffled voices rose in a sparring match on the other side of the closed door. I bit my lip.

"I'll stay until you're home," I heard Colin's raised voice. "But consider this my official resignation."

Seconds later, he emerged, jaw knotted. He glanced around, eyes like a hawk. Hand at my back, he guided me to the elevator.

"You resigned?" My heart shivered.

"Had to." Colin's gaze swept the area continuously until the elevator doors slid open and he escorted me inside. A sliver of uncertainty dug under my skin. "I can't be a part of something I don't agree with. What he's doing to you is wrong. I told him so. I'm sorry Ash." His eyes leveled me. "I told him the truth."

I swallowed. "Truth?"

"That I love you."

Every nerve in my body fluttered with thrill. I brought myself to his chest, smiled up into his eyes. "I hope you told him that I love you, too."

Colin snorted, shook his head. "No. You can tell him that when he's out of here." He touched my cheek. A sharp beat jagged between us. "He told me there's been another threat on your life."

"What?" My stomach hollowed.

"He's lying."

"How do you know?"

"I'd bet the job on it."

The moving motion of the car left my suddenly unsteady legs even weaker. "He doesn't want me to leave him," I murmured. "Ever." I knew what had to be done. "You can't be there when he gets back," I said.

Colin nodded. "You're right."

"He'll see that I can be on my own, that I should be on my own. He won't have any way of stopping it."

The elevator sped downward.

It was easy to pretend everything would work out. With Dad in the hospital, and Mother resigned to moving on, the townhouse was a lighter place. I struggled with feeling relieved that Dad wasn't there. Not that I wanted him out of my life forever, but having him gone, even temporarily, made it obvious that I could live on my own.

Mother seemed to sense that things were different between Dad and me. We didn't discuss it—she became snappy when she talked about Dad, even though she'd accepted their failed marriage. I loved her enough to not go there.

The night before Dad was supposed to be discharged, she and I and Colin were seated in the dining room, eating dinner. Gavin brought out brownies ala mode.

"Brownies?" Mother's brow cocked.

Gavin flushed, and flicked a glance at Colin. "I thought we were celebrating."

"When was the last time I celebrated anything with *brownies*?" Mother droned, disparagingly. "And with ice cream, no less."

"He made them for me," Colin piped. I bit my lip. "I've resigned, Fiona. I'll be leaving tomorrow."

Mother's eyes widened. Her mouth opened and it seemed a million demands dashed across her face, then slowly her expression shifted. A soft smile lit her lips. "I'm not surprised," she said. "We can't keep you forever."

Colin dipped his head, and he picked up his spoon. "This looks great, Gav. Thank you."

Gavin clasped his hands at his chest. "I haven't made brownies since I was ten. I'm a little rusty."

Mother poked at the ice cream, fudge sauce and brownie with her nose crinkled.

I took a spoonful. "It's delicious, Gavin."

Gavin tilted his head back and forth. "It's not cherry claufoits."

"Mmm." Colin's dimples flashed when he chewed. *Cute.*

Gavin excused himself and Mother sampled a bite of dessert. A long silence grew. Colin and I glanced at each other. My cheeks heated every time he looked at me. I caught Mother watching, and she swallowed and set aside her spoon.

"Will you be going back to California, Colin?" she asked.

"For Christmas, yes." He reached for his water goblet, sipped, eyes on me. "But then I'll be back for school."

"That will make Barb and Phil happy." Mother pushed her brownie ala mode away and clasped her hands on the table. "We will miss you," her tone was quiet. "You've told Charles?"

"Yes." Colin put his goblet down on the table. "It's been great being here. But you'll see me again."

Mother glanced briefly at me. "Oh?"

My nerves drew tight. I looked at Colin.

Colin's gaze stayed firmly on Mother. "I love Ashlyn. I want to keep seeing her."

Mother seemed to ponder through the thickening silence. Her gaze shifted to me, then back to Colin.

She pulled her dessert plate back in front of her, picked up her spoon and smiled. "That's the best news I've heard in a long time."

Spring

Sunny rays shot down between the towering buildings on Lexington Avenue. The air was thick, bordering on oppressive. Exhaust fumes rode on the heavy atmosphere, but that just meant people were going places, doing things. Seeing friends.

Like me.

A smile filled my lips.

I walked alone. The pastel floral skirt I wore, flirted around my knees with each step. I'd pushed up the sleeves of the light lemon blouse so the bracelets I'd layered at my wrists glittered like thick, jeweled cuffs. I kept my bag tucked under my arm.

I was used to the presence of eyes watching me, of whispers trailing me wherever I went. I'd learned to ignore stares of curiosity, pointing fingers and the occasional clicking sound of a camera. I was still getting comfortable with being without a bodyguard—the vacancy slowly filling in with confidence. Felicity and I had taken a self-defense class together, and the can of pepper spray Colin had given me had come in handy when one particularly annoying paparazzo hadn't gotten the message to keep his distance.

I wasn't sure how long it would take for anonyminity to return, or if it ever would, but I didn't let the strange celebrity stop me. I'd graduated from Chatham, been accepted to Juilliard and I allowed my heart the freedom it deserved.

Whether or not the guy following me now was someone Dad had hired to keep an eye on me from a distance, I wasn't sure. Dad denied any involvement, but he'd been honest enough to tell me he couldn't promise me that he wouldn't keep an eye on me somehow.

Colin had to move on. I understood that—Colin leaving was as important to my freedom as me holding my own against Dad. I hadn't seen him since he'd left the townhouse, though we'd talked some the phone. Hard as it was for me not to see him, he said he needed to clear his head. We both needed time to think. He said he wouldn't see me until Dad was well on the road to recovery. I didn't blame him—after moving from the townhouse with Mother to her new penthouse, I felt like the last chain had finally been cut from my ankle.

Being in Mother's new place eased some of the longing. I didn't walk by Colin's empty bedroom and wish that I could see him look up from the book he was reading. Or catch him just out of the shower. Or see him in the music room, his shoulder against the wall as he listened to me play. Mother's place held no images of Colin, no memories. It was a new start.

She'd bought me a white baby grand.

Dad had insisted the black grand stay with him. He resigned himself to the fact that living with Mother was my choice. All he asked was that I take his calls and indulge him in lunch and dinner invitations. And that I consider staying with him over the weekend sometime.

I thought that was a good place to start.

Coming to the corner of Fifth Avenue and 59th Street, I stopped with a small crowd; a mix of pedestrians and tourists. I crossed the street and the tourist crowd thickened as I neared Central Park. I caught sight of the vibrant green trees in the distance. The park was one of my favorite places in the city. I loved the bridges, the serene winding paths, the quiet private niches where lovers could meet.

Or reunite.

I turned a glance over my shoulder to see if the suited man was still tailing me. He was. I waved. His head averted the second I made eye contact.

Facing forward, I kept my gaze out ahead. As long as the suited guy kept his distance, we were good. I had more important things on my mind.

Approaching the entrance to the park, I saw him—watching me. His flash of dark hair, straight shoulders—the unforgettable presence of Colin Brennen. My pulse shimmied. He stood at the same entrance I'd run through months earlier the night I'd made him chase after me.

My nerves plucked as I neared. He pressed through the tourists and pedestrians like his life depended on breaking the barrier until he was finally ten feet away. I didn't know if he still owned any of the designer clothes Mother had given him. Somehow, I doubted they mattered. He had on a pair of khakis and a short-sleeved black shirt.

His dimples deepened. "Ash." He wrapped his arms around me and my body fluttered, longing at last contented. "I've missed you," he said, his lips against my temple. Bodies filed around us.

"I've missed you, too."

We held each other. Eyes closed, I fought the impulse to laugh and weep, the joy surging through my uncontainable.

His embrace loosened, and his gentle hands skimmed up my arms to my shoulders. He drew back, and his gaze seemed to say what I felt: looking at you eases everything inside of me. Finger under my chin, he lifted my face to his and kissed me. His mouth left mine and his eyes skimmed my face, my skin tingling as though he'd touched me. His gaze caught on someone behind me. He nodded at the man following my trail. "The new me?"

"No one can replace you." Slipping my hand in his, I grinned. "It's time to ditch him."

About the Author

Jennifer Laurens is the mother of six children, one of whom has autism. She lives in Utah with her family, at the base of the Wasatch Mountains.

Other Titles:

Heavenly
Penitence
Absolution

Falling for Romeo
Magic Hands
Nailed
A Season of Eden
An Open Vein

Visit the website:
www.jenniferlaurens.com